TO JORDAN,
I HOPE YOU ENJOY
THIS LOVING
CONVERSATION.

BEST,

Matt

DEATH

(A Love Story)

By

Matthew J. Pallamary

Mystic Ink Publishing

Mystic Ink Publishing
San Diego, CA
mysticinkpublishing.com

© *2020 Matthew J. Pallamary. All Rights Reserved,*

ISBN 10: 0-9986809-4 (sc)
ISBN 13: 978-0-9986809-4-1 (sc)

Library of Congress Control Number: 2019910265
Mystic Ink Publishing, San Diego, CA

Book Jacket and Page Design: Matthew J. Pallamary / San Diego CA
Author's Photograph: Matthew J. Pallamary — Robert DeLaurentis / Santa Barbara CA
Gibbs Photo / Malibu CA

TABLE OF CONTENTS

Drifting somewhere in the blackness between dreaming and oblivion, a primal directionless voice rang out from the void and pierced my heart, shaking me to my core like the peal of a bell that struck an all-encompassing chord through every fiber, cell, and molecule of my being with profound immediacy. The shock of it startled me into what should have been awake, except that I plummeted down into the depths of an abyss that swallowed me with full awareness.

PLEASE ALLOW ME TO INTRODUCE MYSELF

Hi, I am your Death and I am here for you.

No wait, don't go!

Aside from the fact that you can't get away, I'm not here for you in *that* way, at least not now, although to be honest with you we do have a date and I am *always* with you whether you acknowledge me or not.

Want to know when I am coming in *that* way?

Sorry, I can't tell you. It's part of the Great Mystery. You know. That place where you came from and where you are going.

If you want to know the truth I'm not *your* death, but you are *mine*. Now don't freak out on me. It's only a visit. I want to spend some quality time with you before the big event and seeing as you took the time to stop by and I have you as a captive audience I thought it would be nice to have a little visit and get acquainted.

Sorry, if we got off on the wrong foot, but that happens more often than not, so let's give it another try.

Pleased to meet you. Hope you guess my name, but what's puzzling you is the nature of my game. No, I'm not who you think from that song – well maybe I am. In truth I have many names and many faces. I'm formally introducing myself to you this way, but I'm really just messing with you, hoping that maybe you will lighten up and think of me a little differently. Who knows? You just might learn something.

We are far more intimate than most people care to admit. Whoever came up with the expression love it to death was a lot closer to the truth than those other idiotic sayings you have about me. Not only am

I always with you, but my love for you is unconditional, all consuming, and infinite from your limited perspective. With a love like that you'd think that my feelings would be hurt by the way you portray me, but one of the benefits of being omnipotent and omniscient is that I am beyond those infantile emotions, and if I were affected by them my love for you wouldn't be unconditional, would it?

Yes, I admit to being a know-it-all. That is the definition of omniscient, so forgive me if I go a little overboard at times. It's not my ego, it's just that I sometimes forget myself. I have access to everything there is to know about you, and everyone else for that matter.

I have friends in more places than you can imagine and my eyes and ears are everywhere including all knowledge in each and every molecule and cell of your neurons, dendrites, mitochondria, organs, and anything else you can imagine. Yes, sometimes I get a little too technical and scientific at times, but every thought, emotion, and the collective knowledge of anything humanity has ever thought, imagined, or experienced is at my disposal.

There are no secrets from me.

I'm here to tell you stories and share some science, history, and myths, all of which are your creations that I want to enlighten you with to help you understand me more. You have seen me as Satan, Anubis, Mot, Thanatos, God, the Devil, loving, punitive, dark, light – the list goes on and on!

It is my sincerest hope that our friendly reintroduction here will change the way you think of me, and maybe in some small way reflect the depth of the love I have for you.

One of the most enduring ways you depict me is as the Grim Reaper, a skeleton wearing a shroud holding a scythe who comes to collect you. Yes, there is some truth to that and many of your stories are about people trying to trick, bribe, or avoid me and hold on to the psychopomp who escorts newly deceased souls into the afterlife. When you portray me this way I'm pretty scary looking. No wonder so many people are terrified of me!

I'd much rather have you show me this way which is a far more truthful way to think of me and of how I feel about you.

Sometimes you think of me as male and other times you think of me as female, but I am far beyond any definition as simplistic as that.

Aside from the Grim Reaper, which you have to admit, is not very flattering, can you honestly tell me what is grim about a homecoming? After all, everyone is more than welcome in my domain which is actually your real home.

Mi casa es su casa.

I suggest you enjoy the short visit of your life because when I come for you, you will realize just how short it really is.

You could even die reading this book.

As I mentioned, I have many names and many faces. In the most basic sense, most people know me as Death, which comes from an old English word *dēap*, which comes from the old Germanic *daupuz*, which comes from a Indo-European root that means the process, act, or condition of dying, but I go infinitely further back than that!

Over time, the idea and the signs of my coming have generated a number of euphemisms. When I come for someone, you may say that they have passed away, passed on, expired, or are gone. The dead person becomes a corpse, a body, remains, or a cadaver. I kind of like that last one. Abra Cadaver! Now you see them, now you don't.

Carrion and carcass are also used mostly when talking about animals, and when all of your flesh has rotted away you become skeletons. In the spirit of politeness, people now like to say deceased, and the dead person is referred to as the decedent while the ashes left after a cremation are sometimes called cremains, a clever combination of the words cremation and remains.

Other than this very decidedly special blessing of a visit with you now, from a scientific point of view my mostly once in a lifetime visit can best be defined as the ending of all biological functions that keep a living organism going. I have many ways to do that depending on how you have lived, where you lived, what your parents did, and lots of other things that come into play that affect our fast approaching, intimate meeting.

There are innumerable variations on how I come for you. If you are good, I might let you enjoy the gift of life for longer and let you die of old age, but this can sometimes be slow and painful. Other times I can be fast and terrifying, like when a predatory wild animal decides it wants to act as one of my agents and send you to me as a gift. You can see this instinct in house cats when they bring you an eviscerated bird, mouse, or lizard as a gift. You should be flattered by that because they are giving you the same respect they have for me.

There are many other ways that I come that keep me busy, which is another reason why you should be grateful that I am spending this special time with you right now, although truth be told, I exist far outside the limitations of space and time as you know them.

I've always found it fascinating that like the loyal cat that brings you corpses as gifts, you unwittingly and sometimes purposefully do the same with me like *you* are my loyal pets. I have to admit to having a special place in my heart for cults, serial killers, war mongers, and other misfits who aid me in my work. No disrespect intended here, but I am flattered by the dedication and service of these seemingly misguided souls.

I understand that you don't always get credit in the case of disease, malnutrition, starvation, and dehydration. Sometimes the weather and other natural forces help make this happen, but sometimes, especially in modern times, you assist them with the way you treat your environment, or from your greed when you hoard resources at the expense of others.

I am grateful for your contributions both direct and indirect that help bring so many of my loved ones home to me. Without sounding insensitive to those left behind, I find the self service of suicide particularly charming and a sign of your undying love for me.

It's a paradox, isn't it? Undying love for Death. It sounds kind of eternal, doesn't it? I'm full of what looks like paradoxes and contradictions, but it's all part of the Great Mystery that you're not quite ready to understand yet.

Aside from those who prefer the self service personal introduction to me there is intentional homicide where you help me directly like a midwife into my reality, and then there are the times you help me without realizing it with accidents and traumas from terminal injuries. Sometimes I'm a little embarrassed and overwhelmed by your generosity when it comes to wars, bombings, and mass murders. Even though I don't need your help, among all the living beings in the world you serve me more than any of the others by killing yourselves and everything around you more than all of them combined.

While we are spending this special moment together I want you to know that I understand why you are terrified of me. Given the circumstances, I forgive you for the way you think of and describe me in light of the fact that in most cases the bodies of the formerly living decompose soon after I take them, which I admit is not a pretty sight, not to mention the smell, but maybe it can bring you some small comfort in the fact that what you see as an unsightly stinking mess gives life to my loyal insect, vermin, and other carrion eating clean up crews who help you become food for the plants. Your remains might even contribute to the radiant beauty of a blossoming flower!

I also realize that from your side of things my visit can be sad and unpleasant because of your love for those who leave you to come back to me, and because I am one of the best known faces of the Great Mystery, you know little of me, which is the reason I have come to visit with you now. Most of you fear the dark and what you don't know, and my visits bring emotional pain, melancholy, and longing, but on the bright side I also engender sympathy and compassion.

I feel compelled to tell you that many of you think there is an afterlife and believe that there is a reward, judgment, and punishment for past sins. Suffice it to say that you will discover the real truth of that when I come to take you home.

Although your thoughts, fears, perceptions, and denials of me are unwarranted, when you see them from the bigger picture that I represent, I assure you there is no judgment on my part for how you think and feel about me. I also want to point out that like the sympathy and compassion I inspire when I check in from time to time, and sometimes when I come, I change my mind to keep things interesting, and end up changing lives for the better.

Grim Reaper?

Huh!

If I do decide to let you stick around and enjoy the gifts and the life that I have loaned you for a longer time, it only means that I am coming for you in increments, sometimes just a few cells at a time, but as I mentioned my love for you is all consuming and our final meeting is inevitable, so rest assured, I am still coming, or maybe it sounds better to say waiting. Regardless of how you think about it, *I am always here for you*, and will come whenever I choose.

If you live a long life and manage to survive all the calamities that three dimensional existence has to offer, old age will wear you down and bring you to me. The aging process comes from the deterioration of cellular activity and the destruction of regular cell functions, meaning yes, I am everywhere and in all things big and small. This gradual deterioration and mortality means that cells are naturally sentenced to stable and long term loss of life in spite of their continuing metabolic reactions and viability.

To put things in perspective and give you a sense of how generous I am, how hard I work, and of how busy I am, roughly one-hundred-fifty-thousand people join me from around the world every day, and of those two thirds come to me through the gradual process of old age. Think about how much you contribute to the other third who come home to me through unnatural man made causes.

Who's the Grim Reaper now?

I understand how confusing it is for you to comprehend what I really am, what I really do, and what I represent. After all it *is* a Great Mystery that you only get a fleeting glimpse of as infinity, and even that falls short. It's one of the reasons I came to visit you now. It's my sincere hope that you come to understand me more. Even though I am admittedly incomprehensible, I am also inevitable, so whether you like it or not, in spite of the fact that you do everything to avoid and try to outwit me, at some point you have to accept me, even if I take you kicking and screaming. I would much rather have you embrace me with the Love I have for you when I finally welcome you home because in the end you have no choice but to admit; *you are mine.*

You have studied all of the ways I can take you and searched the signs of my visits in futile attempts to look for ways out, but you must realize now that I am a process, meaning I am perpetually ongoing instead of a one time event the way you are used to seeing and thinking of me as. With the advancement of your science and technology many of my entry points are now reversible, which I find amusing, but patience *is* a virtue, isn't it? I have all the time in the world and I will *always* prevail in the end.

Your inquiries and your divide and conquer approach to understand me have only confused things more by blurring the dividing line between living and joining me in my realm, and it depends on factors beyond the presence or absence of your vital signs. In your modern day and age clinical death is not necessary or adequate for a determination of legal death. If you have a working heart and lungs, but are considered brain dead, then you can be declared legally dead without clinical death.

Who's really calling the shots here, Clinical Doctor Death, Death, Attorney at Law, or Brain Stealing Death?

Of course the answer is always Yours Truly no matter how anyone tries to define me.

You now have many scientific definitions to try and understand me like brain death, which defines my arrival as the point in time when brain activity ceases, respiratory arrest, when breathing stops, and cardiac arrest, when your heart stops. These are followed by what sounds like partners in an otherworldly family law firm; pallor mortis, the paleness that comes fifteen to twenty minutes after I have come and gone, livor mortis, the settling of blood in the lower part of the body, algor mortis, the reduction in body temperature following my visit, and the well known rigor mortis, where the limbs become stiff, and of course at the end of it all there is always decomposition.

All of these definitions highlight one of the challenges in trying to define me, which is distinguishing me from life, the gift that I bless you with. If you look at my arrival as a point in time, then I am the moment when your life ends, but determining when I have come is difficult as the cessation of your life functions don't often happen at the same time across all of your organ systems.

A popular conception which I have an affinity for is to define life as consciousness. When consciousness ceases a living organism can be said to have died, but even this notion is ambiguous in that the concept of consciousness has different definitions given by scientists, psychologists, and philosophers, not to mention all the religious traditions that believe my arrival doesn't signal the ending of consciousness. In many cultures I am thought of as more of a process than a single event that implies a transition from one spiritual state to another.

Does consciousness survive when I come and take you?

Well...

Sorry, as much as I'd like to tell you, that is part of the Great Mystery, but if it is any consolation, I am always here for you.

Waiting.

Amidst all this confusion about when and how I might come and go, many have been confounded or in many cases have taken things into their own hands and wittingly or unwittingly worked for me by becoming my agents and collaborators. I have to admit that no matter which way it turns out, I am indifferent to the outcome because I know that I *always* prevail in the end.

Throughout history many people have been buried alive either by accident, misdiagnosis, or intentionally as forms of torture, murder, or execution. Sometimes it happens with the consent of the victim as part of a stunt with the intention of escaping. Premature burials are invitations for me to visit through suffocation, dehydration, starvation, or hypothermia if it happens somewhere cold.

Many recorded cases of accidental burial go back to the fourteenth century when after reopening his tomb, the philosopher John Duns Scotus was reportedly found outside his coffin with his hands torn and bloody after attempting to escape me. Alice Blunden of Basingstoke was said to have been buried alive twice back in sixteen-seventy-four. These are just recorded instances, but these accidents go much further back than that.

Revivals of corpses have been triggered by dropped coffins, grave robbers, embalming, and attempted dissections. Many people think that reports of live burial are overestimated. The normal physical effects of decomposition are often misinterpreted as signs that the exhumed person had revived in their coffin. Reports are ongoing of people accidentally being sent to the morgue trapped in steel boxes after being declared dead. When a gentleman named Robert Robinson died in Manchester England in seventeen-ninety-one a movable glass pane was inserted into his coffin and the mausoleum had a door for purposes of inspection by a watchman to see if he breathed on the glass. He instructed relatives to visit his grave periodically to check that he had actually left with me.

In eighteen-eighty-two safety coffins were devised to prevent premature burial, but none of them worked and in eighteen-ninety a family designed and built a burial vault with an internal hatch to allow the victim of a premature burial to escape. The London Association for the Prevention of Premature Burial was formed in eighteen-ninety-six.

I found all these antics and the lengths that people went through to avoid meeting me a source of great entertainment. All of these accidents and misdiagnosed burials have contributed to the legions of vampire and zombie mythologies which I find even funnier.

Undead? Seriously? Talk about the ultimate denial of me. Is that like the spiritual equivalent of antimatter?

From my point of view it doesn't matter when you come, and in the bigger scheme of things, days, weeks, months, or years make no difference to me. You are all mine and sooner or later every single one of you is coming home.

There are those who have flirted with me and in that flirtation have seduced me into coming to take them home. On these occasions, many of which are only stories and myths, people have arranged to be buried alive as a demonstration of their egotistic misplaced ability to survive me. In one story that took place around eighteen-forty an Indian fakir was said to have been buried in the presence of a British military officer and put in a sealed bag in a wooden box in a vault which was interred.

The whole location was guarded day and night to prevent fraud and the site was dug up twice in a ten month period to verify the burial before the fakir was finally dug out and revived in the presence of another officer. The fakir is reputed to have said that his only fear during his wonderful sleep was to be eaten by underground worms. According to other sources the entire burial was only forty days long. Either way it's a great story, but I hate to ruin it by the fact that it's impossible to stay alive for that long without food, water, and air.

More silliness!

As recently as two-thousand-ten a Russian man died after being buried alive to try and overcome his fear of me, but he was crushed to death by the earth on top of him. A year later another Russian died after being buried overnight in a makeshift coffin for good luck.

I love the irony in both cases. The first guy succeeded by facing his fear of me. I don't mind telling you that I love Fear and we are in fact very close, and in this man's bravery we embraced. In the second case it was indeed a case of good luck.

Mine.

Going further back, Saint Oran was a druid living on the Island of Iona in Scotland's Inner Hebrides who became a follower of Saint Columba who brought Christianity to Iona from Ireland in five-sixty-three AD. When Saint Columba had problems building the original Iona Abbey because of supposed interference from the Devil, Saint Oran offered himself as a human sacrifice and was buried alive. He was later dug up and found to be still alive, but he uttered words describing the afterlife he had seen and how it involved no Heaven or Hell, so he was ordered to be covered up again and the building of the abbey went ahead untroubled. Saint Oran's chapel marks the spot where he was buried.

Stories like these go all the way back to prehistoric times in addition to many references to people declared dead by physicians and coming back to life, sometimes days later in their own coffin, or when embalming procedures were about to begin. From the mid-eighteenth century on there was an upsurge in the public's fear of being buried alive and a lot of debate about the uncertainty of the signs that I have come. Various brutal methods were devised to test for signs of life before burial, among them pouring vinegar and pepper into the corpse's mouth and applying red hot pokers to the feet or into the rectum.

In your modern day in cases of electric shock and cardiopulmonary resuscitation known as CPR for an hour or longer stunned nerves can recover, allowing an apparently deceased person to survive. People found unconscious under icy waters can also survive if their faces are kept cold until they arrive at an emergency room in what is called a diving response where metabolic activity and oxygen requirements are minimal. As your technology advances your ideas about when or if I have come will have to be re-evaluated in your increasingly clever ways of trying to forestall my fated visit.

I wish you would love me unconditionally the way I love you and stop trying to avoid our date which is set in stone as you say. I look forward to our reunion which in the bigger scheme of things will be here before you know it. For me it is a joyful homecoming and should be cause for great celebration the way the Irish among you often do. I would much rather have you come willingly and hug me back instead of being such scaredy cats, which brings us to Fear.

MEET FEAR, MY LOVER AND PARTNER IN CRIME

Now don't be afraid. I realize you can't help yourself, but I am so very happy to introduce you to Fear, my lover, ally, and constant companion. Like the Great Mystery, Fear is a glorious paradox. Here I am telling you don't be afraid, and in the same breath I am telling you that Fear absolutely revels in the attention and is often spurned and misunderstood right alongside me. To give it the proper respect it deserves I'll quote William James from back in nineteen-o-two.

"The ancient saying that the first maker of the Gods was fear receives voluminous corroboration from every age of religious history; but none the less does religious history show the part which joy has evermore tended to play. Sometimes the joy has been primary; sometimes secondary, being the gladness of deliverance from the fear."

Maybe deliverance comes from running *to* the fear instead of away from it?

Like me, my trusty sidekick wants you to know us better and though it sounds counterproductive, Fear is the happiest when embraced like me. To make the point, Fear never tires of this African proverb that demonstrates how Fear teaches.

When lions hunt on the savannas they position their youngest most able hunters to wait in tall grass on one side of a herd while the older weakest members of their pride who have lost most of their teeth go to the other side where they roar powerfully. Hearing the frightening roars stampedes the herd into the jaws and claws of the waiting hunters.

The moral of the story:

Run *toward* the roar.

Fear and I are inseparable, and whether you know it or not *you* are just as inseparable as we are. You might think of it as a three way unholy alliance, but it is more accurate to think of our collaboration as a holy alliance. Fear and I are intimate in so many ways with each other and with you! Aside from all of our other connections, many of which you have probably never even considered, my dedicated partner-in-crime serves us in many ways, chief among them as my herald.

When I come for what looks to you like my final visit, most of the time Fear announces my coming. It's all part of the Great Mystery, and much like me, Fear has many faces; among them mortal fear, fear of the unknown, and an endless variety of phobias. Fear serves us with the same selfless, unconditional, sometimes all consuming love in one of its more popular forms as Panic in much the same way that I hold my infinite love for you.

Though I would much rather have you embrace me with the same love I have for you, your fear of me is not unfounded. Fear in and of itself helps you to survive even though your survival is illusory because in the physical world you only survive because I allow you to. When it's time for you to come with me I may or my not have Fear announce my presence. Sometimes we're just having a little fun checking in and lurking just to let you know that you *are* alive. I'm a little embarrassed to admit that I find these play times entertaining because the greater truth of it is that I am ever present and in the minds of many all-powerful, but if you get a sense of the bigger picture, a more benign way to see Fear and I is as the face of the mystery, or perhaps better put the faceless face of the mystery.

We are elusive, yet we can come at a moment's notice.

I want to compliment you on sticking around and giving us your attention in the face of what we represent. Whether you acknowledge it or not, Fear is one of your greatest guides and teachers. Many think of our coming as a final visit to leave the life that you've known, but I want to remind you of the possibility that we may just be your escort into the next life if there is such a thing. I'd love to tell you, but then – well you know.

In much the same way that I come to you in any number of ways, my lover Fear also comes in different ways, only Fear visits with you more often, sometimes for the silliest reasons. Where I come mostly uninvited, you literally invite Fear, sometimes consciously and sometimes unconsciously, but the invitation always comes from *you* whether you know it or not. The daredevils among you flirt with Fear often, which we find flattering as it is also a flirtation with me, and I for one love being seduced.

Aside from this special visit we are having now, I may check in with you from time to time, especially when you're older. I know you feel my touch when I do, thanks to Fear's help, but for the most part I only come once in your lifetime while Fear visits all the time. If it weren't for my endless patience that might make me jealous, but it doesn't. Fear honors me like a talented announcer doing a commercial for a movie preview by reminding you of my imminent visit and I am secure in the knowledge that you will always come to me in the end like a lost, faithful dog who longs for and misses his loving master.

Technically speaking, Fear is a feeling induced by a perceived danger or threat that causes a change in metabolic and organ functions that provokes behavior like fleeing, hiding, or freezing in response to a specific stimulus occurring in the present or in anticipation of a future threat to your body or your life. This response comes from the perception of danger leading to a confrontation with or escape from the threat in a fight or flight response which in extreme cases can result in a paralyzing freeze reaction. In humans and in animals Fear is regulated by the process of cognition and learning so it is judged as rational and appropriate or irrational and inappropriate. An irrational Fear is called a phobia.

Fear is closely related to, but different from anxiety which comes from threats perceived as uncontrollable or unavoidable. The Fear response serves survival by generating appropriate behavioral responses, so it has been preserved through evolution.

Flight or fight is an inborn response for coping with danger by accelerating your breathing and widening your central blood vessels as well as increasing muscle tension that includes contracting the muscles attached to each hair follicle resulting in the proverbial goose bumps that Fear is so famous for.

Fear's arrival also causes sweating, increased blood glucose, increased serum calcium and white blood cells, and an alertness that can disrupt sleep and cause butterflies in the stomach, all of which tells you that you are indeed scared. If you are frail of health and have a weak heart, then this can be enough to send you into my waiting arms.

You can cultivate specific fears by learning through experience or by watching a traumatic accident. If a child falls into a well and struggles to get out, they might develop a fear of wells, heights, enclosed spaces, or water. These instincts go deep and are part of a primitive survival system seated deep in the brain in places like the amygdala. This part of the brain is affected both when someone observes another person experiencing an aversive event knowing that the same treatment awaits them, and when the person themselves are put in a fear provoking situation showing that fear can develop from both conditions, not just from personal history. People who have damage to their amygdala cannot experience fear which you might think of as a good thing, after all fearlessness is considered a sign of bravery, but this can result in bringing you closer to me as this lack of fear can put you in dangerous situations where I might step in without warning.

Many fears are learned and the capacity to fear is part of human nature. Certain fears, like fear of animals and fear of heights are more common than others. Much like my appearances, Fear and its associated sensations are considered unpleasant, but like me, Fear is your friend and loves you more than you know. Primitive humans were quick to fear dangerous situations which made them more likely to survive and reproduce. These primal fears were passed on to successive generations reinforcing natural selection in the form of adaptations that have developed during different time periods.

Some deep-seated fears, like fear of heights, fear of snakes, and others like fear of mice and insects are not unfounded. Mice and insects often carry infectious disease and are harmful to crops and stored foods and many snakes are deadly poisonous. As sinister as all these denizens may be to you, I love them all in their own unique ways because they serve as my agents who have dedicated their lives to helping me in my great work which shows how much they appreciate the gift of existence that I grant them all — including you. You might learn something from their devotion to something unquestionably greater than they are.

You know who.

In your modern times, one list of your top ten fears are terrorist attacks, spiders, death, failure, war, criminal or gang violence, being alone, the future, and nuclear war.

Third place? Seriously? You are more afraid of spiders than me? Too funny! Were I an egotist I could be upset about this, but on closer examination terrorist attacks and spiders when they are poisonous are acting as my agents, so I don't mind sharing the spotlight, especially when I think of them as opening acts for my grand appearances.

Another list says flying, heights, clowns, intimacy, death, rejection, people, snakes, failure, and driving. Here I have been lowered to fifth place. What's up with that? I can understand flying and heights as they are real dangers and sometimes have an intimate connection to me, but clowns? Are you kidding? I guess that shows how funny *you* are. Intimacy is almost as bad, but when I think of it in terms of how intimate I am with you it's a little easier for me to accept.

In still another ludicrous survey the most common fears are demons, ghosts, evil powers, cockroaches, spiders, snakes, heights, water, enclosed spaces, tunnels, bridges, needles, social rejection, failure, examinations, and public speaking.

At least I can comfort myself with the knowledge that I am not only more powerful than all of them, but many of them act as my agents, so though you may not consciously acknowledge my part in the collaboration, I am present in the ones that count.

In the bigger picture, thoughts of my arrival in what is called death anxiety is multidimensional, something that more accurately represents my real nature because it covers fears related to your own death, the death of others, fear of the unknown after I take you, fear of obliteration, and fear of the dying process, which includes fear of a slow demise and a painful one. Aside from some of the ridiculous and not so ridiculous fears I mentioned, ask yourself, is your fear of Me reasonable? After all, my arrival is certain.

In what was called a Multidimensional Fear of Death Scale which I think is more accurate and realistic than the other surveys, they listed Fear of Dying, Fear of the Dead, Fear of Being Destroyed, Fear for Significant Others, Fear of the Unknown, Fear of Conscious Death, Fear for the Body After Death, and Fear of Premature Death. The most potent predictors of death fears were beliefs relating to your ability to generate spiritually based faith and inner strength, and beliefs relating to your perceived ability to manage activities of daily living.

Your psychologists have followed the thinking of the brilliant Mr. James and tested the idea that fear of me motivates religious commitment and that assurances about an afterlife alleviate that fear. Religiosity can be related to fear of me when the afterlife is portrayed as a time of punishment. Those who have been firm in their faith who attend weekly religious services are the least afraid of dying. Church centered religiousness and de-institutionalized spiritual seeking are also viable ways of approaching fear of me in old age.

I find it comical the way people get more religious the closer they get to me because they know I am coming sooner every day, but they need not worry in these desperate moments, for my love is unconditional, eternal, and all consuming.

I understand why you fear the unknown, but it's an irrational fear caused by negative thinking that comes from anxiety along with a feeling of dread that engages your nervous system to mobilize your bodily resources in the face of danger, putting you into fight or flight mode for no *real* reason. This irrational fear can extend into many areas like the hereafter, the next ten years, or tomorrow. Chronic irrational fear can wear your health down over time and bring you to me sooner rather than later, since what you think of as the stimulus is usually nonexistent or delusional. This kind of fear creates additional diseases and disorders along with a primary disease or disorder that can also be behavioral or mental.

Being scared can cause you to be so afraid of what lies ahead that you can't plan, pay attention to, or evaluate what is happening in the present moment. Being in situations that are uncertain and unpredictable causes anxiety along with other psychological and physical problems, especially for those who engage in it constantly like in war zones, places of conflict, terrorism, abuse, or other traumatic environments that I like to frequent.

Fear can become a real party animal and grow like wildfire when it is time for a visit, which flatters me, as I know deep down it is another clever way to bring my loved ones home to me.

Back in sixteen-ninety-two some adolescent girls began having fits described as being beyond the power of epileptic fits that triggered the infamous Salem Witch trials that ended with twenty executions and five other deaths.

Well done, Fear. Clever and well done.

Mass hysteria anyone?

Fear works in that way at all levels of society from family and friends to communities, towns, cities, states, countries, and the world in any number of forms, concentrations, and speeds. Politicians, terrorists, and other power brokers use it to manipulate the masses into making bad decisions, or force them to act in ways detrimental to their person, but serve the will of the manipulators.

Aside from that it's one of our favorite ways of bringing people home to me because it gives us a lot of attention, like I am the celebrity and Fear is shining the spotlight on me. I know that sounds narcissistic, but it shows they are giving me the respect I more than deserve, after all, I do rule *all* of them.

Seeing as you have stuck with me this far and have not run off, I've decided to share what you might call a trade secret that Fear and I have, in the same spirit of a magician sharing a trick known only to privileged insiders.

Bugs, fish, birds, lizards, animals, and humans have special smells called pheromones that are alarm substances to defend themselves and inform their groups of danger, throwing them into fight or flight behaviors that spread throughout the group in moments. This is one of our secret triggers.

I don't want to get too scientific on you, but I want to mention neurochemicals because they are great allies who tie in with the amygdala and other fear centers that permeate you. They are intimate with Fear in much the same way that *I* am intimate with Fear; a microcosm in the macrocosm.

I don't take it personal when you deny me. At the same time I have to admire your efforts when you try, even though you are in a no win situation, but you are ingenious in your own studies of yourself and neurochemistry. You've even come up with a drug treatment for Fear conditioning through your amygdala that prevents fear behaviors, but Fear is more complicated than simply forgetting or deleting memories, so your psychologists have come up with what they call cognitive behavioral therapy that gets people to confront their fear over and over again; in other words, running toward the roar!

As I mentioned, Fear and I are intimate and I enjoy lurking behind all these other fears, even if they are often baseless. I enjoy being the be all and the end all. Your fear of the end of your life and its existence is your fear of me and I appreciate the respect. This particular base fear was formalized in the lives of your ancestors in rituals designed to help reduce your fear of my impending visit and they played a big part in the cultural ideas you now carry. This has helped drive changes in your social formations and when you get right down to it communities came about because people lived in fear that forced them to unite to fight dangers together instead of alone.

I've only scratched the surface of how Fear works with me, and much like me, and life in general, it is unpredictable and can come at any time in the blink of an eye. For all intents and purposes, you can think of Fear as sitting in with us from here on out the way a musician sits in with a band, and going forward you can think of us as one and the same. We really are *that* close.

As part of social formations and rituals religion has arisen, and religion itself is filled with fears that humans have clung to for centuries. These fears aren't just physical fears like the problems of life and death, they are also moral.

I am seen, rightfully so in many respects I may add, as a boundary to another world which is always different depending on how each of you have lived your lives. It's quite subjective and something that gives life to the Great Mystery because in the end it is always speculation no matter who or what you may worship. The origins of these intangible fears are not found in your present world. Fear has been a huge influence on things like morality which flies in the face of your concepts of moral absolutism and moral universalism which state that your morals are rooted in the divine natural laws of the universe and are not generated by any human feeling, thought, or emotion.

I am and have been looked at in so many different ways that aside from your present multitudinous religions and beliefs, I thought we might have some fun looking at some of your history to explore where all these fears come from.

FACES OF DEATH

The fact that I am ubiquitous, omniscient, and have infinite access to knowledge far outside your limited perception of history, time, physics, and virtually everything else you *think* you know has its challenges, so I'm working hard to keep things as simple as possible for you.

Seeing as we are getting closer. Yes, pun intended! In getting to know these different sides to me, I thought you might like to see how humanity has referred to me through the ages to get some background into how you think of me now, even though you still can't comprehend me.

I've been part of your life from the beginning and if you want to know the truth, long before that. Life and I are inseparable in the same way Fear and I are, although sometimes Fear acts on its own, but even then it is in cahoots with me and Life in some way. The major difference between Fear and Life for me is that I hold a tighter reign on Life as it is the gift that I bless you with, even though it is only for a short time. Fear does so much for me on so many levels that I pretty much let it do what it wants, but I can step in and intervene whenever I choose.

Strolling down Memory Lane is less than the blink of an eye for me and even less than that in the big picture. My goal is to put things in ways you can relate to, to give you the biggest picture I can of our history together.

More often than not you personify me in a male form, but in some of your cultures you describe me as female. The truth of the matter is that I exist outside of and am far more infinite than any simplistic male female divisions you can conjure. Although I am admittedly incomprehensible and beyond classification, I'm still willing to make an effort to get acquainted in the best way I can by sharing how I have been seen throughout the ages in different parts of the world.

Egypt is a good place to start as the remains of their culture is one of the oldest, most sophisticated, and most mysterious. They called me Anubis, which is the Greek name that gave me a god status associated with mummification and the afterlife.

From around thirty-one-hundred until about twenty-six-eighty-six BC when the dead were buried in shallow graves the Egyptians showed me with a jackal head and body because jackals were associated with cemeteries where they uncovered bodies and ate their flesh. Later they showed me as a canine or a man with a canine head which was the African golden wolf. You could say I was the first werewolf!

I was thought of as a protector of graves and an embalmer. My big job was a god who ushered souls into the afterlife with a scale that weighed their heart to determine whether a soul could enter the realm of the dead. They showed me as being black, a color that symbolized both rebirth and the discoloration of corpses after embalming. At some point they replaced me with Osiris as the Lord of the Underworld, but that didn't matter to me. That was just me wearing another mask. I never change. The only thing that changes is the names and faces you give me. I am eternal.

Around three-fifty to thirty BC Egypt was ruled by Greek pharaohs who merged me with their god Hermes and called me Hermanubis because we both guided souls to the afterlife. They continued to worship me in Rome through the second century and talked about me in this form in the alchemical and hermetical literature of the Middle ages and the Renaissance.

More often than not the Greeks and Romans scorned me as an animal headed god that they thought of as bizarre and primitive, and the Greeks, bless their little hearts, mockingly called me "Barker", but they came a little closer to the truth when they associated me with Sirius in the Heavens and Cerebrus and Hades in the underworld. Plato often had Socrates utter oaths "by the dog of Egypt" both for emphasis and to appeal to me as Anubis, an arbiter of truth in the underworld.

Showing me as a dog or a jackal might seem demeaning, but they did see me as a god. I don't care how anyone sees me, after all I am invisible. I like to think that dogs and jackals are a better image than that silly Grim Reaper, and then there is that whole thing about unconditional love and loyalty that goes with spelling dog backward.

I was called Mot to the Canaanites as a god of death who was the son of the king of the gods El. The Phoenicians also worshiped me as Mot which became Maweth, the devil or angel of death in Judaism. Even back then I was seen as either an angel or devil, depending on who you asked. Is there *really* a difference? If I weren't secure in myself this could have triggered an identity crisis, but those are the kinds of things that happen when you represent the Great Mystery and I love being part of that!

In ancient Greek religion and mythology I was Thanatos, one of the children of Nyx, which meant night. Sometimes they showed me as a bearded, winged man, and less often as a bearded, winged youth. I had a twin, Hypnos, the god of sleep and together we represented a gentle passing where Hermes helped me take the deceased to the near shore of the river Styx where the boatman Charon conveyed them to Hades. I had two sisters called the Keres, blood drinking, vengeful spirits of violent, untimely deaths who had fangs, talons, and wore bloody clothes.

The Greeks called Eros the God of Sensual Love and Desire my older brother and counterpart. The Romans called him by your more popular name of Cupid. Were I a lesser being I would be envious of the fact that he was represented by a bow, arrows, hearts, wings, and kisses while they continued to show me as a rictus grinning skull carrying a scythe. To add insult to injury some myths credit Eros with being a primordial god involved in the beginning of the cosmos, but all of this is vanity because It is still me at the core of it all.

Because I am eternal and enduring I am beyond all that pettiness, but I felt compelled to point out the slight here. As a matter of fact, if Eros gets the credit for the beginning, then I like to think of myself as the end and I am magnanimous enough to share credit as two sides of the same coin joined at the hip as two faces of the Great Mystery.

Eros appeared in ancient Greece under different guises in the earliest sources called the cosmogonies that referred to the mystery religions. In early Greek poetry and art he was shown as an adult male who embodied sexual power, and he was a profound artist. They credited him with being the son of Aphrodite whose mischievous interruptions in the affairs of gods and mortals caused love bonds to form, often illicitly, then he was shown as a blindfolded child which led to the cute, chubby little Cupid you plaster all over your silly Valentine cards.

Eros the god of love was credited with being the fourth god to come into existence after Chaos, Gaia the Earth, and Tartarus the abyss. Though they never quite came out and said it, if you think it through, I am Tartarus, the bad guy characterized as an abyss used as a dungeon of torment and suffering for the wicked and as a prison where souls are judged after leaving the earth plane. It's the place where the wicked receive divine punishment. My old pal Satan would take up this mantle years later.

Because of my intimate connection with the Great Mystery, the ancient Greeks thought of Tartarus as both a deity, thank you very much, and as a place in the underworld. Ancient Orphic sources and the mystery schools credited Tartarus as the unbounded first-existing entity that the Light and the cosmos were born from.

I like that idea better and it might be a little closer to the truth than a grinning skeleton carrying a scythe. After all Satan's other name of Lucifer does mean the bearer of light or morning star and they show *him* as a red guy running around in red underwear with horns and a pointed tail carrying a pitchfork.

In your supposedly modern age, many of you think of the Thanatos Eros partnership as the sex and death connection which validates me as the beginning and the end of one and the same Great Mystery. Tribal cultures still honor this in sacred circles that acknowledge the bigger picture of four seasons where the dead of winter is relatively still and lifeless followed by the birth of spring, the burgeoning life and maturing blossoms of summer, and the dying life of autumn, and all of the life that springs forth at that appropriately named time of year feeds on the death and decay that precede it. That ought to tell you something about the brilliance of the Great Mystery and how intimately connected we are.

Prehistoric cultures embraced the primal truth of this greater reality and honored it in all aspects of their lives, but as you grew in your quest to get smarter, it could be argued that by questioning what is beyond your comprehension and trying to impose your limited definitions on what is incomprehensible to you, you dumbed yourselves down and brought yourself further from the infinite truth of the Great Mystery.

Aristotle, one of the first purveyors of the written word that hastened your separation from the natural world and led you to your present state of chaos and disconnection believed that each sex act had a life-shortening effect. Many centuries later this troubling idea resurfaced in the work of metaphysical poets like John Donne, who famously said, "Since each such act, they say, diminisheth the length of life a day ... I'll no more dote and run to pursue things which hath endamaged me."

If you were to ask the male praying mantis being eaten by his lover during the act of copulation whether the metaphysical poets were right in saying that the orgasm is a little death, he would probably agree. He'd probably even drop the word little. You would most likely get the same answer from the Pacific salmon that spawns once and dies, but does that make it true for you?

Does sex compel me to come for you sooner in your already short life? Are aging and death the price you pay for sex? Does it make sense to think in terms of a reproductive duty to the species, leaving you surplus when duty is done? If this were true, what would you make of post-menopausal women?

As it turns out Aristotle was right. Sort of. There is a relationship between me and sex, but it is even more interesting than he suspected. In eighteen-eighty-one the German naturalist August Weismann realized that in multicellular bodies like yours there is a division of labor between two kinds of cells. On the one hand there is the germ line, the egg or sperm-forming cells of the ovary or testis that transmit your genes into the next generation. Weismann called the rest of the cells that make up the other organs of the body, the soma.

In the early stages of life on earth before the distinction between germ-line and somatic cells evolved, the responsibility for generating new individuals was shared by every cell. Most organisms were unicellular and their descendants are still with us today in the forms of bacteria, amoebae, and other life forms, but as cells came to live in clumps of genetically identical clones, the separation of germ-line and soma offered new opportunities for some of them freed from the need to support procreation to become specialists.

Inside of you are red blood cells that transport oxygen and other nutrients around your body, white blood cells that police it for intruders to destroy them, and brain and nerve cells engineered for the conduction of electrical signals. The cells of the lens of the eye are uniquely translucent so they can transmit and focus light on the retina.

The distinction between germ-line and soma enabled extraordinary advances in the evolution of higher forms of life and it is this, not sex, that causes you to age and come home to me, further proof of how ubiquitous I am. Yes, there are species that age and don't have sex, and there are species that have sex and don't age, like freshwater Hydras that are capable of sex, but often don't bother and make do with vegetative reproduction by budding. Almost any part of a Hydra can generate a new individual because its germ-line permeates its body and it has no real soma to speak of. It is this lack of distinction between germ-line and soma that allows Hydras to evade the aging process.

This immortality of the germ-line is real. If you could trace your ancestry back to the earliest forms of life on earth you would discover an unbroken chain of cell divisions that made you what you are today.

If Aristotle had been right in his assertion that romantic sex had a life shortening effect, and if he had been a fruit fly, he would have been correct. Unmated fruit flies live longer, but in humans there is no evidence that sexual activity shortens life. In fact the reverse has been suggested and there is no proof that having children shortens your longevity, however contrary to parent's experience this may seem, but there is evidence of a trade-off between our genetic tendencies to long life and fertility, so sex and I are indeed deeply connected, but not in the way poets thought.

Sorry for getting off on a scientific tangent, but it's hard to stay focused when everything is so intimately connected. Remember, you come from the Great Mystery through the sex act and the magical portal that is woman, and you come back to the Great Mystery through me.

My intention was to talk about our history together, so let's move forward and escape the cradle of civilization and the beginnings of your misguided thought into more traditional systems of mythological belief in how you have thought of me in different times and parts of the world.

In Breton folklore I was a spectral figure that portended my arrival called the Ankou or Angau in Welsh, which was believed to be the spirit of the last person that died within the community. I appeared as a tall, haggard figure with a wide hat and long white hair or a skeleton with a revolving head who saw everyone everywhere while driving a deathly wagon or cart with a creaking axle piled high with corpses. A stop at a cabin meant instant death for those inside.

In Ireland I was a creature known as a dullahan whose head was tucked under his or her arm. Dullahans were not one, but an entire species, and the head was said to have large eyes and a smile that could reach its ears. The dullahan rode a black horse or a carriage pulled by black horses that stopped at the house of someone about to die, called their name, and the person would die. The dullahan did not like being watched. It was believed that if they knew someone was watching them they would lash that person's eyes with a whip made from a spine, or they tossed a basin of blood on the person as a sign that they were the next to die.

Ireland also had a female spirit known as Banshee who heralded the death of a person by shrieking or keening. The banshee was described in Gaelic lore as wearing red or green, usually with long, disheveled hair. She could appear in lots of different forms, most often as an ugly, frightful hag, but she could also appear as young and beautiful. In Ireland and parts of Scotland a traditional part of mourning is the keening woman who wails a lament. When several banshees appeared at once it indicated the death of someone great or holy. Some tales said that the woman, though called a fairy, was a ghost, often of a specific murdered woman, or a mother who died in childbirth.

In Scottish folklore there was belief in a black, dark green or white dog known as a Cù Sìth that took dying souls to the afterlife, and in Welsh Folklore Gwyn ap Nudd was the escort of the grave, the personification of me and Winter who led the wild hunt to collect wayward souls and escort them to the Otherworld. Sometimes it was Melwas, Arawn or Afallach in a similar position.

In Mexican culture La Calavera Catrina is a female character that symbolizes me. She is an icon of the Mexican Day of the Dead, a holiday that focuses on the remembrance of the dead.

It's nice to finally get a change of image and a little respect in a celebratory day dedicated to me!

Our Lady of the Holy Death, Santa Muerte is a female deity of Mexican folk religion whose faith has been spreading in Mexico and the United States. In Spanish the word *muerte*, which means death in English, is a female noun, so it is common in Spanish-speaking countries for me to be personified as female. This also happens in other Romantic languages like French, *la mort*, Portuguese *a morte* and Italian *la morte*.

Since the pre-Columbian era Mexican culture has maintained a reverence toward me which can be seen in the commemoration of the Day of the Dead. Elements of that celebration include the use of skeletons to remind people of their mortality. The cult of Santa Muerte is a continuation of the Aztec cult of the goddess of death Mictecacihuatl, Nahuatl for Lady of the Dead clad in Spanish iconography.

In Aztec mythology, Mictecacihuatl is the Queen of Mictlan, the underworld, ruling over the afterlife with Mictlantecuhtli, another deity designated as her husband, so the Aztecs saw it as a family affair. Her role was to keep watch over the bones of the dead. She presided over the ancient festivals of the dead that evolved from Aztec traditions into the modern Day of the Dead after synthesis with Spanish cultural traditions. She is said to preside over the contemporary festival as well and is known as the Lady of the Dead since it is believed that she was born, then sacrificed as an infant. Mictecacihuatl was represented with a defleshed body and with jaw agape to swallow the stars during the day.

Wouldn't you know it? Just when I thought they might make me look more flattering with feminine touches and go back to the old skull and bone stuff, although I have to admit, I love the swallowing stars part.

San La Muerte, Saint Death is a skeletal folk saint venerated in Paraguay, the Northeast of Argentina and southern Brazil. Okay, no party here, but at least they see me as a saint instead of a screaming ragged looking hag. As the result of internal migration in Argentina since the nineteen-sixties, the veneration of *San La Muerte* has been extended to Greater Buenos Aires and the national prison system as well. Even jailbirds need love! Saint Death is depicted as a male skeleton usually holding a scythe. Although the Catholic Church in Mexico has attacked the devotion of Saint Death, many devotees consider the veneration of San La Muerte as part of their Catholic faith. The rituals connected to and powers ascribed to San La Muerte are very similar to those of Santa Muerte.

In Guatemala I am San Pascualito, a skeletal folk saint venerated as King of the Graveyard. Sorry to see here that I am seen again as a skeleton with a scythe, sometimes wearing a cape and crown, but at least I am associated with the curing of diseases.

In the Brazilian religion Umbanda, the Orixa Omolu personifies sickness, me, and the cure. Kind of a mixed bag here. The image of me is also associated with Exu, lord of the crossroads, who rules midnight and the cemeteries.

In Haitian Vodou, the Guédé are a family of spirits that embody me and fertility. There's the sex death thing popping up again, but it's more of a family affair with this crew. Gotta love that!

Moving back across the ocean, in Poland they call me *Śmierć*, and I am back to that tired old Grim Reaper look, but instead of a black robe, I have a white one. Also, due to grammar, I am a female as the word *śmierć* is of feminine gender. I am mostly seen as an old skeletal woman, but at least there's a little variety in this one.

In Serbia and other Slavic countries, my Grim Reaper is known as *Smrt*, Death, or *Kosač*, Billhook. Slavic people found this a lot like the Devil and other dark powers. One popular saying about me as the Grim Reaper is, "Death is not choosing a time, place or years," which means she is destiny.

In the Netherlands and to a lesser extent in Belgium, my personification was a guy known as *Magere Hein or* Meager Hein. Historically, I was sometimes referred to as *Hein* or variations like *Heintje*, *Heintjeman* and *Oom Hendrik*, Uncle Hendrik. Related archaic terms refer to me as *Beenderman*, Bone-man, *Scherminkel*, a very meager person, or skeleton, and *Maaijeman*, mow-man, a reference to my trusty scythe.

The concept of *Magere Hein* was pre-Christian and tied to Pagan beliefs, but it was Christianized and gained its modern name and features of the scythe, skeleton, black robe and the rest of it during the Middle Ages. No respect, I tell you! The designation Meager comes from its portrayal as a skeleton, which was influenced by the Christian Dance of Death theme that was prominent in Europe during the late Middle Ages. Hein was a Middle Dutch name originating as a short form of *Heinric*, probably related to the comparable German concept of Freund Hein. Many of the names given to me also refer to the Devil, showing how his status as a feared and evil being led to him being merged into the concept of Satan. I'll talk more about my buddy Satan later.

In Belgium, this personification of me is called *Pietje de Dood*, Little Pete, the Death. As with some of the Dutch names, it can also refer to the Devil.

In Norse mythology I was personified in the shape of Hel, the goddess of death and ruler over the realm of the same name, where she received a portion of the dead. In the times of the Black Plague, I was often depicted as an old woman known by the name of Pesta, meaning plague hag who wore a black hood. Pesta went into towns carrying either a rake or a broom. If she brought the rake, some people would survive the plague and if she brought the broom everyone would die.

Talk about a stereotype that is hard to shake, later Scandinavians adopted the classic Grim Reaper with a scythe and black robe too!

Lithuanians named me *Giltinė*, deriving from the word *gelti*, meaning to sting. Giltinė was an old, ugly woman with a long blue nose and a deadly poisonous tongue. The legend says that Giltinė was young, pretty, and communicative until she was trapped in a coffin for seven years. The goddess of death was a sister of the goddess of life and destiny, Laima, symbolizing the relationship between beginning and end.

About time someone acknowledged the Great Mystery, and big surprise here, the Lithuanians also adopted the Grim Reaper with a scythe and black robe.

The Sanskrit word for me is *mrityu*, which is often personified in Dharmic religions. In Hindu scriptures I am called King Yama up there with a saint. That's more like it! *Yama Rājā* is also known as the King of Karmic Justice, *Dharmaraja* as one's karma at death was thought to lead to a just rebirth. Yama rode a black buffalo and carried a rope lasso to carry the soul back to his home, called Naraka, Pathalloka, or Yamaloka.

The Hindus have many reapers, but some say there is only one who disguises himself as a small child. His agents, the Yamadutas, carry souls back to Yamalok. Much like Anubis of the Egyptians, all the accounts of a person's good and bad deeds are stored and maintained by Chitragupta. The balance of these deeds allows Yama to decide where the soul has to reside in its next life, following the theory of reincarnation. Yama is also mentioned in the Mahabharata as a great philosopher and devotee of the Supreme Brahman. Yama was introduced to Chinese mythology through Buddhism. In Chinese, he is known as King Yan or Yanluo, ruling the ten gods of the underworld Diyu. He is normally depicted wearing a Chinese judge's cap and traditional Chinese robes and appears on most forms of Hell money offered in ancestor worship. From China, Yama spread to Japan as the Great King Enma, ruler of Jigoku; Korea as the Great King Yŏmna, ruler of Jiok; and in Vietnam as *Diêm La Vương*, ruler of Địa Ngục or *Âm Phủ*.

Separately, the *Kojiki* says that the Japanese goddess Izanami was burnt to death giving birth to the fire god Hinokagutsuchi and entered a realm of perpetual night called Yomi-no-Kuni. Her husband Izanagi pursued her there but discovered his wife was no longer beautiful. After an argument, she promised to take a thousand lives every day, becoming a goddess of death. There are also death gods called shinigami who are closer to the Western tradition of the Grim Reaper.

In Korean mythology, the equivalent of the Grim Reaper is the Netherworld Emissary Jeoseung-saja depicted as a stern and ruthless bureaucrat in Yŏmna's service. As a psychopomp he escorted all good or evil souls from the land of the living to the netherworld when the time came.

In Abrahamic religions the Angel of the Lord smited one-hundred-eighty-five-thousand men in an Assyrian camp and when the Angel of Death passed through to smite the Egyptian first-born, God prevented the destroyer from entering houses with blood on the lintel and side posts. The destroying angel raged among the people in Jerusalem and the angel of the Lord was seen by King David standing between the earth and the Heaven having a drawn sword in his hand stretched out over Jerusalem. The Book of Job also uses the general term destroyers, which tradition identifies with destroying angels, and Proverbs uses the term angels of death. The angel Azra'il is sometimes referred as the Angel of Death as well.

At least they are showing me as an angel or angels which I think is closer to the truth than being a simplistic death dealing devil demon.

Jewish tradition refers to me as the Angel of Dark and Light, a name stemming from Talmudic lore, which is even closer to the truth, and it's more encompassing. There is also a reference to Abaddon, The Destroyer, an Angel who is known as the Angel of the Abyss.

In Talmudic lore, I am characterized as archangel Michael.

A promotion?

In Hebrew scriptures I am sometimes personified as a devil or angel of death, so both sides of the road are covered. In the Book of Hosea and the Book of Jeremiah, I am Maweth or Mot a deity Yahweh can turn Judah over to as punishment for worshiping other gods.

The memitim are a type of angel from biblical lore associated with the mediation over the lives of the dying like Anubis did for the Egyptians. That name is derived from the Hebrew word *mĕmîtîm*, meaning executioners, slayers, or destroyers, and refers to angels that brought about the destruction of those the guardian angels no longer protected. While there is some debate regarding the exact nature of the memitim, it is generally accepted that they were killers of some sort.

According to the Midrash, a rabbinic work that interprets Scripture, I appear as the Angel of Death, "who was created by God on the first day. His dwelling is in Heaven, whence he reaches earth in eight flights, whereas Pestilence reaches it in one. He has twelve wings. 'Over all people have I surrendered thee the power,' said God to the Angel of Death, 'only not over this one Moses, which has received freedom from death through the Law.' It is said of the Angel of Death that he is full of eyes. In the hour of death, he stands at the head of the departing one with a drawn sword, to which clings a drop of gall. As soon as the dying man sees Death, he is seized with a convulsion and opens his mouth, whereupon Death throws the drop into it. This drop causes his death; he turns putrid, and his face becomes yellow. The expression 'the taste of death' originated in the idea that death was caused by a drop of gall."

The soul escapes through the mouth, or through the throat, therefore the Angel of Death stands at the head of the patient. When the soul forsakes the body its voice goes from one end of the world to the other, but is not heard. The drawn sword of the Angel of Death shows that the Angel of Death was figured as a warrior who killed off the children of men. "Man, on the day of his death, falls down before the Angel of Death like a beast before the slaughterer". Samuel's father said: "The Angel of Death said to me, 'Only for the sake of the honor of mankind do I not tear off their necks as is done to slaughtered beasts'."

In later representations the knife replaces the sword and reference is made to the cord of the Angel of Death, which indicates death by throttling. Moses said to God, "I fear the cord of the Angel of Death". Of the four Jewish methods of execution, three are named in connection with the Angel of Death, burning by pouring hot lead down the victim's throat, slaughtering by beheading, and throttling. The Angel of Death administers the particular punishment that God has ordained for the commission of sin.

A sword belongs to the equipment of the Angel of Death and the Angel of Death takes on the form that best serves his purpose. He appears to a scholar in the form of a beggar imploring pity. "When pestilence rages in the town, walk not in the middle of the street, because the Angel of Death, pestilence strides there; if peace reigns in the town, walk not on the edges of the road. When pestilence rages in the town, go not alone to the synagogue, because there the Angel of Death stores his tools. If the dogs howl, the Angel of Death has entered the city; if they make sport, the prophet Elijah has come." The destroyer in the daily prayer is the Angel of Death. There are six Angels of Death: Gabriel over kings; Ḳapẓiel over youths; Mashbir over animals; Mashḥit over children; Af and Ḥemah over man and beast."

The Rabbis found the Angel of Death mentioned in Psalms where the Targum translates: "There is no man who lives and, seeing the Angel of Death, can deliver his soul from his hand." In Ecclesiastes, it explained in Midrash Rabbah in the passage: "One may not escape the Angel of Death, nor say to him, 'Wait until I put my affairs in order,' or 'There is my son, my slave: take him in my stead.'" Where the Angel of Death appears there is no remedy but his name. If one who has sinned has confessed his fault, the Angel of Death may not touch him.

By acts of benevolence the anger of the Angel of Death is overcome. When one fails to perform such acts, the Angel of Death makes his appearance. The Angel of Death receives his orders from God. As soon as he has received permission to destroy, he makes no distinction between good and bad. In the city of Luz, the Angel of Death has no power. When the aged inhabitants are ready to die, they go outside the city. A legend to the same effect existed in Ireland in the Middle Ages.

In Islam, Archangel Azrail is the Angel of Death. He and his subordinates pull the souls out of bodies and guide them through the journey of the afterlife. Their appearance depends on the person's deed and actions. Those that did good see a beautiful being and those that did wrong see a horrific monster.

Islamic tradition discusses in great detail what happens before, during, and after my visit. The angel of death appears to the dying to take out their souls. The sinners' souls are extracted in a most painful way while the righteous are treated easily. After the burial two angels, Munkar and Nakir come to question the dead to test their faith. The righteous believers answer correctly and live in peace and comfort while the sinners and disbelievers fail and punishments ensue.

My coming is a significant event in Islamic life and theology and is seen not as the termination of life, but as the continuation of life in another form. In Islamic belief God made this worldly life as a test and a preparation ground for the afterlife, and with death this worldly life comes to an end. Every person has one chance to prepare themselves for the life to come where God will resurrect and judge every individual and entitle them to rewards or punishment based on their good or bad deeds and I am seen as the gateway to and beginning of the afterlife. In Islamic belief, my coming is predetermined by God, and the exact time of a person's death is known only to God.

I like much of what the Islamic traditions have to say, but I feel compelled to remind you that in the end, what I am sharing here about them as well as all the other ways of believing are myths from different cultures which often veer off into ludicrousness through ignorance of the Great Mystery. Yes, it's true that I make no distinction between good and bad, but I cannot be overcome, I have *all* the power, and I have no anger, only my unconditional, all consuming love for you.

I have only touched on the larger, more prevalent systems of belief and the ways that people have represented me throughout your history. There are innumerable belief systems, myths, representations, and practices among lesser known societies that many have never heard of. There is some grain of truth in every one of them, but overall they contain fallacies and fantasies about how I will come for you and how I will appear to you in our special once in a lifetime intimate moment, which in the end is what makes *all* of these beliefs mythical. Only *I* represent the face of the one ultimate truth which you can only grasp at as the inevitable arrival of the Great Mystery that I will bring to you at a time and place that only I know.

TO KNOW ME IS TO LOVE ME – PART I

I am the one constant through the ages which makes me a de facto immortal who outshines all, or is that out darkens all? Regardless of who you ask, in the end it always comes down to perspective. If you could see what I see you would understand what is incomprehensible in your limited three dimensional perception, but you have to pay the price of admission to do that, and the thought of that terrifies you.

Throughout the ages in different parts of the world I have been seen and thought of in many different ways and I had many faces, male, female, animal, other beasts, and any number of unflattering creatures. I am often seen as the face of sheer terror, and I would be remiss if I did not give credit to my beloved partner in crime Fear for contributing to that. All of these ways of characterizing me depend on how well you think you know me and how much effort you have put out to make my acquaintance.

I am both Heaven and Hell, light or dark depending on your perspective, but all the forms, definitions, and images you give me are nothing more than speculations and imaginings.

Not one of you really knows me and my true nature, and the very act of trying to define me diminishes the infinite vastness that I am, but I do appreciate your efforts, even though they are often misguided. The *only* way you can come to know me in the most intimate way will be on my terms at the time and place of *my* choosing.

Within your ponderings lies a flattering irony, for as much as you try to deny me, you cannot stop thinking about me. Unlike animals which for the most part accept their fate, when it is your time you puzzle over my true nature driven by an awareness of your own mortality. It's a major concern of all your religious traditions and philosophical inquiries. Among these concerns are beliefs in resurrection, an afterlife, reincarnation, rebirth, or whether consciousness ceases to exist in what to atheists is eternal oblivion.

Atheists may deny the existence of a God or gods, but they cannot deny me.

Because of all these diverse beliefs regarding me and what happens when I come to bring you home, different cultures each have unique ways of paying their respects to mark this once in a lifetime passing from your world. I am pleased to be celebrated at the center of so many customs and traditions around the world. Much of it revolves around the care of the dead, which I find quaint, mostly because whatever remains behind is just that; remains. The spirit of whoever inhabited that corruptible package of flesh, blood, and bone are gone from your three dimensions and no longer exist in the world as you know it, but this custom is in memoriam to how they appeared to you and I respect that.

In many traditions these customs prepare them for the afterlife, which I have to give you credit for. You have no conception about what it truly entails, but it does honor that transition and it deals with the disposal of bodies after I take the soul.

In Tibet the body is given a sky burial and left on a mountain top. Mummification or embalming are also prevalent in some cultures in an effort to slow down the decay.

Everyone comes to me in the end even if it is through human folly. They often come through ignorance and absurdity, especially in misguided cultures with moralistic views about the death penalty.

They use me as a threat.

What if I'm not the penalty, but the reward?

Depending on your cultural context, sexual crimes like adultery and sodomy carry the death penalty as well as religious crimes like renunciation of your religion. In many cultures drug trafficking is also a capital offense. In China human trafficking and serious cases of corruption are punished by the death penalty and in militaries around the world courts-martial have imposed death sentences for offenses like cowardice, desertion, insubordination, and mutiny.

Death in warfare and in suicide attacks also have cultural links. With the popularity of terrorism and further back in time with suicide bombings, kamikaze missions in World War Two, and suicide missions in a host of other conflicts in history, including the present day mass shootings, death for a cause by suicide attack and martyrdom have served me well.

Suicide, particularly euthanasia are understood differently in divergent cultures. In Japan, ending a life with honor by seppuku was considered a desirable death, whereas in traditional Christian and Islamic cultures, suicide is viewed as a sin.

Talking about me and witnessing the myriad ways I take you is difficult for most cultures. Western societies like to treat my visit with the utmost material respect, with an official embalmer and associated rites, while Eastern societies like India are more open to accepting and honoring my visit with a funeral procession of the corpse that ends in an open air burning-to-ashes. Either way is fine with me because after it is all said and done, I end up with *you* no matter how you end up coming regardless of what happens to your remains after you leave with me.

To the ancient Egyptians I was not the end of life but a transition to another plane of reality. Once the soul successfully passed through judgment by the god Osiris it went on to an eternal Paradise, The Field of Reeds, where everything lost returned and souls lived happily ever after. Even though the Egyptian view of the afterlife was the most comforting of any ancient civilization, people still feared me.

Rituals mourning the dead didn't change much in Egypt's history and are still similar to how people react to death in your present day. One might think that knowing their loved one was on a journey to eternal happiness or living in Paradise would have made the ancient Egyptians feel more at peace with me, but inscriptions mourning the death of a beloved wife, husband, child, or pet all expressed the grief of loss, how they missed the one who left, and how they hoped to see them again in Paradise, but they didn't express the wish to die and join them anytime soon. There are texts that express a wish to die, but they are to end the sufferings of one's present life, not to exchange one's mortal existence for the hope of eternal Paradise.

In Buddhist practice I play an important role. Awareness of me is what motivated Prince Siddhartha to strive to find the deathless and attain enlightenment. In Buddhist doctrine I function as a reminder of the value of having been born as a human being which is the only state one can attain enlightenment in, and they use me to remind themselves that they shouldn't take that for granted. The belief in rebirth among

Buddhists doesn't remove anxiety about me since all existence in the cycle of rebirth is thought to be filled with suffering. Being reborn many times does not always mean that one progresses.

In Judaism I have been seen as tragic and intimidating. People who come into contact with corpses are thought of as ritually impure. There are a variety of beliefs about the afterlife in Judaism, but none of them contradict the preference of life over death. This is partially because the finality of my arrival puts a cessation to the possibility of fulfilling any commandments.

I am far more than the mere ending of life as you know it. Yes, life and I are considered to be two sides of the same coin, but the deeper truth is that life is the gift I bless you with for your brief visit to the three dimensional existence that you cling so tenaciously to.

Your fear of me often brings denial to the greater reality that I represent which is pointless. That very same fear and your mourning rituals hold hope for immortality, if not in this earthly life through reincarnation, ressurection, or some other mythical belief designed to avoid our meeting, then in the hopes of an afterlife that grants you a continued existence on the other side of the portal that I am the keeper of.

Your hope for life after I take you is grounded in the concept that an essential part of your identity or stream of consciousness that you identify with continues to manifest after the cessation of life in your physical body. I would be remiss if I did not give my compatriot Fear credit for helping to stimulate all of this. According to many of your ideas about the afterlife, the essential aspect of the individual that lives on after death might be some partial element, or the entire soul or spirit that carries your personal identity, or it might not in cases like Indian nirvana.

Your belief in an afterlife can be naturalistic or supernatural in contrast to the atheistic belief in oblivion after dying.

In some systems of belief, continued existence takes place in a spiritual realm and in other popular views the individual can be reborn into this world and begin the life cycle over again with no memory of what they did in the past. In this belief rebirths and deaths take place over and over again until the individual gains entry to a spiritual realm or Otherworld.

Abrahamic traditions believe that the dead go to a specific plane of existence after I take them, or they are ordained by God or some other divine judgment based on their actions or beliefs during life. In contrast, in systems of reincarnation the nature of continued existence is determined by the actions of the individual in the ended life rather than through the decision of a different being.

Theists believe some kind of afterlife awaits people when they die. Members of non-theistic religions believe in an afterlife too, but without reference to a deity. In still another spin on beliefs, the Sadducees, an ancient Jewish sect believed that there is a God but no afterlife. Many religions whether they believe in the soul's existence in another world like Christianity, Islam, and many pagan belief systems, or in reincarnation like in Hinduism and Buddhism, believe that your status in the afterlife is a reward or punishment for your conduct during life.

Reincarnation is the idea that someone starts a new life in a different physical body or form after each biological death. It is referred to as rebirth or transmigration and is a part of the *Samsāra* doctrine of cyclic existence. It is also a central tenet of all major Indian religions, namely Buddhism, Hinduism, Jainism, and Sikhism. The idea of reincarnation is found in many cultures. A belief in rebirth was held by Greek historic figures like Pythagoras, Socrates, and Plato. It is also a common belief of ancient and modern religions like Spiritism, Theosophy, and Eckankar and is found in tribal societies around the world in places like Australia, East Asia, Siberia, and South America.

Although the majority of denominations in the Abrahamic religions of Judaism, Christianity, and Islam do not believe that individuals reincarnate, particular groups within them do refer to reincarnation, among them the mainstream followers of Kabbalah, the Cathars, Alawites, the Druze, and the Rosicrucians who speak of a life review immediately after death before entering the afterlife's planes of existence before the silver cord is broken, followed by a judgment that is more like a final review or end report of your life.

The idea of an afterlife played an important role in Ancient Egyptian religion. They believed that when the body died, parts of its soul known as *ka*, a body double, and the *ba*, its personality went to the Kingdom of the Dead. While the soul dwelt in the Fields of Aaru Osiris demanded work as restitution for the protection he provided. Because of this statues were placed in tombs to serve as substitutes for the deceased.

Arriving at your reward in the afterlife was a demanding ordeal requiring a sin-free heart and the ability to recite spells, passwords, and formulas of the Book of the Dead. In the Hall of Two Truths, the deceased's heart was weighed against the *Shu* feather of truth and justice taken from the headdress of the goddess Ma'at. If the heart was lighter than the feather they could pass on, but if heavier they were devoured by the demon Ammit.

The Egyptians believed that being mummified and put in a sarcophagus was the only way to have an afterlife. Only if the corpse had been properly embalmed and entombed in a mastaba could the dead live again in the Fields of Yalu and accompany the Sun on its daily ride. Due to the dangers the afterlife posed, the Book of the Dead was placed in the tomb with the body as well as food, jewelery, and curses.

Egyptian civilization was based on religion and their belief in rebirth after death became the driving force behind their funeral practices. Death was seen as a temporary interruption rather than complete cessation of life, and eternal life could be ensured by means like piety to the gods, preservation of the physical form through mummification, and the provision of statuary and other funerary equipment. Each human consisted of the physical body, the *ka*, the *ba*, and the *akh*. The Name and Shadow were also living entities. To enjoy the afterlife all these elements had to be sustained and protected from harm.

The Greek god Hades was the king of the underworld, where souls lived after death, and the god Hermes was the messenger of the gods who took the dead soul to the underworld which was called Hades or the House of Hades. Hermes left the soul on the banks of the River Styx, the river between life and death.

Charon, also known as the ferry-man, took souls across the river to Hades if the soul had gold, so the family of the dead soul put coins under the deceased's tongue when they buried them. Once they crossed, the soul was judged by Aeacus, Rhadamanthus, and King Minos, then the soul was sent to Elysium, Tartarus, Asphodel Fields, or the Fields of Punishment. The Elysian Fields were for those who lived pure lives, and it consisted of green fields, valleys, and mountains. Everyone there was peaceful and contented, and the Sun always shone.

Tartarus was for the people who blasphemed against the gods, or were rebellious and consciously evil.

The Asphodel Fields were for those whose sins equalled their goodness, were indecisive in their lives, or were not judged. The Fields of Punishment were for people who sinned often, but not so much as to be deserving of Tartarus where the soul was punished by being burned in lava or stretched on racks. Some heroes of Greek legend were allowed to visit the underworld. The Romans had similar beliefs about the afterlife, with Hades being known as Pluto. In the ancient Greek myth about the Labours of Heracles, the hero had to travel to the underworld to capture Cerberus, the three-headed guard dog, as one of his tasks.

In the *Dream of Scipio,* Cicero described an out of body experience of the soul traveling high above the Earth looking down at the small planet from far away.

In Virgil's *Aeneid,* the hero Aeneas traveled to the underworld to see his father. At the River Styx he saw the souls of those not given a proper burial forced to wait by the river until someone buried them. While down there with the dead he was shown the place where the wrongly convicted resided and the fields of sorrow where those who committed suicide and regretted it resided, including Aeneas' former lover. He heard the groans of the imprisoned in Tartarus where the titans and powerful non-mortal enemies of the Olympians lived. He also saw the palace of Pluto and the fields of Elysium where the descendants of the divine and bravest heroes lived, the river of forgetfulness, and Lethe, which the dead had to drink from to forget their life and begin anew. His father showed him all of the future heroes of Rome who would live if Aeneas fulfilled his destiny in founding the city.

The Norse idea of an afterlife has lots of descriptions, but the most well-known are Valhalla, the Hall of the Slain, or the Chosen Ones where half the warriors who died in battle joined the god Odin who ruled over that majestic hall in Asgard. The other half joined the goddess Freyja in a great meadow in a Field of the Host called Fólkvangr. The Covered Hall referred to as Hel, is similar to Hades from the ancient Greeks. There, something like the Asphodel Meadows of the Greeks is where where people who neither excelled in what is good nor excelled in what is bad go after they die to be reunited with their loved ones. Niflhel, The Dark or Misty Hel is a realm analogous to the Greek's Tartarus which is the deeper level beneath Hel. Those who break oaths and commit other vile things are sent there to suffer harsh punishments.

She'ol in the Hebrew Bible is a place of darkness where both the righteous and the unrighteous go regardless of the moral choices made in life. It is a place of stillness and darkness cut off from life and from God. The inhabitants of Sheol are the shades who are entities without personality or strength. Under certain circumstances they are thought to be able to be contacted by the living the way the Witch of Endor contacted the shades of Samuel for Saul.

While the Hebrew Bible described Sheol as the permanent place of the dead, around five-hundred BC to seventy AD a more diverse set of ideas developed where Sheol was considered the home of both the righteous and the wicked separated into respective compartments. In other systems of belief it was considered a place of punishment meant for the wicked dead alone. When the Hebrew scriptures were translated into Greek in ancient Alexandria, the word Hades was substituted for Sheol which was reflected in the New Testament where Hades is both the underworld of the dead and the personification of the evil it represented.

In the Talmud, after death the soul is brought for judgment. Those who led pristine lives entered into the *Olam Haba,* known as the world to come. Most don't enter the world to come immediately, but experience a review of their earthly actions where they are made aware of what they have done wrong. Some view this as a re-schooling with the soul gaining wisdom as one's errors are reviewed. Others view it as a time to include spiritual discomfort for past wrongs.

At the end of this time which is not longer than a year, the soul takes its place in the world to come. Although discomforts are part of some Jewish conceptions of the afterlife, the concept of eternal damnation prevalent in other religions is not a tenet of the Jewish afterlife. According to the Talmud, extinction of the soul is reserved for a smaller group of malicious and evil leaders whose evil deeds go way beyond norms, or who lead large groups of people to utmost evil.

Maimonides described the *Olam Haba* in spiritual terms, relegating the prophesied physical resurrection to the status of a future miracle unrelated to the afterlife or the Messianic era. According to Maimonides, an afterlife continued for the soul of every human being separated from the body it was housed in during its earthly existence.

The Zohar described Gehenna not as a place of punishment for the wicked, but as a place of spiritual purification for souls.

At least they are showing a little bit of leeway here.

There's hope!

There is no reference to reincarnation in the Talmud or any prior writings, but many rabbis recognize it as being part of Jewish tradition. Called *gilgul*, it became popular in folk belief and is found in Yiddish literature among Ashkenazi Jews. A few kabbalists thought that some human souls could end up being reincarnated into non-human bodies. These ideas are found in a number of kabbalistic works from the thirteenth century, and among mystics in the late sixteenth century.

Mainstream Christianity believes in the Nicene Creed that includes the phrase: "We look for the resurrection of the dead, and the life of the world to come." Punishments are part of many Christian conceptions of the afterlife, and the idea of eternal damnation is a widespread tenet of the Christian afterlife.

Jesus maintained that the time would come when the dead would hear the voice of the Son of God and all who were in the tombs who did good deeds would come out to the resurrection of life while those who did wicked deeds would be subject to the resurrection of condemnation.

The Book of Revelation talks about God and the angels fighting Satan and demons in an epic battle at the end of times when all souls would be judged along with ghostly bodies of past prophets and transfiguration. Hippolytus of Rome characterized the underworld of Hades as a place where the righteous dead, waiting in the bosom of Abraham for their resurrection, would rejoice at their future prospect while the unrighteous would be tormented at the sight of the lake of fire they were destined to be cast into.

Gregory of Nyssa championed the possibility of purification of souls after death in connection with purgatorial flames. The noun purgatorium comes from the Latin, meaning place of cleansing, and is used to describe a state of painful purification of the saved after life.

In the eighteenth century which was considered the Age of Enlightenment Emanuel Swedenborg wrote theological works that described the afterlife in detail according to his claimed spiritual experiences. The most famous of these was *Heaven and Hell which* covered topics like marriage in Heaven where all angels are married, children in Heaven raised by angel parents, time and space in Heaven, or the lack of. Swedenborg also wrote about after-death awakening in the World of Spirits in a place halfway between Heaven and Hell where people first wake up after death, and the allowance of free will choice between Heaven or Hell as opposed to being sent to either one by God, as well as the eternity of Hell that one could leave. He asserted that all angels or devils were once people on earth.

I'm glad he got that all figured out.

On the other hand, the Age of Enlightenment produced more rationalist philosophies. Many deist freethinkers held that belief in an afterlife with reward and punishment was a necessity of reason and good morals.

Some Christians deny that entry into Heaven can be properly earned and believe it is a gift that is solely God's to give through his unmerited grace. They credit this belief to a passage from St. Paul. "For it is by grace you have been saved, through faith—and this not from yourselves, it is the gift of God, not by works, so that no one can boast."

Since the Protestant Reformation, Lutheran and Calvinist theological traditions emphasize the necessity of God's undeserved grace for salvation and reject the notion that would make man earn salvation through good works. Other Christians do not accept this doctrine, leading to controversies about grace, free will, and the idea of predestination. The belief that Heaven is a reward for good behavior is a common folk belief in Christian societies, even among members of churches who reject it.

Some Christian believers downplay the punishment of Hell. Universalists teach that salvation is for all. Jehovah's Witnesses and Seventh-day Adventists teach that sinners are destroyed rather than tortured forever. In the New Testamant John says that only those that accept Jesus will be given eternal life, so people who do not accept him cannot burn in Hell for eternity because Jesus has not given them eternal life. Instead it says they will perish.

Talk about exclusivity!

What about all those Buddhists, Islamists, Jews and other "unwashed masses", not to mention all those primitive tribes around ther world? What did they do to be left out of the party?

If I were someone who had Christianity forced on me with these kinds of threats and promises, I would take the stance of Groucho

Marx, the twentieth century comedian, who famously said, "I don't want to belong to any club that will accept me as a member."

Christianity depicts a distinction between *angels*, those divine beings created by God before the creation of humanity that are used as messengers, and *saints*, the souls of humans who received immortality from the grace of God through faith in Jesus Christ of Nazareth, who dwells in Heaven with God.

I'll take Groucho, thank you very much!

Latter Day Saints believe that the soul existed before earth life and will exist in the hereafter. According to them angels are either spirits that have not yet come to earth to experience their mortality, or spirits or resurrected beings that have already passed through mortality and do the will of God. According to LDS Doctrine, Michael the Archangel became the first man on earth, Adam, to experience his mortality. The Angel of Moroni visited the boy Joseph Smith after living out his mortal life in ancient America. Later he received Angelic administrations from the Apostles Peter, James, and John, John the Baptist, and others.

I'll still take Groucho over that exclusive nonsense.

What I really find ludicrous is that all these self-important believers have been laying claim and trying to define and dissect what is *mine*, something far outside any conception they can imagine, but I have to admit to finding infinite humor in the fact that all these constricted delusions are shattered when the reality that I represent fully asserts itself.

In all of these imagined scenarios we cannot forget the idea of Limbo, which was elaborated on by theologians in the Middle Ages. It was never recognized as a dogma of the Catholic Church but it was a popular theological theory within it. The idea of Limbo is that unbaptized innocent souls like those of infants and virtuous individuals who lived before Jesus Christ was born on earth, or those that died before baptism existed in neither Heaven or Hell.

Those souls neither merited the beatific vision, nor were subjected to any punishment because they were not guilty of any personal sin although they had not received baptism, so they still bore original sin and were seen as existing in a state of natural, but not supernatural, happiness until the end of time. In other Christian denominations it was described as an intermediate place or state of confinement in oblivion and neglect.

At least they left the door open.

Beyond the second coming of Jesus, bodily resurrection, and final judgment, Orthodoxy does not teach much else, but unlike Western forms of Christianity, Orthodoxy is traditionally non-dualist and does not teach that there are two separate locations of Heaven and Hell. It acknowledges that the location of one's final destiny, Heaven or Hell, as being figurative and that the final judgment is simply one's uniform encounter with divine love and mercy, depending on the extent that one has been transformed, partaken of divinity, and is compatible or incompatible with God.

Joseph Smith of The Church of Jesus Christ of Latter-day Saints presented an elaborate vision of the afterlife as the scene of an extensive missionary effort by righteous spirits in Paradise to redeem those still in darkness; a spirit prison or Hell where the spirits of the dead remain until judgment. It is divided into two parts: Spirit Prison and Paradise. Together they are known as the Spirit World.

Maybe that's why the Mormons spend so much time knocking on doors.

They believe that Christ visited spirit prison and opened the gate for those who repent to cross over to Paradise, which is similar to the Harrowing of Hell in some mainstream Christian faiths. Both Spirit Prison and Paradise are temporary according to LDS beliefs. After the resurrection, spirits are permanently assigned to three degrees of Heavenly glory, determined by how they lived; Celestial, Terrestrial, and Telestial. The Sons of Perdition, or those who have known and seen God and deny it are sent to the realm of Satan which is called Outer Darkness, where they are destined to live in misery and agony forever.

Somehow I don't think Buddha is going to buy into that one, let alone all the other passed over deities.

The Celestial Kingdom is believed to be a place where we can live eternally with our families, but progression does not end once one has entered the Celestial Kingdom, it extends eternally. According to the *True to the Faith* handbook on doctrines in the LDS faith, the Celestial Kingdom is the place prepared for those who have received the testimony of Jesus and been made perfect through Jesus the mediator of the new covenant, who wrought out this perfect atonement through the shedding of his own blood. To inherit this gift followers have to receive the ordinances of salvation, keep the commandments, and repent of their sins.

We can't forget the Jehovah's Witnesses who sometimes use terms like afterlife to refer to any hope for the dead, but understand it to preclude belief in an immortal soul. Individuals judged by God to be wicked like in the Great Flood or at Armageddon are given no hope of an afterlife, but believe that after Armageddon there will be a bodily resurrection of both the righteous and unrighteous dead, but not the wicked. Survivors of Armageddon and those who are resurrected are expected to gradually restore earth to a Paradise. After Armageddon unrepentant sinners are punished with eternal death defined as non-existence.

Chalk one up for the atheists!

These exclusive claims to divinity have sprung from the same prehistoric roots, and have diverged even further from each other, each claiming to hold the real truth.

Christianity is built on the written word of God alone and see the Bible as the infallible rule of faith that gives them the sure knowledge of the Gospel.

Mormons believe that God was once as we are and is now an exalted man, and that men can become gods. Joseph Smith referred to this as the great secret. They also assert that God's marriage partner is their mother in Heaven and that they are the spirit children of that union and that good works are necessary for salvation. They also believe that if it had not been for Joseph Smith and the restoration of truth, there would be no salvation outside the church of Jesus Christ of Latter-day Saints.

Jehovah's Witnesses, through The New World Translation, claim that their version of the Bible is scholarly and more accurate even though the translators were not biblical scholars or theologians. They believe that salvation comes through works and not faith alone, and that Jesus Christ was a perfect man. In their Bible, Christ is a god, but not *the* God. They don't believe everything that Jesus claimed about Himself. The New World Translation and the Watchtower tracts systematically set out to eliminate evidence for the deity of Christ.

I'll bet that pisses the Christians off!

The Seventh-day Adventists put their own colorful spin on things teaching that the first death, or death brought about by living on a planet with sinful conditions like sickness, old age, accidents and other misfortunes is a sleep of the soul.

Adventists believe that the body and breath of God equals a living soul. Like Jehovah's Witnesses they use key phrases from the Bible like, "For the living know that they shall die: but the dead know not any thing, neither have they any more a reward; for the memory of them is forgotten." Adventists also point to the fact that the wage of sin is death and God alone is immortal and that God will grant eternal life to the redeemed resurrected at Jesus' second coming. Until then, all those who have died are asleep. When Jesus the Christ, who is the Word and the Bread of Life comes a second time, the righteous will be raised incorruptible and will be taken in the clouds to meet their Lord. The righteous will live in Heaven for a thousand years where they will sit with God in judgment over the unredeemed and the fallen angels.

During the time the redeemed are in Heaven the Earth will be devoid of human and animal inhabitation. Only the fallen angels will be left alive. The second resurrection is of the unrighteous, when Jesus brings the New Jerusalem down from Heaven to relocate to Earth. Jesus will call to life all those who are unrighteous. Satan and his angels will convince the unrighteous to surround the city, but Hell fire and brimstone will fall from Heaven and consume them, thus cleansing Earth of all sin. The universe will then be free from sin forever. This is called the second death.

A copycat?

Sorry, but as far as I am concerned, I am the *only* coming, the first *and* the last, even if they do say that imitation is the greatest form of flattery.

According to the Adventists the new earth God will provide an eternal home for all the redeemed and a perfect environment for everlasting life where Eden will be restored. The great controversy will be ended and sin will be no more. God will reign in perfect harmony forever.

In this Adventist view, if you are righteous, you get to sit with God up in the clouds to judge all those poor unredeemed souls. You have to admit, this option is appealing, but I'm afraid I have to invoke the Groucho clause on this one too.

Jesus really gets around and I have to admit, he is special to me. Many have been killed and tortured for not believing in him, in fact wars have been fought over belief in him for hundreds and hundreds of years, so he has been a great help in bringing many of you home to me. He deserves special attention, so I'll be talking about him later, but for now, in the interest of fairness, let's take a look at some other scenarios of different belief systems, which although they would deny it, also stem from the same prehistoric roots.

TO KNOW ME IS TO LOVE ME – Part II

The Islamic belief in the afterlife in the Quran is colorful and more expansive because it takes into consideration other forms of life. The Arabic word for Paradise is *Jannah* and Hell is *Jahannam*. Their comfort level while in the grave depends on their level of *iman* or faith in the one almighty creator or supreme being, God or Allah. To achieve healthy *iman* you have to practice righteous deeds or your level of *iman* chokes, shrinks, and can wither away if you do not practice Islam long enough, so the depth of practicing Islam is in good deeds. You can also acquire *tasbih* and recite the names of Allah in such a way as *Subahann Allah* or Glory be to Allah over and over again like a Hindu or Buddhist mantra to acquire good deeds.

In the Quran God warns about grievous punishment to those who do not believe in the afterlife and He lets mankind know that Hell is prepared for those who deny their meeting with him. I can relate to that as many of you try to deny your meeting with me, but as you know, I refuse to take no for an answer when the time comes.

Islam teaches that the purpose of Man's creation is to worship Allah alone, which includes being kind to other human beings and life including bugs and trees by not oppressing them.

That's my favorite part of it!

Islam also teaches that the life you live on Earth is a test for you and to determine each individual's ultimate abode, whether it's punishment or *Jannat* in the afterlife, which is eternal and everlasting.

Jannah and *Jahannam* both have different levels. *Jannah* has eight gates and seven levels. The higher the level the better it is and the happier you are. *Jahannam* has seven deep terrible layers and the lower the layer the worse it is. Individuals will arrive at both everlasting homes during Judgment Day which commences after the Angel Israfil blows the trumpet the second time. Islam also teaches the continued existence of the soul and a transformed physical existence after death. Muslims believe there will be a day of judgment when humans will be divided between the eternal destinations of Paradise and Hell. A central doctrine of the Quran is the Last Day, when the world will be destroyed and Allah will raise all people and jinn from the dead to be judged.

Sounds familiar.

Until the Day of Judgment, deceased souls remain in their graves awaiting the resurrection, but they begin to feel a taste of their destiny to come. Those bound for Hell will suffer in their graves while those bound for Heaven will be in peace until that time.

The resurrection on the Last Day is physical and explained by suggesting that God will re-create the decayed body.

On the Last Day, resurrected humans and jinn will be judged by Allah according to their deeds. A soul's eternal destination depends on the balance of good to bad deeds in their life and they are either granted admission into Paradise to enjoy spiritual and physical pleasures forever, or they will be condemned to Hell to suffer spiritual and physical torment for eternity. The day of judgment is described as passing over Hell on a narrow bridge in order to enter Paradise. Those who fall, weighted by their bad deeds are destined to remain in Hell forever.

Looks like there's no parole there!

Ahmadi Muslims believe that the afterlife is not material, but spiritual. According to the founder of the Ahmadiyya sect, in Islam the soul will give birth to another rarer entity that will resemble the life on earth. This entity will bear a similar relationship to the soul that the soul has with the human existence on earth. On earth if a person leads a righteous life and submits to the will of God, his or her tastes become attuned to enjoying spiritual pleasures as opposed to carnal desires, and with this an embryonic soul takes shape. Different tastes are said to be born that those given to carnal passions find no enjoyment in, like when the sacrifice of one's own rights over that of others becomes enjoyable, or when forgiveness becomes second nature. In such a state a person finds contentment and peace at heart, and according to

Ahmadiyya beliefs, at this stage a soul within the soul has begun to take shape.

Sufi scholars define Barzakh as the intermediate realm or isthmus between the world of corporeal bodies and the world of spirits, and it's a means of contact between them. Without it there would be no contact between the two and both would cease to exist. Described as simple and luminous like the world of spirits it is also able to take different forms the way the world of physical bodies can. In broader terms Barzakh is anything that separates two things and has been called the dream world where the dreamer is in both life and death.

The teachings of the Bahá'í Faith say that the nature of the afterlife is beyond the understanding of the living just as an unborn fetus cannot understand the nature of the world outside the womb.

I have to say, this one has the ring of truth for me.

It also states that the soul is immortal and after death it will continue to progress until it attains God's presence. In Bahá'í belief, souls in the afterlife continue to retain their individuality and consciousness and can recognize and communicate spiritually with other souls they have made deep friendships with like their spouses.

The Bahá'í scriptures make distinctions between souls in the afterlife, and that souls will recognize the worth of their deeds and understand the consequences of their actions. Those souls who have turned toward God will experience gladness, while those who have lived in error will become aware of the opportunities they lost. Souls can also recognize the accomplishments of souls that have reached the same level as themselves, but not those of a higher rank.

In Hindu beliefs the Upanishads describe reincarnation. In the Bhagavad Gita, Krishna says that just as a man discards his old clothes and wears new ones, the soul discards the old body and takes on a new one. Hindus believe that the body is nothing but a shell and that the soul inside it is immutable, indestructible, and takes on different lives in cycles of birth and death. The end of this cycle is called *mukti,* and staying with the supreme God forever is *moksha* or salvation.

The Garuda Purana deals solely with what happens to a person after death where the God of Death Yama sends his representatives to collect the soul from a person's body when he is due to take the soul to Yama. A record of each person's timings and deeds is kept in a ledger by Yama's assistant, Chitragupta.

At least I'm getting some recognition here and they gave me an assistant!

After leaving the body a soul travels through a long dark tunnel toward the South. An oil lamp is lit and kept beside the head of the corpse to light the dark tunnel and allow the soul to travel comfortably.

The soul, called *atman* leaves the body and reincarnates according to the deeds or *karma* done in its last birth. Rebirth can be in the form of animals or other lower creatures if bad karmas were done, and in human form in a good family with a joyous lifetime if you were good in your last birth. In between the two births a human is required to face punishments for bad karmas in Hell, or enjoy the good karmas in Heaven. Whenever their punishments or rewards are over, they are sent back to earth.

A person stays with the God or ultimate power only when they discharge *yajna karma;* work done for the satisfaction of the supreme lord only in last birth which is also called *moksha* or *nirvana*, the ultimate goal of a self realized soul. *Atma* moves with *Parmatma* or the greatest soul. According to the Bhagavad Gita an *Atma* or soul never dies, but what does die is the body that is made of five elements, Earth, Water, Fire, Air, and Sky, while Soul is believed to be indestructible. None of the five elements can harm or influence it. Hinduism also describes the various Hells where a person is punished after death for bad *karmas*.

Hindus also believe that *inkarma is* the accumulated sums of one's good or bad deeds. *Satkarma* means good deeds and *vikarma* means bad deeds. According to Hinduism the concept of karma is as you sow, you shall reap, so if a person lived a good life they will be rewarded in the afterlife, and if not, their sum of bad deeds will be mirrored in their next life. Good karma brings good rewards and bad karmas lead to bad results. There is no judgment here. People accumulate karma through their actions and thoughts.

Buddhists say that rebirth happens without an unchanging self or soul passing from one form to another and the type of rebirth will be conditioned by the moral tone of the person's actions or karma. If a person has committed harmful actions of body, speech, and mind based on greed, hatred, and delusion, rebirth in a lower realm like the animal realm, a hungry ghost or a Hell realm is expected. On the other hand if a person has acted with generosity, loving kindness, compassion and wisdom, rebirth is in a happy realm; a human one, or one of many Heavenly realms. The mechanism of rebirth with karma depends on differing levels of karma. The most important moment that determines where a person is reborn into is their last thought. According to Theravada Buddhism, there are thirty-one realms of existence one can be reborn into.

Pure Land Buddhism of Mahayana believes in a special place apart from the thirty-one planes of existence called Pure Land. It is believed that each Buddha has their own pure land, created out of their merits for the sake of sentient beings who recall them mindfully so they can be reborn in their pure land and train to become a Buddha there. The main practice of Pure Land Buddhism is chanting a Buddha's name.

The Tibetan Book of the Dead explains the intermediate state of humans between death and reincarnation. The deceased will find the bright light of wisdom that shows a straightforward path upward and leave the cycle of reincarnation, but there are numerous reasons why the deceased don't follow that light. Some had no briefing about the intermediate state in the former life. Others follow their instincts like animals, and some have fear resulting from foul deeds in the former life or from insistent haughtiness. In the intermediate state the awareness is flexible, so it is important to be virtuous, adopt a positive attitude, and avoid negative ideas.

Ideas arising from the subconscious can cause extreme tempers and cowing visions. In this situation they have to understand that these manifestations are reflections of their inner thoughts. No one can hurt them because they have no physical body. The deceased get help from different Buddhas who show them the path to the bright light. The ones who don't follow the path will get hints for a better reincarnation. They have to release the things and beings that they still hang onto from the life before. It is recommended to choose a family where the parents trust in the Dharma and to reincarnate with the will to care for the welfare of all beings.

In spite of its quirks, this is a nice idea.

Buddhists say that, "Life is the cosmic energy of the universe and after death it merges with the universe again, and as the time comes to find the suitable place for the entity that died in the life condition, it gets born. There are ten life states of any life: Hell, hunger, anger, animality, rapture, humanity, learning, realization, bodhisattva and buddhahood. The life dies in its particular life condition and reborn into the same life condition."

Shinto, the traditional religion of Japan focuses on ritual practices carried out diligently to establish a connection between present-day Japan and its ancient past. It's common for families to participate in ceremonies for children at a shrine and have a Buddhist funeral at the time of death. In old Japanese legends the dead go to a place called *yomi,* a gloomy underground realm with a river separating the living from the dead that is similar to the Greek Hades. Shinto holds negative views on Me and corpses as a source of pollution called *kegare,* but I am also viewed as a path to deification in Shintoism as can be seen by how legendary individuals become enshrined after I take them.

Zoroastrianism says that the *urvan,* the disembodied spirit, lingers on earth for three days before departing downward to the kingdom of the dead ruled by Yima. For the three days that it rests on Earth, righteous souls sit at the head of their body, chanting the Ustavaiti Gathas with joy, while a wicked person sits at the feet of the corpse, wailing and reciting the Yasna. Zoroastrianism says that for righteous souls, a beautiful maiden, the personification of the soul's good thoughts, words, and deeds appears. For a wicked person, an old, ugly, naked hag appears. After three nights the soul of the wicked is taken by the demon Vizaresa to Chinvat bridge, and is made to go to darkness which is Hell.

Yima is believed to have been the first king on earth as well as the first man to die. Inside of Yima's realm spirits live a shadowy existence and are dependent on their own descendants still living on Earth who satisfy their hunger and clothe them through rituals done on earth.

Rituals done on the first three days are vital as they protect the soul from evil powers and give it strength to reach the underworld. After three days the soul crosses Chinvat bridge which is its Final Judgment where Rashnu and Sraosha are present. Rashnu is like Anubis of the Egyptians who holds the scales of justice. If the good deeds of the person outweigh the bad the soul is worthy of Paradise. If the bad deeds outweigh the good the bridge narrows down to the width of a blade-edge, and a horrid hag pulls the soul into her arms and takes it down to Hell with her. Misvan Gatu is the place of the mixed ones where the souls lead a gray existence lacking both joy and sorrow. A soul goes there if their good deeds and bad deeds are equal.

Depending on who you ask, Sikhism may or may not believe in the afterlife. Sikhs believe that the soul belongs to the spiritual universe which has its origins in God, but it's a matter of debate about the afterlife. Many endorse it and the concept of reward and punishment. There are verses in their *Guru Granth Sahib*, but many Sikhs believe otherwise and treat those verses as metaphorical or poetic.

The Guru Granth Sahib includes poetic renditions from multiple saints and religious traditions like those of Kabir, Farid and Ramananda. Their essential doctrine is to experience the divine through simple living, meditation, and contemplation. Sikhism also has the belief of being in union with God while living. Accounts of an afterlife are considered to be aimed at the prevailing views of the time to provide a reference without establishing a belief in the afterlife, so while it acknowledges that living the life of a householder is above the metaphysical truth, overall Sikhism is agnostic about the question of an afterlife.

If you study the Sikh Scriptures you will find the existence of Heaven and Hell mentioned in the *Guru Granth Sahib* and in *Dasam granth*. Sikhism believes in the existence of Heaven and Hell, but Heaven and Hell are created to temporarily reward and punish, and one will at some point be born again until they merge in God. According to the Sikh scriptures the human form is the closet form to God and the best opportunity for a human being to attain salvation and merge back with God. Sikh Gurus say that nothing dies, nothing is born, and everything is ever present, it just changes forms. Like standing in front of a wardrobe, you pick up a suit or a dress and wear it, then discard it and wear another one. In this view of Sikhism, your soul is never born and never dies. It is a part of God that lives forever.

Jainism believes in the afterlife and that the soul takes on a body based on previous karmas or actions performed by that soul through eternity. Jains also believe the soul is eternal and that the freedom from the cycle of reincarnation is the way to eternal bliss.

Wiccan afterlife is described as The Summerland where souls rest, recuperate from life, and reflect on the experiences they had during their lives. After a period of rest they are reincarnated and the memory of their previous lives is erased. Many Wiccans see The Summerland as a place to reflect on their life actions, not as a place of reward, but as the end of a life journey at an end point of incarnations.

Traditional African religions are diverse in their beliefs. Hunter-gatherer societies like the Hadza have no belief in an afterlife and the death of an individual is a straightforward end to their existence.

Ancestor cults are found throughout Sub-Saharan Africa, including cultures like the Yombe, Beng, Yoruba, and Ewe. The belief that the dead come back into life and are reborn into their families is given concrete expression in the personal names given to children. What is reincarnated are some of the dominant characteristics of the ancestor and not his soul. Each soul remains distinct and each birth represents a new soul. The Yoruba, Dogon, and LoDagoa have ideas similar to Abrahamic religions, but in most African societies there is an absence of clear-cut notions of Heaven and Hell, although there are notions of God judging the soul after death.

In some societies like the Mende, multiple beliefs coexist. The Mende believe that people die twice: once during the process of joining the secret society, and again during biological death when they become ancestors. Some Mende believe that after people are created by God they live ten consecutive lives, each in progressively descending worlds. One theme is that the ancestors are part of the world of the living and interact with it regularly.

In the hundreds of distinct American Indian languages, there is no single world that can be translated as religion, but this doesn't mean that they didn't have religion. It shows that religion was not a separate category of life but was closely integrated with their culture. Spirituality is a better word to describe how they believe. At the beginning of the European invasion there was no single Native American religion which makes it impossible to make broad generalizations about traditional American Indian beliefs about Me.

Many of the books written about American Indian beliefs by non-Indians are not about their traditional beliefs, but are filtered through Christianity and Christian concepts. As an example, the idea of a happy hunting-ground is modern and borrowed or invented by the white man.

For many American Indian cultures the focus of religion, particularly their ceremonies, was on maintaining harmony with the world with a focus on living in harmony *today*, not in the afterlife. For many Indians there is an awareness of Me and a vague concept of something happening after I come, but this is not dogmatic. They felt that they would find out when they die and in the meantime it's something they have no way of knowing anything about and therefore shouldn't waste time thinking about it.

Pretty smart, if you ask me.

While Christian missionaries were convinced that all religions had to have some concept of Heaven and Hell and some form of judgment after death, these were alien concepts to most American Indians. The missionaries took this as additional evidence that the Indians didn't have religion.

Among many of the Indian nations in Massachusetts there was the idea that after I came the soul would go on a journey to the southwest, eventually arriving at a village to be welcomed by the ancestors. In the same way, the Narragansett in Rhode Island viewed my coming as a transition between two worlds when the soul would leave the body and join the souls of relatives and friends in the world of the dead which lay to the southwest.

Among some of the tribes like the Beothuk and the Narragansett, it was felt that communication between the living and the dead was possible. Among the Narragansett the souls of the dead could pass back and forth between the world of the dead and the living and the dead could carry messages and warnings to the living. Among the Caddo on the Southern Plains, the living could send messages to their deceased relatives by passing their hands over the body of someone recently deceased from feet to head, then over their own body. In this way messages could be sent by the deceased to other dead relatives.

One common theme in many of the Indian cultures in North America is the idea of reincarnation and the idea that life and death are part of an ongoing cycle. Many Indians believed that one could be born more than once and some spoke of having full knowledge of a former incarnation.

In the Northwest Coast area many Indians believed in the reincarnation of people and animals, that the dead could visit this world, and that the living could enter the past. They also believed that memory survived from generation to generation and that their elders remembered the past because they lived it.

Among the Lenni Lenape female elders examined babies looking for signs of who they had been in an earlier life. These signs included keeping the body relaxed and the hands unclenched and reacting favorably to places and things associated with the dead relative.

Reincarnation was often seen as something that happened not just to humans but to animals too, so hunters thanked the animals they harvested so the soul of the animal would be reborn with good feelings toward the hunter and allow its physical form to be harvested again.

In many Indian cultures throughout North America, the names of the deceased were not, and in many cases are not, spoken. The deceased can be spoken about, but in an indirect way that doesn't use their name. Among the Navajo the name of the deceased was not mentioned for a year following my visit and after that the name of the deceased was rarely mentioned. The possibility of naming a place after a dead person was considered unthinkable and would have negative consequences for the soul of the deceased.

In South and Central American Indian tribal cultures the axis mundi is the world tree that extends from the earth up into the sky worlds and straight down into the underworlds framed by a strong east-to-west orientation that starts when the sun emerges out of primordial water on the edge of the earth to begin its journey over land. It moves north to cross the apex of the vertical axis at the center, then west where it goes underwater at the other edge, then south, followed by east at night.

The axis mundi represents the center of the universe constituted by a people's territory, village, house, and body, all of which are represented as a dynamic living structure in particular times and places. It is often thought of as the tree-of-life that grows and branches, creating a diversity of fruits and other beings that when violently cut down peppers the earth with a variety of life giving plants, animals, and human beings that transform into today's people and their living environments. It is also represented as a ladder or stairway coming out of deep earth from underwater extending up into sky worlds.

What indigenous people take to be salient in their pasts is bound to the landscape which is a sacred and cosmic phenomenon embodying everything that people identify with as themselves and other. Shamans travel the routes of these landscapes and mythopoetic history where they visit crystal castles and other locations to commune with any number of exotic beings and landscapes to see what can only be known by direct experience. The shaman is one who knows. Both male and female shamans exist, though males predominate. All fully human beings and some animals have shamanic power in them represented as their own life force that gives meaning to the cosmos, landscape, kin, enemies, home, and self.

In South America special totem animals include the anaconda of the water domain, the jaguar or puma of the earth domain, and the harpy eagle or condor of the sky domain. Great powers abide in the sky, earth, water, and under the earth they are concentrated in special places and objects. Control of these powers lies in the ability of shamans and their counterpart artists, speakers, dancers, and ritual specialists to move in and out of the world of spirits to cure body, soul, and psyche, and to see the everyday world and the cosmos in aesthetic patterns communicated through ritual, art, design, speech, drama, poetics, rhythm, and song. These prehistoric traditions are the most pure as they originate at the roots of all religious thought that has grown out of and splintered off into the multitude of conflicting systems of belief that make up the modern religions of the world.

Stepping forward into contemporary beliefs is a movement called Unitarian Universalists who believe that all souls will be saved and that there are no torments of Hell. Unitarian Universalists differ widely in their theology so there is no agreed upon stance on the issue. Although Unitarians believe in a literal Hell and Universalists believe that everyone goes to Heaven, modern Unitarian Universalists can be categorized into those believing in a Heaven, reincarnation, and oblivion like the atheists. Most Unitarian Universalists believe that Heaven and Hell are symbolic places of consciousness and their faith is largely focused on the worldly life rather than an afterlife.

According to Edgar Cayce who was known as the sleeping prophet, the afterlife consists of nine realms equated with the nine planets of astrology. The first, symbolized by Saturn, was a level for the purification of the souls. The second, Mercury's realm, gives the ability to consider problems as a whole. The third of the nine soul realms is ruled by Earth and associated with the Earthly pleasures. The fourth realm is where love is discovered and is ruled by Venus. The fifth is where limitations are met and is ruled by Mars. The sixth realm is ruled by Neptune, where creative powers are discovered that frees souls from the material world, and the seventh is symbolized by Jupiter, which strengthens the soul's ability to depict situations and analyze people, places, things, and conditions. The eighth afterlife realm is ruled by Uranus and develops psychic ability and the ninth afterlife realm is symbolized by Pluto, the astrological realm of the unconscious. This afterlife realm is a transient place where souls can travel to other realms or solar systems. It is the soul's liberation into eternity and the realm that opens the doorway from our solar system into the cosmos. I have to give Cayce some credit here as his system is not as ludicrous as some of the others that bigger numbers of people follow and believe in, and it includes the bigger cosmos!

Mainstream spiritualists postulate a series of seven realms not unlike Cayce's nine realms ruled by the planets. In these the soul moves higher as it progresses until it reaches the ultimate realm of spiritual oneness. The first realm, equated with Hell is the place where troubled souls spend a long time before being compelled to move up to the next level. The second realm where most souls move to is considered an intermediate transition between the lower planes of life and Hell, and the higher perfect realms of the universe. The third level is for those who have worked with their karmic inheritance and the fourth is where evolved souls teach and direct those on Earth. The fifth is where the soul leaves human consciousness behind and at the sixth the soul is aligned with cosmic consciousness and has no sense of separateness or individuality. At the seventh level the goal of each soul is to transcend its own sense of soulfulness and reunite with the World Soul and the universe.

All of these literal soul searching beliefs and inquiries into the Great Mystery and what happens when you pass through my portal into it is an attempt to look into the beyond. As you have progressed in the evolution of your societies things have moved beyond surrendering and abandoning to the mysticism of faith, which is a complete trust in something, whether in a God, gods, or the doctrines of religions without any tangible proof.

The prefix para means to go beyond and in the case of parapsychology it means to go beyond psychology to try and bridge and link the rational thinking and scientific method of psychology with what lies outside of it in the same way that metaphysics represents what lies beyond the laws of physics while remaining connected to it.

The Society for Psychical Research was founded in eighteen-eighty-two with the intention of investigating phenomena relating to Spiritualism and the afterlife. Its members still conduct scientific research on the paranormal. Some of the earliest attempts to apply scientific method to the study of phenomena relating to an afterlife were conducted by them.

Parapsychological investigation of the afterlife includes the study of hauntings, apparitions of the deceased, instrumental trans-communication, electronic voice phenomena, and mediumship as well as the study of near death experiences.

In an attempt to connect the spiritual with the physical, a study was conducted in nineteen-o-one to measure the weight lost by a human when the soul departed the body with Me to prove that the soul was material, tangible, and measurable. Although the results varied considerably from twenty one grams, for some people this figure became synonymous with the measure of a soul's mass. The results from this experiment have never been reproduced and are regarded as having no scientific merit.

In your present philosophy there remains the question of personal identity called open individualism which is similar to an old belief that individual existence is illusory, and our consciousness continues existing after death in other conscious beings. Problems arise with the idea of a particular person continuing after death, among them the idea that the materialist must have some kind of physical continuity, and then there is the question of personal identity. How can a person cease to exist in one place while an exact replica appears in another. If the replica had all the same experiences, traits, and physical appearances of the first person, you could attribute the same identity to the second.

In the panentheistic model of process philosophy and theology where the belief that the divine pervades and interpenetrates every part of the universe and extends beyond time and space, philosophers reject that the universe is made of substance. Instead they believe that reality is composed of living experiences, but in their view people don't experience subjective, personal immortality in the afterlife. They have objective immortality because their experiences live on forever in God who contains all that was. Other philosophers believe that people have subjective experience after death.

From a scientific viewpoint regarding the mind–body problem, most neuroscientists take the physicalist position that consciousness derives from and/or is reducible to physical phenomena like neuronal activity in the brain. The implication of this is that once the brain stops functioning at brain death, consciousness fails to survive and ceases to exist.

Psychological proposals for the origin of belief in an afterlife include cognitive disposition, cultural learning, and as an intuitive religious idea. In one study children were able to recognize the ending of physical, mental, and perceptual activity in death, but were hesitant to conclude the ending of will, self, or emotion in death.

After all this time throughout your history and all your faith, speculations, beliefs, and scientific approaches, you still do not know if there is an afterlife or if I bring you to one, or will you embrace oblivion, and if I did bring you to a Heaven, Hell, Limbo, Purgatory, or a Happy Hunting Ground, what would it be like? Is it one of these or maybe all of these, depending on what you believe, or maybe it is something that is simply beyond your limited comprehension of the infinite? Maybe the smartest thing to do is to follow Groucho's example.

If you ever did find out there would be no Great Mystery and I would lose my treasured fascination and mystique, but I know you will never stop trying to figure it out and you will never stop trying to outwit and avoid me.

You don't give up easily even when I do come for you.

All of these deities, wild imaginings, and the unquestionable certainties of so many faiths along with the many masks that people put on me to try and make sense out of my arrival, and the subsequent inexplicable disappearance of their loved ones after I take them from your precious three dimensional prison add to the power of my omniscience because I hold all the cards and I have all the answers which I will bless you with.

When you show up for our appointment.

IMMORTALITY

I admire your persistence and ingenuity in trying to deny me what is mine. I don't take it personal, in fact it's fascinating to watch how as time passes you try harder and harder with more complicated far-fetched schemes to put off the inevitable. I find it both endearing and entertaining, and would be remiss if I did not give my compadre Fear kudos for doing such an excellent job as a driving force behind the scenes.

The myths and fantasies around this impossibility go back far into prehistory. One of my favorites is the Fountain of Youth, a spring that was supposed to restore the youth of anyone who drank or bathed in its waters. Tales of fountains like this have been recounted across the world for thousands of years. Stories of similar waters were big among the indigenous people of the Caribbean who beleived in the restorative powers of the water in the mythical land of Bimini.

The legend became more popular when it was connected to the Spanish explorer Ponce de León. According to that story he was searching for the Fountain of Youth when he traveled to what is now Florida and was told by Native Americans that the Fountain of Youth was in Bimini.

Similar, but more credible because it employed the scientific approach, even if it is still an unrealistic fantasy, is the science of alchemy which aims to purify, mature, and perfect objects. Its common aims were the transmutation of base metals like lead into noble metals, particularly gold, and the creation of an elixir of immortality and panaceas that could cure any disease, as well as the development of a universal solvent. The perfection of the human body and soul was thought to result from the alchemical *magnum opus* in the Hellenistic and Western mystery traditions in the achievement of gnosis.

This also gave rise to the myth of the elixir of life, or elixir of immortality which was said to be a potion that granted the drinker eternal life and eternal youth and was said to cure all diseases. Alchemists have spent lifetimes trying to formulate it.

In China many emperors tried to discover the fabled drink with varying results. In the Qin Dynasty, Qin Shi Huang sent Taoist alchemist Xu Fu with five-hundred young men and five-hundred young women to the eastern seas to find it and they never came back. When Shi Huang Di visited, he brought 3000 young girls and boys, and none of them ever returned.

The ancient Chinese believed that ingesting long-lasting precious substances like jade, cinnabar or hematite brought longevity to the person who consumed them. Gold was considered particularly potent because it was a non-tarnishing precious metal. The idea of drinkable gold was found in China by the end of the third century BC. The most famous Chinese alchemical book known as Essential Formulas of Alchemical Classics was credited to Sun Simiao, a medical specialist called the King of Medicine by later generations. In it he discussed the creation of elixirs for immortality that included mercury, sulfur, the salts of mercury, and arsenic, as well as those for curing diseases and the fabrication of precious stones.

Many of those substances were toxic and resulted in Chinese alchemical elixir poisoning, so I have to give a nod to Sun Simiao for helping me. The Jiajing Emperor in the Ming Dynasty died from ingesting a lethal dosage of mercury in an Elixir of Life conjured by alchemists. Many more Chinese emperors came home to me from elixir poisoning.

In India, Amrita is referred to in the Hindu scriptures where it was believed that anybody who consumed even a tiniest portion of it gained immortality. The legend says that in early times when the inception of the world had just taken place, evil demons called Ashur gained strength. They were seen as a threat to the Devas who feared them, so Indra, the god of sky, Vayu, the god of wind, and Agni, the god of fire went to seek help from the three primary gods; Vishnu the preserver, Brahma the creator, and Shiva the destroyer who suggested that Amrit could only be gained from churning the ocean because the ocean's depths hid mysterious and secret objects. Vishnu agreed to take the form of a turtle on whose shell a huge mountain was placed to be used as a churning pole.

With the help of a long, mighty serpent named Vasuki, the churning process began. The gods pulled the serpent which had coiled itself around the mountain from one side while the demons pulled it from the other. The churning needed immense strength, so the demons were persuaded to do the job in return for a portion of Amrit. Finally with the combined efforts of gods and demons, Amrit emerged from the ocean depths. All the gods were offered the drink, but the gods tricked the demons who didn't get any.

The Vedas are the oldest Indian Hindu sacred scriptures and have the same hints of alchemy as ancient China in its connection between gold and long life. The idea of transmuting base metals into gold appeared in the second to the fifth century AD Buddhist texts around the same time it did in the West.

In European alchemical tradition, the Elixir of Life was related to the creation of the philosopher's stone and certain alchemists had reputations as its creators, including Nicolas Flamel and St. Germain.

Immortality in ancient Greek religion included an eternal union of body and soul which was seen in Homer, Hesiod, and other ancient texts. The soul was thought to have an eternal existence in Hades, but without the body it was considered dead, so most had nothing to look forward to but an eternal existence as a disembodied soul. There were a number of men and women believed to have gained physical immortality and brought to live forever in Elysium or the Islands of the Blessed. Some were thought to have died and been resurrected before they achieved physical immortality. In some versions of the Trojan War myth, Achilles was snatched from his funeral pyre by his divine mother Thetis, resurrected, and brought to an immortal existence. According to Herodotus the sage Aristeas of Proconnesus was found dead, then his body disappeared from a locked room. Later he was found to have been resurrected, and to have gained immortality.

The philosophical idea of an immortal soul was advocated by Plato and his followers, but most traditional Greeks thought that some people were resurrected from the dead and made physically immortal and others could only look forward to an existence as disembodied and dead, but everlasting souls. The parallel between these beliefs and the later resurrection of Jesus was adopted by the early Christians.

Christian theology says that Adam and Eve lost physical immortality and that of all their descendants in the Fall of Man. Christians in the Nicene Creed believe that every dead person whether they believed in Christ or not will be resurrected from the dead at the Second Coming. This belief is known as Universal resurrection.

At least these guys give everyone a fair shake. It's hard not to bite my tongue with all this talk of resurrection and the second coming.

Like you're going to get away.

If people invest their lives in this, it begs the question of who or what is the *real* second coming.

Guess who?

Maybe it's more like the first coming, or better still, the last.

Hindus believe in an immortal soul that reincarnates after death. According to them people repeat a process of life, death, and rebirth in a cycle called *samsara*. If they live their life well their *karma* improves and their station in the next life will be higher or lower if they live their life poorly. After many life times of perfecting its karma, the soul is freed from the cycle and lives in perpetual bliss. There is no place of eternal torment in Hinduism, although if a soul consistently lives evil lives it can work its way down to the bottom of the cycle.

Good for them. They left the door open.

In Judaism the concept of an immaterial and immortal soul distinct from the body came about as a result of interaction with Persian and Hellenistic philosophies. The Hebrew word *nephesh* is translated as soul, but has a meaning closer to living being and refers to a living, breathing conscious body instead of an immortal soul. In the New Testament, the Greek word traditionally translated soul has the same meaning as the Hebrew without reference to an immortal soul.

In a Taoist book titled Lüshi Chunqiu it repeatedly states that I am unavoidable.

At least, those guys got it right!

Many see Taoism as being focused on the quest for immortality, but it is better understood as a way of life instead of a religion. Its believers do not view Taoism the way non-Taoist historians do. In its traditional teachings, spiritual immortality can be rewarded to people who do good deeds and live a simple, pure life. A list of good deeds and sins are tallied to determine whether or not a mortal is worthy. Spiritual immortality in this definition allows the soul to leave the earthly realms of afterlife and go to pure realms in the Taoist cosmology.

Zoroastrians believe that on the fourth day after death the soul leaves the body and the body remains an empty shell. Souls go to either Heaven or Hell. These concepts of the afterlife in Zoroastrianism influenced Abrahamic religions. The Persian word for immortal is associated with the month *Amurdad*, meaning deathless in Persian. In the Iranian calendar near the end of July the month of Amurdad is celebrated in Persian culture as ancient Persians believed the Angel of Immortality won over the Angel of Death in this month.

Like *that's* going to happen!

Aside from all these myths and beliefs there are philosophical arguments for the immortality of the soul. Plato had four. The first was the Cyclical or Opposites Argument that says forms are eternal and unchanging, and as the soul always brings life then it must not die and is imperishable. If the body is mortal and subject to physical death, the soul has to be its indestructible opposite. Plato suggested the analogy of fire and cold. If cold is imperishable and its opposite fire is within close proximity, it has to withdraw intact like the soul does during death. This was likened to the idea of opposite charges in magnets.

The second is Plato's Theory of Recollection which said that humans possess non-empirical knowledge at birth which implies that the soul existed before birth to carry that knowledge.

In the third Affinity Argument, invisible, immortal, and incorporeal things are different from visible, mortal, and corporeal things. Your soul is of the former while your body is of the latter, so when your bodies die and decay your souls continue living.

Last is the Argument from Form of Life, or The Final Argument that explains that Forms and incorporeal and static entities are the cause of all things in the world, and all things participate in Forms. For example, beautiful things participate in the Form of Beauty; the number four participates in the Form of the Even, and so on. The soul participates in the Form of Life, which means it can never die.

In broader terms you think of immortality as eternal life, being exempt from death, and having unending existence. Scientists, futurists, and philosophers have theorized about the immortality of the human body with some suggesting that human immortality could be achieved in the future. I'll believe that when I see it, but I'm willing to bet *your* life that though admirable, this is nothing more than another futile attempt at denying what is due me.

In religious contexts immortality is seen as a promise of God or other deities to human beings who show goodness and follow divine law. What form an unending human life would take or whether an immaterial soul exists and possesses immortality has been a major focus of religion as well as the subject of speculation, fantasy, and debate.

I know in your present time you prefer hard scientific evidence, so let's take a look at some other things in your three dimensional reality that your imaginations have come up with in your quest to avoid my visit.

Physical immortality is seen as a state of life that allows someone to avoid me and maintain conscious thought. It can also mean the unending existence of someone from a physical source other than organic life like a computer. Your present pursuit of physical immortality is based on cryonics, digital immortality, breakthroughs in rejuvenation, predictions of an impending technological singularity, or spiritual beliefs like those held by Rastafarians and Rebirthers.

There are three main ways that I will come to take you; slower like aging and disease, faster like physical trauma, or the ever-popular instantaneous flash which can come from anywhere.

Life extension researchers define aging as a collection of cumulative changes to the molecular and cellular structure of adult organisms that result in essential metabolic processes, but once they progress far enough they increasingly disrupt metabolism resulting in pathology and death. Aging in humans comes from many of my inroads, among them cell loss without replacement, DNA damage, oncogenic nuclear mutations and epimutations, cell senescence, mitochondrial mutations, lysosomal aggregates, extracellular aggregates, random extracellular cross-linking, immune system decline, endocrine changes, and the loss of molecular fidelity. Eliminating aging would require finding a solution to each of these causes in what is called engineered negligible senescence.

Some believe that life extension technologies promise a path to complete rejuvenation and cryonics holds the hope that the dead can be revived in the future following sufficient medical advancements. Life extension might be a more achievable goal in the short term, but it won't confer invulnerability to disease or physical trauma, and if you did manage to achieve that lofty goal, I would still win in the end when your numbers increase and your resources dwindle.

Life extension refers to an increase in maximum lifespan by slowing down or reversing the aging process. Average lifespan is determined by vulnerability to accidents and age or lifestyle afflictions like cancer or cardiovascular disease. Good diet, exercise, and avoidance of hazards like smoking can extend lifespans. Maximum lifespan is also determined by the rate of aging inherent in your genes.

Life extension researchers try to understand the nature of aging and develop treatments to reverse aging processes or at least slow them down. Some researchers believe that future breakthroughs in tissue rejuvenation, stem cells, regenerative medicine, molecular repair, gene therapy, pharmaceuticals, and organ replacement will enable humans to have indefinite lifespans through complete rejuvenation to a healthy youthful condition.

Even if they do, I'll still be there waiting.

Disease is often surmountable through technology and your understanding of genetics has been leading to cures and treatments for previously incurable diseases and the mechanisms of how other diseases do damage are becoming better understood. Sophisticated methods of detecting diseases early are being developed all the time. Neurodegenerative diseases like Parkinson's and Alzheimer's might be curable using stem cells and breakthroughs in cell biology and telomere research are leading to treatments for cancer. Vaccines are also being researched for AIDS and tuberculosis. Genes associated with type one diabetes and certain cancers have been discovered allowing new therapies to be developed. Artificial devices attached directly to the nervous system might restore sight to the blind while drugs are being developed to treat other diseases and ailments.

Physical trauma will always remain a threat to physical life, so an otherwise immortal person would still be subject to unforeseen accidents or catastrophes. A body that could automatically repair itself from severe trauma through strategies like nanotechnology would mitigate this factor. Being the seat of consciousness, the brain cannot be risked to trauma if a continuous physical life is to be maintained. Severe trauma to the brain would result in significant behavioral changes that would render physical immortality undesirable.

Organisms unaffected by these traumas still face the problem of obtaining sustenance from currently available agricultural processes or hypothetical future technological processes in the face of changing availability of resources as environmental conditions change. After avoiding aging, disease, and trauma, you can still die of starvation.

I always win in the end. It simply comes down to a matter of patience and I have an infinite amount of that.

Biological immortality is an absence of aging which is the absence of a sustained increase in the rate of mortality as a function of chronological age. A cell or organism that doesn't experience aging or ceases to age is considered biologically immortal.

Biologists have chosen the word immortal to designate cells that are not limited by the what's called the Hayflick limit where cells no longer divide because of DNA damage or shortened telomeres. Every time a cell divides the telomere becomes shorter and when it finally wears down, the cell is unable to split and dies. Telomerase is an enzyme that rebuilds the telomeres in stem cells and cancer cells allowing them to replicate an infinite number of times. Scientists hope to grow organs with the help of stem cells, allowing organ transplants without the risk of rejection. These technologies are the subject of ongoing research, but even if you have any success, one way or another you will still end up meeting me.

I promise.

Some scientists believe that boosting telomerase in the body can prevent cells from dying and could lead to extended healthier lifespans. When tested on mice, those that were genetically engineered to produce 10 times the normal levels of telomerase lived fifty percent longer than control mice.

Under normal circumstances without telomerase, if a cell divides repeatedly, at some point all the progeny will reach their limit to the number of times a human cell population will divide before cell division stops. With the presence of telomerase each dividing cell can replace the lost DNA, and any single cell can then divide unbounded. While this unbounded growth has excited lots of researchers, exploiting this property of unbounded growth is a crucial step in enabling cancerous growth. If an organism can replicate its body cells faster it would stop aging.

Embryonic stem cells express telomerase that allows them to divide and form the individual. In adults, telomerase is high in cells that need to divide regularly like those in the immune system while most other cells express it at low levels in a cell-cycle dependent manner.

Technological immortality holds the prospect of longer life spans by scientific advances in fields like nanotechnology, emergency room procedures, genetics, biological engineering, regenerative medicine, microbiology, and others. Your present life span is already longer than those of the past because of better nutrition, availability of health care, standard of living, and biomedical advances. An important aspect of scientific thinking about immortality is that some combination of human cloning, cryonics, or nanotechnology will play an essential role in extreme life extension. Some scientists think that nanorobots can be created that will go through human bloodstreams, find dangerous things like cancer cells and bacteria, and destroy them. Future advances in nanomedicine might facilitate life extension through the repair of many processes responsible for aging.

Cryonics is the practice of preserving organisms for future revival by storing them at cryogenic temperatures where metabolism and decay are almost stopped, and used to pause for those who believe that life extension technologies will not develop sufficiently within their lifetime. Ideally cryonics would allow clinically dead people to be brought back in the future after cures to their diseases have been discovered and aging is reversible, not something *I* would bet on. Cryonics procedures use a process called vitrification that creates a glass-like state rather than freezing when the body is brought to low temperatures. This process reduces the risk of ice crystals damaging cell-structures which would be detrimental, especially in the brain.

Some scientists think that therapeutic cloning and stem cell research might provide a way to generate cells, body parts, or entire bodies that would be genetically identical to a prospective patient. Dog and primate brain transplantation experiments were conducted in the mid-20th century but failed due to rejection and the inability to restore nerve connections, but the implantation of bio-engineered bladders grown from patients' own cells has proven to be a viable treatment for bladder disease.

The use of human stem cells, particularly embryonic stem cells has been controversial because of religious teachings or ethical considerations and controversies over cloning are similar. Some believers of therapeutic cloning predict the production of whole bodies, lacking consciousness, for eventual brain transplantation.

In that case the lights are on but nobody's home in more than one case.

Regardless of the humor I find in your ludicrous schemes to put me off, I still admire your cleverness. A large number of genetic modifications have increased lifespans in model organisms like yeast, nematode worms, fruit flies, and mice. The longest extension of life caused by a single gene manipulation was around fifty percent in mice and ten-fold in nematode worms.

There's also an approach that involves fooling genes into thinking the body is young. The idea is that you have genes that activate throughout your life. You possess more lethal genes that activate in later life than in early life, so to extend life, you try to prevent them from switching on by identifying changes in the environment of your body that takes place during aging and simulating the superficial chemical properties of young bodies.

It is very ingenious of you to try and thwart me at this level if I say so myself, but remember, my eyes and ears are everywhere, including every cell of your neurons, dendrites, mitochondria, organs, and anything else you can imagine.

In still another futile scheme, science fiction stories fantasize the idea of mind uploading, the transference of brain states from a human brain to an alternative medium like a computer that can provide similar functionality. That fantasy is never going to happen either. These intellectually arrogant science fiction dreamers think they can avoid my visit by eliminating the complications related to physical bodies by copying or transferring conscious minds from biological brains to non-biological computer systems.

They are delusional enough to think that by uploading someone's habits and memories by some kind of direct mind-computer interface that their memory can be loaded to a computer or to a new organic body. Some of them think it's possible to upload human consciousness into a computer where they can exist indefinitely in a virtual environment by using advanced cybernetics and computer hardware installed in the brain to help sort memory or accelerate thought processes. Components would be added until the person's entire brain functions were handled by artificial devices, avoiding sudden transitions that would lead to identity issues and running the risk of the person being declared dead and not being a legitimate owner of his or her property.

The human body would be treated as an optional accessory and the program implementing the person could be transferred to a powerful computer. Another mad scheme for mind uploading is to perform a detailed scan of an individual's original, organic brain and simulate the entire structure in a computer. What level of detail such scans and simulations would need to emulate awareness, and whether the scanning process would destroy the brain is unknown, but I'm willing to take bets on how far this egotistical fantasy gets. Whatever the imaginative and impossible route to mind uploading, so called people in that state would be considered immortal, short of loss or destruction of the machines that maintained them.

Finally, stretching this science fiction fantasy to its limits, there is talk of transforming humans into cyborgs that include brain implants, or extracting a human processing unit and placing it in a robotic life-support system. Depending on the definition, many technological upgrades to the body like genetic modifications or the addition of nanobots would qualify an individual as a cyborg. Some people believe that such modifications would make them impervious to aging and disease and theoretically immortal unless killed or destroyed.

Beam me up, Scotty. There's no intelligent life down here!

All of these fantasies are what you call transhumanism, another one of your misguided philosophical movements that attempts to transform your human condition by developing sophisticated technologies to enhance human intellect and physiology.

Transhumanists study the potential benefits and dangers of emerging technologies that could overcome fundamental human limitations as well as the ethical limitations of using them. The most common transhumanist concept is that human beings may eventually be able to transform themselves into different beings with abilities so greatly expanded that they will become posthuman gods that could grow physically and mentally powerful enough and become so intelligent and technologically sophisticated that their behavior would not be comprehensible to normal humans trapped by their limited intelligence and imagination; in other words the ultimate ego trip that I can't help but laugh at.

As if you could do a better job than the Cosmic design of the Great Mystery!

This ludicrous notion is another twist on your godlike delusions of immortality like your futile quests for the Fountain of Youth, the Elixir of Life, and any other efforts to stave off aging and our appointment that you are obligated to keep, regardless of how my lover Fear plays with you.

In the early twentieth century your scientists predicted great benefits from the application of advanced sciences to human biology and were partially correct in thinking that every advance would first appear indecent and unnatural, not to mention the fact that it added to the supposed science of eugenics.

You get so caught up in your intellectual arrogance and look to your technology as a savior failing to see that it actually takes you further from the truth. You think you can invent a technology that can surpass all your intellectual activities in the form of an ultraintelligent machine that could design even better machines creating an intelligence explosion, that leaves mere mortals behind.

Artificial intelligence, the key word here being *artificial*, is nothing more than your ongoing narcissistic longings for transcending your human bodies in a quest for more exquisite ways of being.

As if the gift of the miracle of life and expansive consciousness is not enough.

In a real stretch of science fiction imagination some transhumanists think that the collapse of the Universe billions of years in the future could create the conditions for the perpetuation of humanity in a simulated reality within a megacomputer and achieve a form of posthuman godhood.

As if the infinite, ineffable universe is going to collapse.

Religious critics have faulted the philosophy of transhumanism as offering no eternal truths or a relationship with the divine and say that a philosophy bereft of these beliefs leaves humanity adrift in a foggy sea of cynicism.

Amen to that!

Transhumanists support the convergence of technologies including nanotechnology, biotechnology, information technology and cognitive science as well as hypothetical future technologies like simulated reality, artificial intelligence, superintelligence, three-D bioprinting, mind uploading, chemical brain preservation and cryonics. They believe that humans can and should use these technologies to become more than human, and support the recognition and protection of cognitive liberty, morphological freedom, and procreative liberty as civil liberties to guarantee individuals the choice of using human enhancement technologies on themselves and their children.

Did you happen to notice that there is an interesting use of words here describing technology; hypothetical, simulated, artificial, all of which indicate that this has no basis in reality.

I am reality.

The twentieth century philosopher Mary Midgley traced the notion of achieving immortality by transcendence of the material human body by characterizing those ideas as quasi-scientific dreams and prophesies involving visions of escape from the body with self-indulgent, uncontrolled power-fantasies based on pseudoscientific speculations and irrational fear-of-death-driven fantasies.

That's what I'm talking about. Let's get real!

Your hubris in thinking you can do a better job than the Great Mystery which you cannot even comprehend let alone improve on doesn't take into account the issue of biocomplexity and the unpredictability of attempts to guide the development of biological evolution. Cloning and genetic engineering of animals are error-prone and disruptive of embryonic development and creates unacceptable risks to human embryos. Aside from that, improvements in experimental outcomes in one species are not automatically transferable to a new one.

Transhumanism is just another of a long line of utopian movements that seek to create Heaven on earth to avoid my claim on you, as if my plans for you are lacking. Yes, its a mystery, but you have to admit, surprises are thrilling!

If these fantasies ever came to fruition, human enhancement technologies would be disproportionately available to those with greater financial resources which would aggravate the gap between rich and poor and create a genetic divide that would create a two-tiered society of genetically engineered haves and have nots.

As if you don't already have enough conflict and chaos amongst yourselves, future eugenics wars would erupt as well as coercive state-sponsored genetic discrimination and human rights violations like compulsory sterilization of people with genetic defects, the killing of the institutionalized, and segregation and genocide of those thought of as inferior.

All of your efforts to subvert the natural order and skip out on our appointment are doomed to failure, and any possibility of physical immortality raises medical, philosophical, religious, and ethical questions. How would you deal with patients who have severe brain damage in a state of partial arousal rather than true awareness? Send them to me? What about the nature of personality over time?

Though it won't happen, how would you manage technology that mimicked or copied the mind or its processes, and what about the social and economic differences created by longevity? What would you do when you continue to reproduce on a planet that cannot support a population that grows out of control with no checks and balances? Who decides who lives and who dies?

You don't realize it, but by trying to get around me you are creating more problems for yourselves, and the more you deny me, the more I will gain in the end when it all comes crashing down because the very fact that I am here is serving you and the Great Mystery. In many respects it is my very reason for being.

Physical immortality could be a form of eternal torment. How would you deal with having to watch everyone you care about dying around you?

Aside from that, if all of you did achieve immortality time would become infinite and you would struggle to find motivation for any kind of action.

If you are honest with yourself immortality would be undesirable. Either your characters would remain the same in an immortal afterlife or they would not. If they remained the same and you kept the desires, interests, and goals that you have now, then over an infinite stretch of time you would find eternal life tedious. If you changed you would be too different from your current self to care much what happens to you. The best you can hope for is to live as long as you wanted and accept the blessing I bring that rescues you from the unbearable tedium that immortality would bring.

The extension of life has been a mainstay in the history of scientific pursuits throughout history, from the Sumerians and Egyptians, through the Taoists, Ayurveda practitioners, alchemists, hygienists and philosophers with a resurgence at the end of the nineteenth and the beginning of the twentieth centuries.

On a global scale immortality would strengthen your nasty habit of destroying the natural order of your environment. Among other things, I am an essential component of any healthy ecosystem. Without me you run the risk of overpopulation which adds to your already rampant global decay.

Ever noticed how time seems to pass more quickly as you age? This comes from the fact that the older you are, the smaller proportion of your life a period of time is perceived to be. At ten years old, a year is one tenth of your entire life, while at at one hundred a year is one hundredth of your life.

Would you perceive days as becoming progressively shorter into infinity? Regardless, your memories would eventually fade into one convoluted mess. You would be unable to distinguish non-notable memories created ten thousand years ago from those formed nine thousand years ago.

Your body is not designed to last forever, especially with something as complex as your brain which is another reason why I am built in. You do indeed start dying the moment you are born. I am everywhere in every part of your entire makeup.

Imagine what your existence would be like if your capacity for reason, emotion, memory and self control eroded over time. You could become a prisoner in your own mind and nothing would be more true in an immortal society than the saying that the rich get richer and the poor get poorer. Any society that builds itself up on a system of rule with class divides will experience severe social rifts as time goes on, with wealth tending to 'pool' at the top. The only solution is to force a classless society. Many of you believe that immortal beings would revert back to anarchy to achieve true equality. If not, you could expect an endless and chaotic cycle of revolution and replacement where each class reinvents itself to fulfill its desires, unless the world descended into a perpetual civil war between classes on its own.

Your knowledge of my fast approaching imminence often provokes you into fulfilling your dreams. Trips to magnificent locations to see legendary art and participation in life-changing events holds extreme value because you know you might not get another chance, but if eternity was available to you along with the possibility of experiencing all that life has to offer, many experiences would lose their value. What's the point of mastering the sciences learning the arts and engaging in humanities if you have an eternity to do so? With your history you would no doubt end up in extreme forms of hedonism to give your existence meaning.

Immortal life would develop into a monotonous schedule based around needs, habits, and commitments. Day in and day out you would expect the same tedious activities with no end in sight. Holidays, psychedelic trips, and other novel experiences would become part of the same tired old schedule and depths of emotion would become shallow with the passage of time leading to cold-hearted apathy and bitterness. In spite of your urge to survive for as long as possible, many of you would still choose to come home to me after millenniums of boredom.

If everyone from the eighteenth century and earlier lived today, you'd be segregating races and practicing misogyny. I am the only means you have that can permanently rid yourselves of the tyranny of the elders and progress ethically. The views held by those who achieved immortality would be the views held for the rest of eternity. I would still take you by murder and other ways, but that would happen too slowly for social progression. The only solution would be mass psychological conditioning and reprogramming, but who would decide once and for all what is just?

Pensions and other forms of social welfare would become too much of a burden on your governments and the lack of retirement would lead to stagnation in all of your industries. People would spend thousands of years in the same job with no prospect of promotion because people higher up the chain wouldn't be moving on.

There would also be a massive surge in crime. Thirty years imprisonment is not an adequate deterrent for someone looking forward to a lifespan of tens of thousands of years or more, and true life sentences would be immoral. Being stuck in a cell for eternity would be Hell.

You could make heavy use of the death penalty, but given the ethical problems so many of you see in it, it would be multiplied tenfold if you were immortal. There's a big difference between taking the life of someone who would eventually die anyway, and taking the life of someone destined to life forever. Life would hold more value and you would have to rely on rehabilitation and prevention techniques to prevent chaos.

In reality immortality is nothing more than mortality with no foreseeable end. Unfortunately, having transcended natural deaths, you would have to face the reality of one day perishing violently. Other than starvation or dehydration, there would be no passing away quietly in your sleep. It would take a lot more than simple physical decay or disease to destroy a truly immortal being. If you didn't drown in rising water levels or freeze in future ice ages, you could count on shuffling off your mortal coil by being stabbed, shot, poisoned, immolated, asphyxiated, crushed, electrocuted, or by being blown up.

If not any of these, the death of a star would eventually engulf you and your planet. You could escape into space, but not much awaits you there unless you enjoy drifting in endless darkness until the end of time.

What all of these absurd notions of life extension and immortality proves is that they are nothing more than flashy distractions to what is inevitable.

Me.

As far as I am concerned, dying is part of living, and when the time comes, I hope you are prepared to embrace me for the gift of the magical, transformative moment that I have waiting for you, and I hope you realize by now that even if you did manage to achieve immortality in your three dimensional physical plane you would *still* be serving me.

I have to give my lover Fear credit where credit is due for all the great work done to add to the suspense, drama, mystery, and anticipation of our intimate, inescapable date. It has a way of making that magic moment all the more special.

In the end it all comes down to a waiting game and I am ever patient because I have all the time in the world – and then some.

ALWAYS WITH YOU, ALWAYS WITH ME

Immortality, life extension, and all those possessions that many of you have worked your entire life for are meaningless when I come for you. They have been mine all along and only on loan to you for the brief moments of your existence in what you think of as time; something else that I rule over.

Whether you admit it or not I am always very close to you, or maybe a better way to put it is that you are close to me, which makes you especially dear to me. You might even say I love you more than life itself, although we are really two sides of the same coin.

In much the same way that Fear and I are inseparable, you and I are inseparable. I'm there waiting for you between every beat of your heart and in that that pause between every breath that you take, and I can step in whenever I want. Life is my gift to you, but in the grander scheme of things it is more like a short term loan.

In spite of my dark reputation I am your best friend and I love you with every aspect of my being and with every ounce of *your* being which is also mine.

Call me what you will, but you can't stop me and you can't escape the depths of my love. You are mine, my dear one, my beloved, my lover. Don't worry Fear is beyond jealousy. I will take you whenever the time is right and there are any number of ways that I might come for you. I don't care what you think you are, Christian, Muslim, Jewish, Buddhist, Atheist, or in some kind of cult. It might look ugly to you when I take someone home, but you have no idea what it looks like from this side.

Mind you all of my claims over everything you think you own may come across as greedy and possessive and I suppose there is some truth in that, but in reality I am multidimensional and exist outside of your limited linear conceptions of time and space far beyond anything you can conceive.

Instead of seeing me as greedy and possessive, if you look at it from a higher perspective I am quite generous because I let you have and collect as much as you think you need, but there are those who think of it is a cruel joke because I take it all back in the end.

He who dies with the most toys wins?

Now *that* is funny!

I talked about the ways you have thought of me in different times and cultures and all the names and masks you have given me, and I talked about how you think your existence will be after I take you back into the Great Mystery in what you think of as the afterlife. No, I'm not going to spoil the surprise I have in store for you, but I do appreciate the respect you show to me and those who have left you to come back to me.

In your present time your ceremonies of burial, cremation, and interment encompasses beliefs and practices from many cultures to remember and respect the dead from interment to monuments, prayers, and rituals in their honor. Common motivations for funerals include mourning the deceased, celebrating their life, and offering support and sympathy to the bereaved. They usually have religious elements intended to help the soul reach the afterlife, resurrection, or reincarnation, depending on what they think the Great Mystery holds for them.

The word *funeral* comes from the Latin *funus* which had a variety of meanings, including the corpse and the funerary rites themselves. Your funerary art has evolved in connection with burials, including tombs and objects specially made for burial like flowers with a corpse.

These practices usually include a ritual where corpses receive a final disposition. Depending on the belief it can involve the destruction of the body by cremation or sky burial, or it is preserved by mummification or interment. Differing beliefs about cleanliness and the relationship between body and soul are reflected in these practices. In modern times you usually have a memorial service or celebration of life without the remains of the person I have taken.

With all these diverse rituals and beliefs from different origins and ideas about what you think happens when I visit and after I take your loved ones home, what you often see as somber, sorrowful going away events, from *my* perspective are homecoming parties, and seeing as you go through so much trouble to celebrate them and honoring me and my work, I want to acknowledge the respect and point out how many of you honor my once in a lifetime visit.

I confess that I am partial to the Bahá'í Faith because it teaches the essential worth of all religions and the unity and equality of all people. I'm not so sure about the worth of all religions, but I do like the idea of unity and equality of all people.

Even Groucho can't deny the appeal of this one!

The Bahá'í Faith has its roots in the mid-nineteenth-century Bábí religion, whose founder taught that God would send a prophet like Jesus or Muhammad. It initially grew in Iran and parts of the Middle East where it still faces persecution, but to its credit it has spread into most of the world. Though I have some quibbles with its belief system, I find it tragically comical and oh so human, that a belief system that embraces everyone and their beliefs to be the subject of persecution from the start.

Bahá'í Faith funerals are characterized by not embalming, a prohibition against cremation, using a chrysolite or hardwood casket, wrapping the body in silk or cotton, and burial not more than an hour away from the place of my arrival. They put a ring on the deceased's finger saying, "I came forth from God, and return unto Him, detached from all save Him, holding fast to His Name, the Merciful, the Compassionate."

Bahá'í funeral services contain the only prayer permitted as a group congregational prayer, although most of it is read by one person. The Bahá'í decedent often controls some aspects of the funeral, since leaving a will and testament is a requirement for the Bahá'í. Since there are no Bahá'í clergy, services are conducted with the assistance of a Local Spiritual Assembly.

Among Buddhists my visit is regarded as an occasion of major religious significance, both for the deceased and for the survivors. For the deceased it marks the moment when the transition begins to a new mode of existence within the round of rebirths. Buddhists believe that when I come all the karmic forces that the dead person accumulated during the course of their lifetime become activated to determine the next rebirth. For the living I am a powerful reminder of Buddha's teaching on impermanence. It also provides an opportunity to assist the deceased person on to their new existence.

Not bad!

Christian burials usually happen on consecrated ground. Burial rather than a destructive process like cremation was the traditional practice with Christians because of the belief in the resurrection of the body. Cremations later became more widespread, although some denominations forbid them. Congregations of different denominations perform different ceremonies. Most involve prayers, scripture reading from the Bible, a sermon, homily, eulogy, and music.

In Hinduism, Antyesti, the last rites or last sacrifice is the rite-of-passage ritual associated with funerals. Dead adults are cremated and dead children are buried. The rite of passage is performed in harmony with the sacred premise that the microcosm of all living beings is a reflection of a macrocosm of the universe.

I like this notion too!

The individual soul Atman goes to Brahman the universal soul, and is believed to be the immortal essence that is released at this ritual, but the body and the universe are vehicles and transitory in different schools of Hinduism. The last rite of passage returns the body to the five elements of air, water, fire, earth and space, and its origins. The final rites of a burial in the untimely death of a child is rooted in the Rig Veda where hymns mourn the death of the child, praying to the deity Mrityu to neither harm their girls or boys, and pleads the earth to cover and protect the deceased child as soft wool.

Among Hindus the corpse is usually cremated within a day of death and washed and wrapped in white cloth for a man or a widow, and red for a married woman. The two toes are tied together with a string and a red mark is placed on the forehead. The dead adult's body is carried to the cremation ground near a river or water by family and friends and placed on a pyre with the feet facing south. The eldest son, a male mourner, or a priest then bathes it before leading the cremation ceremony by walking around the dry wood pyre with the body, saying a eulogy or reciting a hymn and placing sesame seed in the dead person's mouth. After that they sprinkle the body and the pyre with clarified butter and draw three lines signifying Me, who they call *Yama, Kala*, the time deity of cremation and the dead. The pyre is set ablaze while the mourners mourn and the ash from the cremation is consecrated to the nearest river or sea.

After the cremation a period of mourning is observed for ten to twelve days, then the immediate male relatives or the sons of the deceased shave their heads, trim their nails, recite prayers with the help of a priest or Brahmin and invite all relatives, kin, friends, and neighbors to eat a simple meal in remembrance of the deceased. This day in some communities also marks a day when the poor and needy are offered food in memory of the dead, a nice gesture, if I say so myself.

Funerals in Islam are called Janazah in Arabic and follow specific rites. Sharia Islamic religious law calls for the burial of the body preceded by a ritual involving bathing, shrouding the body, and prayer. Burial rituals take place as soon as possible and include bathing the dead body with water, camphor, and the leaves of the ziziphus lotus, except in extraordinary circumstances like battle. Other practices include enshrouding the body in a white cotton or linen cloth, reciting the funeral prayer, burying the body in a grave, and positioning the deceased so that the face or body turned to the right side faces Mecca. They mourn for forty days.

Funerals in Judaism share many features with Islam. Jewish religious law called *Halakha* calls for preparatory rituals involving bathing and shrouding the body accompanied by prayers and readings from the Hebrew Bible and a funeral service marked by eulogies and brief prayers, followed by the lowering of the body into the grave and the filling of the grave. Traditional law and practice forbid cremation and burial rites take place as soon as possible, including bathing the dead body and enshrouding it. Men are shrouded with a white robe and a shawl while women are shrouded in a plain white cloth. The filling of the grave is done by family members and other participants at the funeral. In many communities the deceased is positioned so that the feet face the Temple Mount in Jerusalem in anticipation that the deceased will be facing the reconstructed Third Temple when the messiah arrives and resurrects the dead.

In Sikhism my visit is not considered a natural process, so I guess that makes me unnatural, but they have it more right than most. They see my coming as an event that has absolute certainty and only happens as a direct result of God's Will. To a Sikh, birth and death are closely associated, because they are both part of the cycle of human life of coming and going which is seen as transient stages toward Liberation and total unity with God.

Sikhs believe in reincarnation and that the soul itself is not subject to the cycle of birth and death. I am only part of the progression of the soul on its journey from God through the created universe and back to God again. In life a Sikh is expected to constantly remember Me so that he or she can be sufficiently prayerful, detached, and righteous to break the cycle of birth and death and return to God.

The public display of grief by wailing or crying out loud at the funeral is discouraged and kept to a minimum and cremation is the preferred method of disposal, although if it is not possible other methods like burial, or burial at sea, are acceptable. Markers like gravestones and monuments are discouraged because the body is considered to be only the shell. The person's soul is their real essence.

On the day of the cremation the body is washed, dressed, and taken to the home where hymns are recited by the congregation. Kirtan may also be performed by Ragis while the relatives of the deceased recite *Waheguru* sitting near the coffin. At its conclusion a prayer is said before the coffin is taken to the cremation site.

At the point of cremation a few more Shabads may be sung and final speeches are made about the deceased person, then the eldest son or a close relative lights the fire. The ashes are later collected and disposed of by immersing them in one of the five famous rivers in India.

The Greek word for funeral comes from the verb that means attend to and take care of someone. In present times the body is placed in a casket that is always open in the house where the deceased lived. Mournful songs are sung by their family and the deceased is watched over by their beloved the night before the burial.

Ekphorá is the process of transport of the remains of the deceased from their residence to the church and afterward to the place of burial. Usually certain favorite objects of the deceased are placed in the coffin to go along with them. In some regions coins to pay Charon, who ferries the dead to the underworld are also placed inside the casket. A last kiss is given to the beloved dead by the family before the coffin is closed.

The Roman orator Cicero described the habit of planting flowers around the tomb as an effort to guarantee the repose of the deceased and the purification of the ground, a custom that is still practiced. After the ceremony mourners return to the house of the deceased for a dinner after the burial. According to archaeological findings, traces of ash, bones of animals, shards of crockery, dishes and basins from dinner during the classical era were also organized at the burial spot.

Two days after the burial a ceremony called The Thirds is held, and eight days after the burial the relatives and friends of the deceased assemble at the burial spot where The Ninths take place. In addition to this, memorial services take place forty days, three months, six months, nine months, and one year after my visit, and from then on every year on the anniversary of the death. The relatives of the deceased, for a length of time that depends on them are in mourning, during which women wear black clothes and men wear black armbands.

In ancient Rome the eldest surviving male of the household was summoned to the death bed where he attempted to catch and inhale the last breath of the decedent.

Funerals of the socially prominent were performed by professional undertakers. These rites included a public procession to the tomb or pyre where the body was to be cremated. The surviving relations bore masks bearing the images of the family's deceased ancestors. The right to carry the masks in public was eventually restricted to prominent families. Mimes, dancers, and musicians hired by the undertakers and professional female mourners also took part in these processions. Less well-to-do Romans joined funerary societies that performed these rites on their behalf.

Nine days after the disposal of the body by burial or cremation a feast was given and a libation poured over the grave or the ashes. Since most Romans were cremated, the ashes were usually collected in an urn and placed in a niche in a collective tomb. During this nine day period the house was considered tainted and hung with cypress branches to warn passersby. At the end of the period the house was swept out to symbolically purge it of the taint of death.

In most East Asian, South Asian and many Southeast Asian cultures the wearing of white is symbolic of death. In these societies white or off-white robes are worn to symbolize that someone has come with me and can be seen worn by their relatives during funeral ceremonies. In Chinese culture red is forbidden as it is a traditionally symbolic color of happiness. Exceptions are made if the deceased has reached an advanced age in which case the funeral is considered a celebration where wearing white with some red is acceptable. Western influence has made dark-colored or black attire acceptable for mourners to wear, particularly for those outside the family. In such cases mourners wearing dark colors can also wear white or off-white armbands or white robes.

South Korean funerals mix western culture with traditional Korean culture, largely depending on socio-economic status, region, and religion. In most cases all related males in the family wear woven armbands representing seniority and lineage in relation to the deceased and have to grieve next to the deceased for a period of three days before burying them. During this period it is customary for the males in the family to personally greet all who come to show respect. While burials have been preferred historically, recent trends show an increase in cremations due to shortages of burial sites and difficulties in maintaining traditional graves. The ashes of the cremated corpse are kept in a vault called a columbaria for the storage of their urns.

In Korea funerals are normally held for three days and different things are done each day. On the day a person dies the body is moved to a funeral hall. They prepare clothes for the body and put them into a chapel of rest, then food is prepared for the deceased made up of three bowls of rice and three side dishes. There also has to be three coins and three straw shoes, but this can be canceled if the family of the dead person have a particular religion.

On the second day the funeral director washes the body and shrouding is done, then a family member puts uncooked rice in the mouth and the body is moved into a coffin, then family members and close relatives wear mourning clothing. Mourning for a woman usually includes Korean traditional clothes and mourning for a man includes a black suit. The ceremony begins when they are done with changing clothes and preparing food. After the ceremony family members greet guests.

On the third day the family decides whether to bury the body or cremate it. If they bury it three people from the family sprinkle dirt on the coffin three times. If cremated, the only thing needed is a jar to place burned bones in and a place to keep them. People who come to the funeral bring condolence money and a food called Yukgaejang is served to guests often with Korean alcohol called soju.

Most Japanese funerals are conducted with Buddhist and/or Shinto rites. Many ritually bestow a new name on the deceased. Funerary names typically use obsolete or archaic kanji and other words to avoid the likelihood of the name being used in ordinary speech or writing. New names are usually chosen by a Buddhist priest after consulting the family of the deceased. Most Japanese are cremated.

Religious thought among the Japanese is generally a blend of Shintō and Buddhist beliefs. In modern practice specific rites concerning an individual's passage through life are ascribed to one of these two faiths. Funerals and follow-up memorial services fall under the purview of Buddhist ritual and ninety percent of Japanese funerals are conducted in a Buddhist manner. Aside from the religious aspect Japanese funerals usually include a wake, the cremation of the deceased, and inclusion within the family grave. Follow-up services are performed by a Buddhist priest on specific anniversaries after death.

Funeral practices and burial customs in the Philippines encompass a wide range of personal, cultural, and traditional beliefs and practices that Filipinos observe in relation to death, bereavement, honoring, interment, and remembrance of the dead. These practices have been shaped by the many religions and cultures that entered the Philippines throughout its complex history.

Most if not all present-day Filipinos believe in some form of afterlife and give considerable attention to honoring the dead. Other than Filipino Muslims who are obliged to bury a corpse less than twenty four hours after death, a wake is held from three days to a week. Wakes in rural areas are held in the home while in urban settings the dead are displayed in funeral homes. Friends and neighbors bring food to the family, but leftovers are never taken home by guests because of superstition against it. Although the majority of Filipino people are Christians they have kept some traditional indigenous beliefs concerning Me.

Like many other cultures, funeral practices in Mongolia are the most important rituals that they follow and they have mixed their rituals with Buddhists. For Mongolians who are strict when it comes to their traditions there are three different ways of burial, the main one being open-air burial, and the others being cremation and embalming. Many factors go into deciding which funeral practice to do that consist of the family's social standing, the cause of death, and the specific location of their demise. The people chosen to be embalmed are separate from the Lamaistic Church, and by choosing this practice they are buried in a sitting position to show that they would always be in the position of prayer. More important people like nobles are buried with weapons, horses, and food in their coffins to help them prepare for the next world.

The coffin is specially designed by three or four male relatives. In order to determine its size the builders bring planks to the hut where the corpse is and put together the box and the lid. The same people who made the coffin also help decorate the funeral. Most of this work is done after the sun goes down and they work on decorations inside the youngest daughter's house so the deceased is not disturbed at night.

In Vietnam Buddhism is the most commonly practiced religion, but most burial methods do not coincide with the Buddhist belief of cremation. The body of the deceased is moved to a loved one's house and placed in an expensive coffin for a few days, allowing time for people to visit and place gifts in the mouth which stems from the Vietnamese belief that the dead should be surrounded by family. If somebody is dying in Vietnamese culture they are rushed home from the hospital so they can die there because if they die away from home it is believed to be bad luck to take a corpse home.

Many services are held in Vietnamese burial practices. One is held before moving the coffin from the home, and the other is held at the burial site. After the burial incense is burned at the grave site and respect is paid to all the nearby graves. Following this family and friends return to the home and enjoy a feast to celebrate the life of the recently departed and after they have been buried, the respect and honor continues. For the first forty nine days after burying the family holds a memorial service every seven days where family and friends come back together to celebrate. After this they meet again on the one hundredth day after I come, then two hundred sixty five days after I come, and finally they meet on the anniversary of my visit a year later to continue celebrating the glorious life of their recently departed.

African funerals are open to many visitors. The custom of burying the dead in the floor of dwelling-houses has been prevalent on the Gold Coast of Africa and the ceremony depends on the traditions of the ethnicity the deceased belonged to. The funeral can last for as long as a week. Another memorial custom takes place seven years after the person's death. These funerals and memorials can be expensive for the family, so cattle, sheep, goats, and poultry are offered and consumed.

The Ashanti and Akan ethnic groups in Ghana typically wear red and black during funerals. For special family members there is often a funeral celebration with singing and dancing to honor the life of the deceased. Afterward the Akan hold a somber funeral procession and burial with intense displays of sorrow. Other funerals in Ghana are held with the deceased in elaborate fantasy coffins colored and shaped after objects like fish, crabs, boats, and even airplanes!

Some diseases like Ebola can be spread by funerary customs including touching the dead, but safe burials are performed by following simple procedures like letting relatives see the face of the dead before body bags are closed. Taking photographs can also reduce the risk of infection without impacting the customs of burial.

In Kenya funerals are expensive. Keeping bodies in morgues to allow for fund raising is common in urban areas. Some families bury their dead in countryside homes instead of urban cemeteries and spend more money on transporting the dead.

Within the United States and Canada funeral rituals are pretty much divided into three parts; visitation, funeral, and burial.

At the *visitation,* also called a viewing, wake, or calling hours, the body of the deceased is put on display in the casket and the viewing takes place one or two evenings before the funeral. The body is traditionally dressed in the decedent's best clothes and is often adorned with jewelry which can be taken off and given to the family prior to burial, or buried with the deceased. The body may or may not be embalmed depending on the amount of time since my visit, religious practices, or requirements of the place of burial and the decedent's closest friends and relatives who are unable to attend frequently send flowers.

The viewing is either open casket with the embalmed body clothed and treated with cosmetics for display, or closed casket. The coffin may be closed if the body was too badly damaged from an accident, fire, or other trauma, deformed from illness, if someone is emotionally unable to cope with viewing the corpse, or if the deceased did not wish to be viewed. In those cases a picture of the deceased is put on top the casket, except in the case of Judaism.

Jewish funerals are held soon after death and the corpse is never displayed. Torah law forbids embalming. Traditionally flowers and music are not sent to grieving Jewish families as it is thought of as a reminder of the life that is lost. The Jewish tradition discourages family members from cooking, so food is brought by friends and neighbors.

Overall, funeral viewings take place at a funeral home with gathering rooms where the viewing can be conducted. The viewing might also take place at a church and can end with a prayer service. In a Roman Catholic funeral this might include a rosary. The funeral is officiated by clergy from the decedent's or bereaved's church or religion and can take place at either a funeral home, church, crematorium, or cemetery chapel, and is held according to the family's choosing which can be a few days after my visit to allow family members to attend the service. This type of memorial service is most common for Christians. Roman Catholics call it a mass when communion is offered, the casket is closed, and a priest says prayers and blessings. Roman Catholic funerals take place in parish churches, but if the service takes place in the funeral home's chapel it can be directed by clergy or hosted by a close family member.

The deceased is normally transported from the funeral home in a hearse with private cars traveling in a procession to the church or other location where the services are held. After the funeral if the deceased is to be buried the funeral procession will proceed to a cemetery if not already there, or to a crematorium.

During the funeral and burial service the casket may be covered with a large arrangement of flowers, called a casket spray. If the deceased served in a branch of the armed forces, the casket is covered with a national flag and in the US, nothing should cover it. If the service is held in a church the casket is normally covered in a white pall, recalling the white garments of baptism. At a religious burial service conducted at the side of the grave, tomb, mausoleum or cremation, the body of the decedent is buried or cremated at the conclusion. In many traditions pallbearers, usually males who are relatives or friends of the decedent carry the casket from the chapel to the hearse and from the hearse to the site of the burial service.

Most religions expect coffins to be closed during the burial ceremony, but in Eastern Orthodox funerals the coffins are reopened just before burial to allow mourners to look at the deceased one last time to give final farewells. Greek funerals are an exception, as the coffin is open during the whole procedure unless the state of the body doesn't allow it.

Some cultures place their dead in tombs, either individually, or in specially designated tracts of land. In some places burials are impractical because the groundwater is too high, so tombs are placed above ground like in New Orleans. Elsewhere, a separate building for a tomb is reserved for the socially prominent and wealthy. Grand, above ground tombs are called mausoleums. The socially prominent sometimes have the privilege of having their corpses stored in church crypts, but in recent times this is often forbidden by hygiene laws. Burial was not always permanent, so in some places burial grounds need to be reused due to limited space. In these areas, once the dead have decomposed to skeletons, the bones are removed and placed in an ossuary.

The first emperor of the Qin dynasty, Qin Shi Huang's mausoleum is in the Lintong District of Xi'an, Shaanxi Province in China. Its remarkable features and size made it one of the most important historical sites in China. More than eight thousand life-sized figures composed of clay and fragments of pottery surrounding the emperor's tomb. The Terracotta Army resembles soldiers, horses, government officials, and even musicians. All of the figures were made with great attention to detail and the arrangement and weapons they carry resemble the real weapons they had at that time and their facial features all have unique features.

The three Imperial Tombs of Qin Dynasty were all built in the seventeenth century and constructed to praise the emperors and their ancestors. In tradition, the Chinese followed Feng Shui to build and decorate the interiors. Harmony between the architecture and the surrounding topographical structure were seen as an integral part of nature. According to the Feng Shui theory, to build a tomb there has to be a mountain on the northern side and low land on the south and a river had to be located in the west and east.

In Chinese culture tombs were considered portals between the world of the living and the dead. The Chinese believed that the portal divided the soul into two parts. Half the soul would go to Heaven and the other half would remain within the physical body.

In recent times more of you are donating your bodies to medical schools for research and education. Medical students study anatomy from donated cadavers and they are useful in forensic research. Some medical conditions like amputations or other surgeries can make the cadaver unsuitable for these purposes. In other cases the bodies of people who had certain medical conditions are useful for studying them. It is also possible to donate organs and tissue after death for treating the sick or for research.

There's a lot to be said for spare parts!

I know you miss your loved ones, but instead of sorrow and morbidity I am enamored with recent trends that I enjoy as homecoming parties. These celebrations of life are held outside of funeral homes or places of worship and are celebrated in restaurants, parks, pubs, and sporting facilities, depending on the interests of the deceased. They focus on a life that was lived, including the person's best qualities, interests, achievements and impact, rather than mourning my visit, which I *always* see as joyful. They should be happy parties instead of traditional doom and gloom of somber funerals. These celebrations discourage wearing black and focus on the deceased's individuality, often with fully stocked open bars and catered food.

That's the way to do it!

Along these same lines are Jazz funerals that originated in New Orleans alongside the emergence of jazz music. The jazz funeral is a traditional African-American burial ceremony and celebration of life unique to New Orleans that involves a parading funeral procession accompanied by a brass band playing somber hymns followed by upbeat jazz music. Traditional jazz funerals begin with a procession led by the funeral director, family, friends, and the brass band, who march from the funeral service to the burial site while the band plays slow dirges and Christian hymns. After the body is buried they cut loose and play up-tempo, joyful jazz numbers and parade through the streets, dancing and marching along, transforming the funeral into a street festival.

Though I love these celebrations, I do favor more organic giving back to the earth approaches. One of the most ancient is burial at sea which disposed of the corpse wrapped and tied with weights. This has been a common practice in navies and seafaring nations. A burial at sea also refers to the scattering of ashes in the ocean while the whole body burial refers to the entire uncremated body being dropped in the ocean at great depths.

I'm also a fan of one of your newer hi-tech innovations called promession, an ecological funeral designed to return the body to soil while minimizing pollution and resource consumption. Promession consists of separating the body from the coffin, freezing it with liquid nitrogen, vibrating it into small particles, freeze drying it, separating any metals, and placing the dry powder remains in a biodegradable casket in top soil.

These two approaches are among the oldest and the newest of modern times, but my utmost favorite recent innovation is a green or natural burial that returns the body to the earth with little to no use of artificial, non-biodegradable materials.

As a concept, the idea of uniting an individual with the natural world after they die is as old as humanity itself and was widespread before the rise of the funeral industry. In North America, the opening of the first explicitly green burial cemetery took place in the state of South Carolina. The Green Burial Council based out of California is working to officially certify burial practices for funeral homes and cemeteries to make sure appropriate materials are used.

Those concerned about the effects on the environment of traditional burial or cremation can be placed into a bio-degradable green burial shroud that gets put into a simple coffin made of cardboard or other biodegradable material. Individuals can choose their final resting place in a specially designed park or woodland sometimes known as an ecocemetery. They can even have a tree or other greenery planted over their grave as a contribution to the environment and a symbol of remembrance.

Though you may find the concept hard to grasp, one I love with equal fervor for the same reasons include exposure to the elements, particularly to scavenger animals. After all, most of you have been eating them all of your life and plants too for that matter. Why not return the favor? This practice includes various forms of excarnation where the corpse is stripped of the flesh, leaving only the bones, which are either buried or stored in ossuaries or tombs which is what was done by some Native Americans in prehistoric times.

Ritual exposure of the dead without preservation of the bones is practiced by Zoroastrians in Mumbai and Karachi where bodies are placed in Towers of Silence where vultures and other carrion-eating birds dispose of the corpses. In present day structures the bones are collected in a central pit where assisted by lime they eventually decompose. Exposure to scavenger birds with preservation of some, but not all bones is also practiced by high-altitude Tibetan Buddhists where practical considerations like the lack of firewood and a shallow active layer have led to the practice known as giving alms to the birds.

In my opinion, that's how things should be.

Natural.

LET ME COUNT THE WAYS

I've already talked about the big three, respiratory arrest, cardiac arrest, and brain death, and touched on a few others. I find it tremendously gratifying to have these elements working for me in so many different ways.

They say variety is the spice of life, and life and I *are* two sides of the same coin, so I can honestly say that in all these ways that my minions come for you, Fear is with me pretty much every step of the way, faithfully working behind the scenes to spice things up.

One of my biggest allies in developing countries is infectious disease and my best agents in developed countries are atherosclerosis, heart disease, stroke, cancer, and other diseases related to obesity and aging. Quite the lineup if I say so myself, but the largest unifying cause of death in the developed world is biological aging that leads to complications that end in cardiac arrest, loss of oxygen, and nutrient supply, causing deterioration of the brain and other tissues. I appreciate how all of my loyal helpers not only work alone, but will collaborate at every opportunity.

Of the roughly one-hundred-fifty-thousand people who come home to me every day around the world, two thirds die of age-related causes. In industrial nations the proportion approaches ninety percent. As an added bonus, in developing nations unsanitary conditions and lack of medical technology makes passage to me from infectious diseases more common than in developed countries.

In a year's time mortality from malnutrition accounted for about fifty eight percent of the total mortality rate. Worldwide roughly sixty two million people died from all causes. Of those more than thirty six million died of hunger or diseases from deficiencies in micronutrients. Tobacco smoking killed one hundred million people worldwide in the twentieth century.

If you doubted my omniscience what do you think of me now?

Sometimes you can postpone my visit by diet and physical activity, but the accelerating cases of disease with age still imposes limits on your longevity, and I have all the time in the world.

Suicide has overtaken car crashes for leading causes of my visits in the United States followed by poisoning, falls, and murder. Calls for my visits are different in different parts of the world.

From my perspective suicide is a very thoughtful gesture that I find endearing. I like to think that you miss me that much and can't wait to be with me again, but I am also willing to admit that it is a selfish way to look at it; thinking only of myself. I also find it an interesting paradox because many who take their own lives are also selfish as they too are only thinking only of themselves with no consideration for the loved ones they leave behind.

Is this a win/win?

For me it is, but then again I always win, so it's not really a victory. I never have a victory because everything is mine anyway, so how can I win what is already mine? When someone takes their life and leaves their loved ones behind in grief and sorrow to wait for their turn with me it is a no win.

I just love paradoxes!

I also take into consideration exceptions to the rule that are not necessarily motivated by selfishness. Granted, some suicides are impulsive acts due to stress from financial problems, troubles with relationships, or bullying, and those who have attempted suicide are at a higher risk for future attempts. Effective suicide prevention includes limiting access to firearms, drugs, poisons, and treating mental disorders and substance misuse, but if someone is determined to come home to me they can easily succeed.

I would be remiss if I did not acknowledge the work of doctor Jack Kevorkian aka Doctor Death who spent part of his life in prison because of his service to me, and more importantly because of his dedication to ending suffering. Sure, I didn't need his help but as my ambassador who strove to end the pain and misery of those eager to join me, he has my gratitude.

Roughly twelve out of every one hundred thousand of you take your own lives every year and three quarters of you are from low and middle income countries. Suicide is more common among those over the age of seventy because they get tired of life and the downhill slope that aging brings, but in some countries those between the ages of fifteen and thirty have the highest risk.

Abrahamic religions view suicide as an offense to God and at the other end of the spectrum the samurai of Japan thought of it in the form of seppuku or *harakiri* as a means of making up for failure or as a form of protest. Sati, a practice outlawed by the British Raj, expected Indian widows to kill themselves on their husband's funeral fire.

Suicide attacks are political, religious actions, or some kind of personal vendetta where an attacker carries out violence against others which they understand will result in their own death. Some suicide bombers are motivated by a desire to obtain martyrdom. Kamikaze missions were carried out as a duty to a higher cause or moral obligation and thousands of Japanese civilians took their own lives in the last days of the Battle of Saipan in nineteen forty four with some jumping from Suicide Cliff and Banzai Cliff.

In a more honorable twist on taking one's life for the benefit of others is altruistic suicide, like an elder ending his or her life to leave greater amounts of food for younger people in a community. Suicide in some Inuit cultures has been seen as an act of respect, courage, or wisdom.

In extenuating situations where continuing to live is intolerable, some of you used suicide as a means of escape. Some inmates in Nazi concentration camps killed themselves by deliberately touching electrified fences. The leading method of suicide varies among countries includes hanging, pesticide poisoning, and firearms.

Another burgeoning modern day practice is murder-suicide where individuals take the life of others at the same time, and then there are those suffering from mental disorders, drug misuse, other psychological states, cultural, family, social situations, genetics, and family histories of suicide as well as traumatic brain injury.

Finally, war veterans have a higher risk of suicide due in part to higher rates of mental illnesses like post traumatic stress and other health problems related to war.

Aside from your propensity to kill each other, many of your creations have added to the ways you can join me sooner rather than later.

Substance misuse is the second most common risk factor for suicide after depression and bipolar disorder. Both chronic substance misuse as well as acute intoxication are big contributors, and when combined with personal grief like bereavement the risk is increased. Substance misuse is also associated with mental health disorders, and antidepressants of the SSRI type increase the frequency of suicide among children.

Most people are under the influence of sedative-hypnotic drugs like alcohol or benzodiazepines when they die by suicide with alcoholism present in something like fifteen to sixty percent of cases. Prescribed benzodiazepines are associated with an increased rate of attempted and completed suicides. Countries that have higher rates of alcohol use and a greater density of bars also have higher rates of suicide.

Aside from all the well known endings from heroin overdoses, the misuse of cocaine and methamphetamine have a big connection with suicide. In those who use cocaine the risk is greatest during withdrawal. Those who use inhalants are also at risk with around twenty percent attempting suicide at some point, and more than sixty five percent considering it, and believe it or not, smoking cigarettes is also connected with a bigger risk of suicide.

In ancient Athens a person who committed suicide without the approval of the state was denied the honors of a normal burial and would be buried alone on the outskirts of the city without a headstone or marker. In Ancient Rome suicide was initially permitted, but was later deemed a crime against the state due to its economic costs. Aristotle condemned all forms of suicide and Plato was ambivalent about it. In Rome reasons for suicide included volunteering death in gladiator combat, guilt over murdering someone, to save the life of another, as a result of mourning, from shame from being raped, and as an escape from intolerable physical suffering, military defeat, or criminal pursuit.

Suicide came to be seen as a sin in Christian Europe and was condemned at the Council of Arles as the work of the Devil. In the Middle Ages the Church had drawn-out discussions about the desire for martyrdom, but Catholic doctrine wasn't settled on the subject of suicide until later in the seventeenth century. A criminal ordinance issued by Louis XIV of France stated that the dead person's body be drawn through the streets, face down, then hung or thrown on a garbage heap. Additionally, all of their property was confiscated.

I have to admit to finding that punishment humorous.

Everyone comes home to me in the end. I literally have all the time in the world, but I do appreciate the sentiment of mass suicides like the Jonestown killings of the twentieth century, and I have to give Fear credit for the great work motivating nine hundred and nine members of the Peoples Temple led by Jim Jones who ended their lives by drinking grape Flavor Aid laced with cyanide and prescription drugs.

On a smaller more imaginative scale were the thirty nine Heaven's Gate cult members led by Marshall Applewhite who were all found dead in a hilltop mansion outside San Diego in a carefully orchestrated suicide with sedatives, vodka, and plastic bags used to suffocate. The victims believed they were going to meet a UFO hiding behind the Hale-Bopp comet. Every one of the members left a statement saying they were going to a better place.

It's awfully hard to ignore a compliment like that!

Many instances of suicide are acts of self sacrifice, so in these instances you come back to me through your own actions. It is an entirely different issue when you have no say in the matter and are sent to me through the decisions and actions of others.

I like to think of this as another thoughtful sentiment, even if it is at the expense of others. It's not that I don't appreciate the gifts, but are they really gifts without an agenda, or are they simply bribes that are stalling tactics to buy more time. It's flattering but in the end it doesn't matter. I'm coming for everybody and everything that's living. After all, it is mine for the taking whenever and whatever way I choose.

On a more sinister note there are those who have worked for me as helpers who think they will get some kind of special treatment because they helped my cause, but I have a surprise for them. I don't play favorites. They are coming with me into the Great Mystery just like everybody else.

Human sacrifice has been practiced throughout history. Victims were ritually killed to appease gods, spirits, or the deceased like what was done as offerings or retainer sacrifices when a king's servants were killed so they could continue to serve their master in the next life.

Cannibalism and headhunting are two closely related practices in tribal societies. Headhunting maintained the illusion of dominance over the body and soul of the hunter's enemies in life and afterlife as a trophy and proof of killing, and a show of greatness and prestige by taking on a rival's spirit and power. It was also considered a means of securing the services of the victim as a slave in the afterlife, but it's primary function was ritual and ceremonial with the belief that the head contained soul matter or life force that could be harnessed through its capture.

From my point of view this egotistical illusion of power is a fruitless attempt to hijack what is already mine. It serves no purpose other than sending these souls to me sooner rather than later and in the bigger picture that has no relevance, because they're already mine. In serving themselves they are unwittingly serving me.

Human sacrifice has been practiced throughout your history and is intended to bring good fortune and pacify the gods in the same way you dedicate a building, a temple, or a bridge. In ancient Japan maidens were buried alive at the base or near constructions to protect the buildings against disasters or enemy attacks. For the re-consecration of the Great Pyramid of Tenochtitlan, the Aztecs killed about eighty-thousand-four-hundred prisoners over the course of four days.

Human sacrifice was often intended to win the gods' favor in warfare. Mongols, Scythians, early Egyptians, ancient Chinese, and Mesoamerican chiefs took their households, including servants and concubines with them to the next world so they could serve them in the afterlife. A great going away party for them, and a great homecoming party for me!

The ever inventive Celts stabbed their victims with swords to divine the future from their death spasms and different gods required different sacrifices. Victims meant for Esus were hanged, those meant for Taranis immolated, and those for Teutates drowned.

Norse warriors were buried with enslaved women with the belief that they would become their wives in Valhalla. After days of festivities they were stabbed to death by an old woman priestess referred to as Völva or "Angel of Death", and burnt together with the deceased in his boat.

I've always found your sacrifices to me oddly endearing, no matter how misguided. It created a bond in the sacrificing community, especially when combined with capital punishment to remove those who had a negative effect on society. Your sense of justice was not always justified when you focused on religious heretics, foreign slaves, or prisoners of war, and you have gotten a little carried away at times when your zeal came in outbursts of blood frenzy and mass killings.

Pre-Columbian Americans sacrificed prisoners and had voluntary sacrifices. In the case of volunteers they were celebrated and pampered as royalty, then crowned with flowers on a bed prepared in a ditch full of flowers and sweet herbs where they were laid with piles of dry wood on both sides and set on fire. The Mixtec players of the infamous Mesoamerican ballgame were sacrificed when the game was used to resolve a dispute between cities. The rulers would play a game instead of going to battle and the losing ruler would be sacrificed. The Maya also held the belief that the limestone sinkholes called *cenotes* were portals to the underworld and sacrificed human beings by tossing them down into them to please the water god Chaac.

Not to be outdone, the Aztecs practiced human sacrifice on a large scale as an offering to Huitzilopochtli because they believed that the sun was engaged in a daily battle and sacrifices would prevent the end of the world that could happen every fifty-two years. The Aztec also periodically sacrificed children. It was believed that the rain god Tlāloc, required their tears.

Who thought that one up?

The number of people sacrificed in central Mexico in the fifteenth century was something like two-hundred-fifty-thousand a year. With so many coming it's hard to keep track and I can't help but feel gratified by so much attention.

Further South the Incas practiced human sacrifice at festivals or royal funerals where retainers also died to accompany the dead into the next life. The Moche of Eastern Peru sacrificed teenagers in large numbers. Their most important ceremonies started with ritual combat and ended in the sacrifice of those defeated in battle. Dressed in fine clothes and adornments, armed warriors faced each other in ritual combat in hand-to-hand encounters aimed at removing the opponent's headdress instead of killing him. The losers were stripped, bound, and led in procession to the place of sacrifice where the priests and priestesses prepared them. Sacrifices varied, but at least one of the victims would be bled to death. His blood was offered to the principal deities, me, myself, and I. As many as four thousand servants, court officials, favorites, and concubines were killed upon the death of the Inca Huayna Capac.

I noted these more dramatic examples to get the point across, but this kind of thing has happened all over the world over time. In many ways these going away parties, or in my case coming home parties that honored me in my many names, faces, and guises have been the ultimate flattery, but in the end it is all meaningless, and though thoughtful, it doesn't make any points with me. Anyone who sacrifices anybody else will come home soon enough; much sooner than they might imagine in the bigger scheme of things.

Many cultures have sacrifices in their mythologies and religious texts that stopped before historical records began. The story of Abraham and Isaac in Genesis is an example of a myth that explains the abolition of human sacrifice. The story ends with an angel stopping Abraham at the last minute and providing a ram to be sacrificed instead.

The Vedic *Purushamedha* literally means human sacrifice is a symbolic act in its earliest references. In Ancient Rome human sacrifice was abolished, replaced by animal sacrifices or mock-sacrifices of effigies.

In a milder version of these traditions, Eastern Orthodox and Roman Catholic Christians believe that the pure sacrifice of Christ is present in the sacrament of the Eucharist, a practice of ritual cannibalism where bread and wine becomes the Real Presence representing the body and blood of the Risen Christ.

Most Protestant traditions do not share the belief in the Real Presence but otherwise believe that in the bread and wine Christ is present spiritually, not in the sense of a change in substance or that the bread and wine of communion are symbolic reminders. Early Christians in the Roman Empire were accused of being cannibals called *theophages*, the Greek word for god eaters.

Ritual murders still happen, but on a much smaller scale than the grand pageantries of blood orgies practiced by the Inca, Maya, Aztecs, and others. Ritual killings by individuals or small groups in modern societies are mostly seen as simple murder and are difficult to classify as human sacrifice, or simple pathological homicide because they lack the societal integration of proper sacrifice.

Instances closest to ritual killing in the criminal history of modern society are mostly pathological serial killers like the Zodiac Killer and mass suicides with doomsday cult backgrounds like the Peoples Temple and the Heaven's Gate incident.

An interesting variation on these practices is the idea of a scapegoat, an animal that is ritually burdened with the sins of others and driven away. The word scapegoat is an English translation from Hebrew that means the sender away of sins, the goat that departs, goat sent out, emissary goat, or better still e - scape goat, although in your ever present inventiveness, you have practiced this with fellow humans you chose to ostracize and blame for holding different beliefs whether political, spiritual, cultural, or for being different in some way perceived as threatening to society.

The story of Jesus Christ is a well known example of this.

Ancient Greeks practiced scapegoating based on the belief that the sacrifice of one or two individuals would save the whole community, but it was mainly used during circumstances like famine, drought, or plague. In their mythologies someone of high importance had to be sacrificed if the whole society was to benefit from the aversion of the catastrophe, but no king or person of importance was willing to sacrifice himself or his children, so the scapegoat came from lower society. In these situations a poor man was feasted and led around the walls of the city once before being stoned, beaten, and driven from the community.

In other variations, German tribes practiced two forms of capital punishment; the first where the victim was hanged from a tree, and another where they were tied to a wicker frame, pushed face down into mud and buried. The first was used to make an example of traitors; the second for punishment of shameful vices like cowardice. Ancient Germans thought that crime should be exposed and infamy should be buried out of sight.

In ancient Rome Vestal Virgins convicted of violating celibacy vows were sealed in a cave with a small amount of bread and water so the goddess Vesta could save them if they were innocent, but in reality they were walled up and left to die instead of being subjected to premature burial.

In Denmark female thieves were buried alive and adulterous women were punished with premature burial and beheaded.

In the Holy Roman Empire rape, infanticide, and theft were punished with live burial. The rape of a virgin was punished by live burial and rapists of non-virgins were beheaded. Female murderers of their employers were also buried alive and sometimes those buried alive were impaled through the heart afterward. This combined punishment of live burial and impalement was practiced in Nuremberg until fifteen–o-eight. The city council decided in fifteen-fifteen that the punishment was too cruel, and opted for drowning instead.

In the sixteenth century Netherlands live burial was used as punishment for women found guilty of heresy.

In seventeenth century feudal Russia live burial as an execution method was known as the pit and used against women condemned for killing their husbands. In sixteen-eighty-nine the punishment was changed to beheading.

In terms of modern mass executions, Serbian officials buried living Bulgarian civilians during the Balkan Wars and in World War Two Japanese soldiers buried Chinese civilians alive. This method of execution was also used by German leaders against Jews in Ukraine and Belarus during World War Two.

Lest you think yourself more civilized in your modern day and age, live burials occurred during the Vietnam War and in the Gulf War where Iraqi soldiers were buried alive by American tanks of the First Infantry Division shoveling earth into their trenches.

Aside from all this unnecessary but appreciated help from you, I have many allies in instruments who are more than willing to help me. Some of them are microscopic life forms that burn through the human body and spirit like wildfire like the Ebola virus and others that aid me in other ways. They can be Beasts of the Wild or something miniscule like a flea on a rat carrying the plague, but my major allies are humans who can wipe out hundreds and thousands with bombs and weapons of war and destruction, or I have help from simpler things like unsanitary conditions that bring cholera or other diseases.

Sometimes I come creeping in increments, the subtle details lost in a slow erosion of vision and the gradual loss of hearing where I come inch by inch, piece by piece taking you on the installment plan, or I might come in the sudden blast of a stroke, embolism, or blood clot. I am after all the face of the Great Mystery and if I am honest about it mass destruction events like Hiroshima and Nagasaki are like orgasms to me, not to mention the help I get from Mother Nature herself in the form of earthquakes, tidal waves, volcanic eruptions, hurricanes, tornadoes, landslides and other natural events.

Talk about instant gratification.

In the end everything conspires to serve me, and why not? You who are human are allies who help me in my work and unwittingly lead yourselves to me. War and ecological destruction bring you to me in masses. All I have to do is sit back and wait for you to give me back the gift of your lives in the mindless pollution of your environment that leaves you drowning in your own shit.

MY IMPORTANT WORK MAINTAINING THE BALANCE

Part of the Great Mystery that I can share with you if you are paying attention is that it always seeks balance, and whether you realize it or not much of my work is in service to that. In spite of what you might think, I really am all loving, all encompassing, and devoted to you.

You have a magical gift of life with all the beauty I bless you with and you mostly speak of me in dark and sorrowful terms. I can take hundreds and thousands of you in an instant with help from your weapons of mass destruction or in more natural ways like storms, floods, and fires, or in less direct ways through famine and disease. I can creep up on you one moment at a time in the slow throes of cancer and other diseases or I can sneak up on you in the middle of the night, and in a flash you're gone before you know it.

When I do come I bring with me the end of life as you know it, but in the bigger scheme of things an end is also a beginning because everything goes full circle in the Great Mystery. Day turns into night, night turns into day, the moon circles the earth, the earth circles the sun, and life succumbs to Me.

You don't know any better and continue to reproduce beyond what is sustainable while poisoning your environment which obligates me to take large scale housecleaning measures in service to the balance that the Great Mystery demands, and it is all in service to the greater good.

My allies in the plant, animal, insect, germ, virus, and other forms of life are more than eager to serve me in this mission as well as the elemental forces of nature. Earth, air, fire, and water work together in weather, earthquakes, volcanoes, and other natural forces, and my compatriot Fear is ever present behind the scenes quickening things when these events come into play.

As an example of how natural forces work when they are not interfered with by humans I want to acknowledge my loyal allies, wolves who prey on hoofed mammals like deer, elk, and moose. By preying on the most vulnerable that are young, diseased, old, weak, or injured, wolves keep their populations healthy and vigorous by regulating group sizes that impact local biodiversity. When deer and elk become too abundant they overgraze vegetation leading to habitat degradation and damaging effects on other wildlife.

In the Southeastern United States, elimination of red wolves resulted in increased coyote and raccoon populations that caused a reduction in wild turkeys, and expanding coyote populations suppressed smaller predators like foxes that prey on smaller mammals responsible for infecting ticks with Lyme disease.

After an absence of close to a hundred years from Yellowstone National Park reintroduced wolves triggered a positive impact on species diversity and abundance across the ecosystem. By reducing prey numbers and altering the behavior of Elk, the Elk became wary of wolves and browsed on different species of vegetation at a different intensity when wolves were present. With less grazing pressure from elk, stream bank vegetation like willow and aspen regenerated after decades of over-browsing creating habitat for birds, fish, beaver, and other species. It also improved aquatic habitat by helping to stabilize channels and control erosion.

Competition with wolves reduces coyote numbers and the impact they have on species like pronghorn. In some areas wolves contributed to reductions in coyote population by as much as half and pronghorn survival increased from twenty to seventy percent while populations of smaller predators like the red fox grew.

Scavenging species also benefit from wolves. Carrion feeders like eagles, bears, and magpies thrive on remains left by them. Ravens also follow wolves as a primary feeding strategy and the remains of kills left by wolves help other species survive food-stressed winters.

Populations change all the time among algae, invertebrates, fish, frogs, birds, and mammals. When resources like food, nesting sites, or refuges are limited, populations decline which helps regulate them around what is sustainable. Predators like wolves also influence the size of the prey population and the interaction between these two forms of population control work together to drive changes in populations over time. I also work with other factors like parasites and disease to further fine tune and influence these balances.

Like the wolves in Yellowstone, red foxes in northern Sweden prey on voles, grouse, and hares that feed on vegetation, and the availability of their food influences their population. When it's abundant their populations grow and when scarce they turn to less desirable foods causing them to grow slower and reproduce less reducing their population. As predator populations increase they act as a top-down control pushing prey populations lower. Aside from these herbivore-prey plant balances and predator-prey interactions, my little minion parasites play a role in regulating populations.

Parasites with complex life cycles require two hosts. In some systems prey function as intermediate hosts with predators acting as primary hosts. Parasites can manipulate the behavior of intermediate hosts to make transmission to primary hosts more likely when the parasite is at a stage of its life cycle when it can successfully infect the primary host. Behavioral changes favoring parasite transmission involve unusual foraging behavior on the part of the intermediate host in locations that make them more susceptible to predation by the primary host, so parasites can change the size of prey populations during times of heavy infestation when they infect the primary host making predator populations diminish.

As part of complex ecological communities, predators, prey, plants, and parasites all influence changes in population size over time. Simple systems can experience large cyclical changes and communities with more complex food webs have more subtle shifts in response to changes in parasite load, predation pressure, and herbivory. Humans have impacted far too many ecological communities by removing predators or reducing the availability of resources.

All of these interactions work together as forces of nature at my command in the service of the Great Mystery to do their part in restoring the balance of nature to maintain sustainability.

When food becomes scarce organisms switch to less-desirable alternatives. The point that they make this shift at depends on a number of factors, including the availability of food, the costs associated with it, and other factors like the risk of exposure to predators while eating.

It should come as no surprise that humans who are also mammals are no different. Being the ever-clever strategists that you are in your wily ways of trying to avoid me, combined with your history of scapegoats and sacrifices, you have been known to make some interesting choices of less-desirable alternatives when you find yourselves challenged by hunger and scarcity.

Cannibalistic behavior is a common ecological interaction in the animal kingdom, and along with that human cannibalism has occurred since prehistoric times. The rate of cannibalism increases in nutritionally poor environments as individuals turn to other individuals as additional food sources. It's a bit of a two-edged sword in that cannibalism regulates population numbers making resources like food, shelter, and territory more available with the decrease of competition. Although it can benefit the individual, cannibalism decreases the expected survival rate of the whole population. Other negative effects include the increased risk of pathogen transmission as the encounter rate of hosts increases.

In some cultures, especially in tribal societies, cannibalism is a cultural norm. Consumption of a person within the same community is called endocannibalism. Ritual cannibalism of the recently deceased can be part of the grieving process or as a way of guiding the souls of the dead into the bodies of living descendants. Exocannibalism is the consumption of a person from outside the community, usually as a celebration of victory against a rival tribe. Both types of cannibalism can be fueled by the belief that eating a person's flesh or internal organs will endow the cannibal with some of the characteristics of the deceased.

In most parts of the world cannibalism is not a societal norm, but is sometimes resorted to in situations of extreme necessity where survivors eat the corpse of someone already dead as opposed to homicidal cannibalism where someone is killed for food.

Cannibalism was practiced in New Guinea and in parts of the Solomon Islands and flesh markets existed in parts of Melanesia. Cannibalism has also been practiced from Fiji to the Amazon Basin to the Congo to the Māori people of New Zealand, and was practiced in ancient Egypt, Roman Egypt, and during famines like the great famine in twelve-hundred-one.

Many instances of cannibalism occurred during World War Two like in the eight-hundred-seventy-two-day Siege of Leningrad after all birds, rats and pets were eaten by survivors. Two-point-eight million Soviet POWs died in Nazi custody in less than eight months during nineteen-forty-one to nineteen-forty-two, and by the winter of nineteen-forty-one starvation and disease resulted in massive deaths which led to many incidents of cannibalism.

German soldiers in the besieged city of Stalingrad cut off from supplies resorted to cannibalism and following the German surrender soldiers were taken prisoner and sent to POW camps in Siberia or Central Asia where due to being underfed by their Soviet captors resorted to cannibalism.

There were several instances of cannibalism in World War Two of Allied prisoners by their Japanese captors. In September nineteen-forty-two, Japanese daily rations on New Guinea consisted of eight-hundred grams of rice and tinned meat. By December it fell to fifty grams and cannibalism was conducted by whole squads under the command of officers. Every day one prisoner was taken out, killed and eaten by soldiers.

During Mao Zedong's Cultural Revolution public events for cannibalism were organized by Communist Party officials and people took part in them to prove their revolutionary passion.

In still another absurd scheme to delay my visit Indian ascetics who believe that eating human flesh confers spiritual and physical benefits like prevention of aging eat those who have voluntarily willed their body to the sect when I take them, so I get their essence. At the risk of sounding insensitive they only get leftovers, which are literally lifeless.

Cannibalism was practiced in several wars in Liberia and the Democratic Republic of the Congo, and still practiced in Papua New Guinea for cultural reasons in ritual and in war in Melanesian tribes. It has also been practiced as a last resort by people suffering from famine like the ill-fated Donner Party, and more recently, the crash of a Uruguayan Air Force Flight where survivors ate the bodies of dead passengers, and then there are the isolated but spectacular cases of the mentally ill like Jeffrey Dahmer.

When things get to the point of becoming unsustainable, more drastic balancing forces have to be brought into play in service to the greater good. I have legions of them that are invisible to the naked eye and can spread across large areas bringing millions of souls home to me in short periods of time so the survivors can have a better stay during their short visit to your third dimension.

There have been a number of mass exoduses who came home to me in history, most of which came with the domestication of animals in forms like influenza and tuberculosis.

In the four-hundred-thirty BC Plague of Athens typhoid fever killed a quarter of Athenian troops and a quarter of the population over the next four years, fatally weakening the dominance of Athens. Its virulence prevented a wider spread because it killed off its hosts faster than they could spread it. In one-hundred-sixty-five to one-hundred-eighty AD the Antonine Plague brought to the Italian peninsula by soldiers returning from the Near East killed a quarter of those infected, up to five million in all. At the height of a second outbreak, in the Plague of Cyprian from two-hundred-fifty-one to to-hundred-sixty-six, five thousand people a day died in Rome.

In another major housecleaning and homecoming from five-hundred-forty-one to seven-hundred-fifty the Plague of Justinian was the first recorded outbreak of the bubonic plague that started in Egypt and reached Constantinople the following spring killing ten thousand a day at its height, going on to eliminate a quarter to a half of the human population throughout the known world causing Europe's population to drop by about half between five-hundred-fifty and seven hundred.

From thirteen-thirty-one to thirteen-fifty-three I raged as the infamous Black Death and brought seventy five million souls home. Starting in Asia, I reached Mediterranean and western Europe in thirteen-forty-eight and killed twenty to thirty million Europeans in six years, a third of the total population and up to a half in the worst-affected urban areas. It was the first of a cycle of European plagues that continued until the eighteenth century.

There were more than a hundred epidemics in Europe in this period and it recurred in England every two to five years from thirteen-sixty-one to fourteen-eighty. By the thirteen-seventies England's population was reduced by half. The Great Plague of London of sixteen-sixty-five to sixteen-sixty-six was its last major outbreak in England when we took about one-hundred-thousand souls; twenty percent of London's population.

A third plague started in China in eighteen-fifty-five and spread to India where ten million people died. During this eruption the United

States saw its first outbreak in the San Francisco plague of nineteen-hundred to nineteen–o-four.

Encounters between European explorers and populations in the rest of the world often introduced local epidemics of extraordinary virulence. Disease killed part of the native population of the Canary Islands in the sixteenth century. Half the native population of Hispaniola in fifteen-eighteen were killed by smallpox which also ravaged Mexico in the fifteen-twenties, killing one-hundred-fifty-thousand in Tenochtitlán alone, including the emperor, and in Peru in the fifteen-thirties, measles killed a further two million natives in the seventeenth century. From sixteen-eighteen to sixteen-nineteen smallpox wiped out ninety percent of the Massachusetts Bay Native Americans.

During the seventeen-seventies smallpox killed at least thirty percent of the Pacific Northwest Native Americans and smallpox epidemics in seventeen-eighty to seventeen-eighty-two and eighteen-thirty-seven to eighteen-thirty-eight brought devastation and drastic depopulation to the Plains Indians. The death of ninety-five percent of the Native American population of the New World was caused by Old World diseases like smallpox, measles, and influenza.

Smallpox also devastated the native population of Australia, killing about half of Indigenous Australians in the early years of British colonization. It also killed many New Zealand Māori. As late as eighteen-forty-eight to eighteen-forty-nine, forty thousand out of one-hundred-fifty-thousand Hawaiians died of measles, whooping cough, and influenza. Introduced diseases, notably smallpox, nearly wiped out the native population of Easter Island and in eighteen-seventy-five measles killed over forty thousand Fijians, about a third of their population. It also devastated the Andamanese population and Ainu population decreased drastically in the nineteenth century due to infectious diseases brought by Japanese settlers pouring into Hokkaido.

In another approach from a different community of microbial allies, syphilis was carried from the New World to Europe after Columbus' voyages and became a major killer in Europe during the Renaissance. Between sixteen-o-two and seventeen-ninety-six, the Dutch East India Company sent almost a million Europeans to work in Asia. Less than a third made their way back to Europe. The majority died of diseases and diseases killed more British soldiers in India than war.

By eighteen-thirty-two the federal government of the United States established a smallpox vaccination program for Native Americans and from the beginning of the twentieth century onward the elimination or control of disease in tropical countries became a driving force for all colonial powers.

The sleeping sickness epidemic in Africa ended due to mobile teams screening millions of people. In the twentieth century the world saw the biggest increase in its population in human history due to lessening of the mortality rate in many countries from medical advances. As a result the world population grew from one-point-six billion in nineteen hundred to an estimated seven billion in the twenty-first century.

If you haven't figured it out by now, I not only rule over every aspect of your life, but the forces of nature are at my command in all its forms from microbes to mammals. In your cleverness you outwit my allies, but I have a vast array to call on.

Since cholera became widespread in the nineteenth century it has brought me tens of millions of souls. Previously restricted to the Indian subcontinent, from eighteen-seventeen to eighteen-twenty-four, starting in Bengal, cholera spread across India and by eighteen-twenty, ten thousand British troops and countless Indians died from it. It extended as far as China and in Indonesia more than one-hundred-thousand people succumbed on the island of Java alone, then to the Caspian Sea before receding. My work in the Indian subcontinent between eighteen-seventeen and eighteen-sixty exceeded fifteen million souls and another twenty-three million died between eighteen-sixty-five and nineteen-seventeen.

From eighteen-twenty-six to eighteen-thirty-seven cholera reached Russia, Hungary, Germany in eighteen-thirty-one, London in eighteen-thirty-two, France, Canada, and the United States in the same year, making it to the Pacific coast of North America by eighteen-thirty-four.

Flu viruses have also erupted over time that trimmed back your numbers like the Russian Flu, the Spanish Flu, the Asian Flu, and in the last part of the twentieth century the Hong Kong Flu, all of which brought millions of souls home to me. These continue to mutate and adapt to help me get the natural world back into a more sustainable balance.

Aside from my star performers I have typhus, measles, tuberculosis, leprosy, malaria, yellow fever, and more recently SARS, Ebola, and Zika viruses. Mind you, these are just my microbial armies that work closely with my insect and animal kingdoms to reduce their numbers in the name of restoring balance in the service of the Great Mystery.

Modern day viral hemorrhagic fevers like Ebola, Lassa fever, Rift Valley fever, Marburg virus, and Bolivian hemorrhagic fever are highly contagious and deadly, but their ability to cause a massive outbreak is limited because their transmission requires close contact with an infected vector that only has a short time before I end it. The short time between a vector becoming infectious and the onset of symptoms lets medical professionals quarantine vectors and prevent them from breaking out elsewhere. Genetic mutations can also occur that increase their potential for widespread harm.

Antibiotic-resistant microorganisms called superbugs can cause the re-emergence of diseases that are currently controlled. Cases of tuberculosis resistant to traditionally effective treatments remain a big threat. Every year nearly half a million new cases of multidrug-resistant tuberculosis occur worldwide with China and India having the highest rates. About fifty million people worldwide are infected with multidrug-resistant TB, seventy-nine percent of which are resistant to three or more antibiotics. In two-thousand-five, one-hundred-twenty-four cases were reported in the United States and extensive drug-resistant TB was identified in Africa in two-thousand-six and subsequently discovered in forty-nine other countries including the United States. There are about forty thousand new cases every year.

Common infectious bacteria have developed resistance to whole classes of antibiotics. Antibiotic-resistant organisms have also become an important cause of healthcare-associated infections and infections caused by community-acquired strains of methicillin-resistant *Staphylococcus aureus* known as MRSA in otherwise healthy people.

I'm impressed with how quickly you emulated the way my microbial armies work with my insect and animal kingdoms to reduce populations and harness it to your advantage. Your man made methods of self-destruction are effective, but they cannot sustain your growing numbers. Your cleverness in adopting these natural relations to that end is not only brilliant, it serves the Great Mystery in helping to restore an ecological balance of forces.

You have been practicing rudimentary biological warfare for some time now. During the sixth century BC the Assyrians poisoned enemy wells with a fungus that made them delirious. In thirteen-forty-six the bodies of Mongol warriors of the Golden Horde who died of plague were thrown over the walls of the besieged Crimean city of Kaffa preceding the spread of the Black Death into Europe, Near East, and North Africa, bringing me about twenty-five million Europeans.

British Army commanders approved the use of smallpox as a biological weapon in the French and Indian War to target Native Americans causing a smallpox outbreak by giving two blankets and a scarf taken from a Small Pox Hospital to them.

By nineteen hundred the germ theory and advances in bacteriology brought a new level of sophistication to the use of bio-agents in war. Biological sabotage in the form of anthrax and glanders was undertaken on behalf of the Imperial German government during World War One, then the Geneva Protocol of nineteen-twenty-five prohibited the use of chemical and biological weapons.

With the onset of World War Two the Ministry of Supply in the United Kingdom established a biological warfare program where tularemia, anthrax, brucellosis, and botulism toxins were weaponized. Although the British never used the biological weapons it developed, its program was the first to successfully weaponize a variety of deadly pathogens and bring them into industrial production. Other nations like France and Japan began their own biological weapons programs.

When the United States entered the war Allied resources were pooled at the request of the British and the U.S. established a large research program at Fort Detrick, Maryland. The biological and chemical weapons developed there were tested at the Dugway Proving Grounds in Utah generating facilities for the mass production of anthrax spores, brucellosis, and botulism.

The most notorious program of that time was run by a secret Imperial Japanese Army Unit based in Manchuria that conducted fatal human experiments on prisoners and produced biological weapons for combat use.

Although the Japanese lacked the technological sophistication of American and British programs, it outstripped them in its widespread application and indiscriminate brutality. Biological weapons were used against Chinese soldiers and civilians in several military campaigns. In nineteen-forty the Japanese Army Air Force bombed Ningbo with ceramic bombs full of fleas carrying the bubonic plague. Many of these operations were ineffective due to inefficient delivery systems, although up to four-hundred- thousand people died. During the Zhejiang-Jiangxi Campaign in nineteen-forty-two, around one-thousand-seven-hundred Japanese troops died out of a total ten thousand soldiers who fell ill with disease when their own biological weapons attack rebounded on them.

During the final months of World War Two Japan planned to use plague as a biological weapon against civilians in San Diego, California during Operation Cherry Blossoms. The plan was set to launch on the twenty-second of September nineteen-forty-five, but was not executed because of Japan's surrender on the fifteenth of August nineteen-forty-five.

In Britain the nineteen-fifties saw the weaponization of plague, brucellosis, tularemia, equine encephalomyelitis, and vaccinia viruses, but the program was canceled in nineteen-fifty-six while the United States Army Biological Warfare Laboratories weaponized anthrax, tularemia, brucellosis, Q-fever and others.

The United States also developed an anti-crop capability during the Cold War that used plant diseases to destroy enemy agriculture. Biological weapons also targeted fisheries as well as water-based vegetation. Diseases like wheat blast and rice blast were weaponized in aerial spray tanks and cluster bombs for delivery to enemy watersheds in agricultural regions to initiate epidemics among plants. Biological warfare can also specifically target plants to destroy crops or defoliate vegetation. The United States and Britain discovered plant growth regulators during the Second World War and initiated a herbicidal warfare program that was used in Malaya and Vietnam in counterinsurgency operations.

In the nineteen-eighties the Soviet Ministry of Agriculture developed variants of foot-and-mouth disease, rinderpest against cows, African swine fever for pigs, and psittacosis to kill chickens that were prepared to be sprayed from tanks attached to airplanes over hundreds of miles.

Japan and several other nations have developed and been accused of using entomological warfare by employing insects in a direct attack or as vectors to deliver biological agents like plague. Entomological warfare exists in three varieties. One type involves infecting insects with a pathogen and dispersing them over target areas where they act as a vector infecting any person or animal they bite. Another is a direct insect attack against crops where the insect is not infected with any pathogen but represents a threat to agriculture, and the final method uses uninfected insects like bees and wasps to directly attack the enemy.

Biological weapons can be used to gain an advantage over an enemy, either by threats or actual deployments and can be easily developed and stockpiled allowing nations to pose a credible threat of mass casualty that can alter the terms of how other nations interact with them. They also have the potential to create a level of destruction and loss of life far in excess of nuclear, chemical, or conventional weapons relative to their mass, cost of development, and storage.

Biological weapons are difficult to detect, economical, and easy to use, making them appeal to terrorists. The cost of a biological weapon is estimated to be about point-o-five percent of the cost of a conventional weapon to produce similar numbers of mass casualties per kilometer square and their production is simple. Common technology can produce biological warfare like that used in production of vaccines, foods, spray devices, beverages, and antibiotics. A major factor of biological warfare that attracts terrorists is that they can easily escape before government agencies or secret agencies can start investigations because the potential organism has a short incubation period of three to seven days.

A technique called Clustered, Regularly Interspaced, Short Palindromic Repeat known as CRISPR is now cheap and widely available. In this technique a DNA sequence is cut off and replaced with a new sequence that codes for a particular characteristic that can show up in an organism that can be extremely dangerous if used with wrong intentions. These weapons can backfire and harm more than the intended victims and could have even worse effects than on the target. Additionally agents like smallpox or other airborne viruses can spread worldwide and ultimately infect the user's home country.

In your competitions to find different ways to destroy each other the only one who wins is Me, and in the bigger scheme of things even that is irrelevant, because there is no winning here. All I have to do is come for you whenever I feel. No matter which way you cut it your homecoming is inevitable.

Aside from playing around with nature which does keep us closer, I still have to bring in forces bigger than you, or to be more precise forces that you call in when your consumption outgrows what your environment can handle. In terms of extending your time in the third dimension and your clever schemes and goals of gaining more while you are there, you are your own worst enemy, and knowingly or not, all that you do plays into the inescapable goal of the Great Mystery bringing things into balance.

Sometimes the forces of nature, your manipulation of them, greed, pollution, and even the elemental forces of earth, air, fire, and water form into weather patterns that come from your disruption of the natural order. Any combination of these can negatively impact the food supply that sustains you, resulting in famine, war, inflation, crop failure, population imbalance, or government policies accompanied by malnutrition, starvation, epidemic, and increased mortality. Every inhabited continent in the world has experienced famine.

In the nineteenth and twentieth century it was mostly Southeast and South Asia as well as Eastern and Central Europe that suffered the most deaths from famine, but the numbers dying from it began to fall from the two thousands, ultimately creating more unseen problems.

The cyclical occurrence of famine has been a mainstay of societies engaged in subsistence agriculture since the dawn of agriculture itself and its frequency and intensity has fluctuated throughout history depending on changes in food demand, population growth, and supply-side shifts caused by changing climate. Famine was first eliminated in Holland and England during the seventeenth century from the commercialization of agriculture and the implementation of improved techniques to increase crop yields.

By the mid-nineteenth century governments could alleviate the effects of famine through price controls, large scale importation of food products from foreign markets, stockpiling, rationing, and regulating production and charity. The Great Famine of eighteen-forty-five in Ireland was one of the first to feature such intervention, although the government response was lackluster. Confronted by widespread crop failure in the autumn of eighteen-forty-five, Ireland's Prime Minister purchased one-hundred-thousand pounds worth of maize and cornmeal from America. Due to weather conditions the first shipment did not arrive in Ireland until the beginning of February eighteen-forty-six when the maize corn was re-sold for a penny a pound.

A systematic attempt at creating a regulatory framework for dealing with famine was developed by the British Raj in the eighteen-eighties. The British created an Indian Famine commission to address the issue of famine to recommend steps for the government to take in the event of one. The commission issued a series of guidelines and regulations on how to respond to famines and food shortages called the Famine Code which was one of the first attempts to scientifically predict famine to mitigate its effects.

During the twentieth century around seventy million people died from famines across the world. An estimated thirty million of them died during the famine of nineteen-fifty-eight to nineteen-sixty one in China. Other notable famines included the Bengal famine of nineteen-forty-three caused by the Japanese occupation of Burma, famines in China in nineteen-twenty-eight and nineteen-forty-two, and a sequence of famines in Russia and elsewhere in the Soviet Union, including the Russian famine of nineteen-twenty-one and the Soviet famine of nineteen-thirty-two.

A few of the great famines of the late twentieth century were: the Biafran famine in the nineteen-sixties, the Khmer Rouge-caused famine in Cambodia in the nineteen-seventies, the North Korean famine of the nineteen-nineties and the Ethiopian famine of nineteen-eighty-three to nineteen-eighty-five.

Until two-thousand-seventeen worldwide deaths from famine had been falling. From the eighteen-seventies to the nineteen-seventies famines killed an average of nine-hundred-twenty-eight-thousand people a year. Since nineteen-eighty annual deaths dropped to an average of seventy-five-thousand, less than ten percent of what they had been until the nineteen-seventies. That reduction came despite the one-hundred-fifty-thousand lives lost in the two-thousand-eleven Somalia famine.

The total number of humans currently living reached around seven-point-seven billion in November two-thousand-eighteen. It took over two-hundred-thousand years of human history for the world's population to reach one billion, and only two hundred years to reach seven billion. World population has experienced continuous growth since the end of the Great Famine of thirteen-fifteen to thirteen-seventeen and the Black Death in thirteen-fifty when it was near three-hundred-seventy million. The highest population growth rose over one-point eight percent a year between nineteen-fifty-five and nineteen-seventy-five, peaking to two-point o-six percent between nineteen-sixty-five and nineteen-seventy. The growth rate has declined to one-point-one-eight percent between two-thousand-ten and two-thousand-fifteen and is projected to decline further in the course of the twenty-first century.

World population reached one billion for the first time in eighteen-o-four and it was another one-hundred-twenty-three years before it reached two billion in nineteen-twenty-seven. It took only thirty-three years to reach three billion in nineteen-sixty, fourteen years to reach four billion in nineteen-seventy-four, thirteen years to reach five billion in nineteen-eighty-seven, twelve years to reach six billion in nineteen-ninety-nine, and twelve years to reach seven billion in October two-thousand-eleven.

How many people can your world hold with diminishing resources that are consumed at ever increasing rates to remain sustainable in support of this burgeoning life?

Your rapidly expanding numbers aggravates environmental problems, including rising atmospheric carbon dioxide, global warming, pollution, and the situation grows worse. Continued human population growth and over-consumption are the primary drivers of mass species extinction. By twenty-fifty population growth and wasteful consumption could result in oceans containing more plastic than fish by weight. All of this is to say that rapid population growth is the biggest driver behind many ecological threats.

To your credit you have recognized the problem and made efforts to fix it, but they are insufficient. Not only is your overpopulation more complex than you can resolve, but in the end it won't stop me from coming. It's only a matter of when and how many I decide to take at a time, and that is driven by how much is sustainable.

Of all the twentieth century's great humanitarian ventures none has accomplished more than your campaign to control world population. Fertility rates have declined in every region of the world, but your efforts account for only a small share of the decline. Aid levels for family planning have been flat or declining since the mid-nineteen-nineties, even though birthrates remain high in many countries. Tens of millions of women in sub-Saharan Africa and other regions still lack birth control and safe abortions.

After World War Two, the movement to reduce population growth encountered unexpected practical and moral problems. What should be done when ordinary people are reluctant to do what's good for them or humanity? In the nineteen-sixties and nineteen-seventies in the heyday of population control, the movement gave many wrong answers.

Family planning grew out of two contradictory movements. The eugenics movement attracted those who were concerned not just about the numbers, but the kind of people who might inherit the earth. Eugenicists aimed to breed better people by sterilizing the unfit and encouraging fitter parents to have more children. After World War One feminists promoted birth control as a means of liberating women and preventing poverty and war, but many progressives sympathetic to eugenics and its promise to attack the most basic causes of poverty and conflict, and an alliance between feminists and eugenicists formed under the banner of family planning left out who would do the planning.

At first family planning involved voluntary efforts, but high birthrates in poor countries combined with declining death rates due to improved nutrition and health fueled rapid increases in population.

No government went further than India from nineteen-seventy-five to nineteen-seventy-seven when they raised incentive payments, ratcheted up disincentives, and encouraged states to consider compulsory sterilization for Indians with more than three children. To many the population effort looked like a war on the poor, especially when an aggressive slum clearance program and displaced Indians were told they could not build new homes elsewhere unless they consented to sterilization. In several towns and cities the police and army fired on crowds to keep sterilization camps running.

Population control met its formal end in nineteen-ninety-four in what was called the Cairo Consensus, where one-hundred-sixty-two states rejected the use of population targets and the incentives and disincentives used to reach them, embracing instead a new focus on the well being of individuals, including full reproductive rights, education for women, and health care for mothers and infants.

The United States gives more than four-hundred-million dollars to family planning efforts worldwide, more than any other country, but younger people committed to the cause cared most about extending reproductive rights with the idea that women should have the same freedom to control their fertility, regardless of what size family they choose to have.

Family planning accounts for about a quarter of the worldwide decline in fertility rates since the nineteen-fifties. Women can choose from pills, IUDs, implants, and injectables that might not exist had family planning organizations not pushed to develop them, but women had the means to regulate the number of children they bore long before these methods. What was lacking was the economic security, education, and basic health needed to persuade couples to have smaller families. Where those conditions occur birthrates decline. Brazil, Algeria, and Turkey, all made minimal efforts in family planning in the second half of the 20th century, yet fertility rates in all three declined dramatically.

I also want to give a nod to those engaging in same sex relationships. Your love of each other halts procreation and contributes to keeping things in balance without my having to intervene. Yes, you will all come home to me just like everybody else, but you can feel good about your part in contributing to the work.

In spite of all your efforts to stem your rising population, you cannot keep up with your growing numbers, and at some point you will reach a threshold where your environment can no longer support so many lives. When that time comes I'll be patiently waiting for you to come home to me as I always have, and as always there will be many ways for you to return to me.

YOU CAN RUN, BUT YOU CAN'T HIDE

Yes, I'm coming for you, or you're coming for me. It's all a matter of perspective. I could come at any moment no matter how old or how young you are. I can take you in a heartbeat, a breath, a flash, or I can take you slowly on the installment plan. I can even take you before you ever get into the world.

I can be gentle and slip you away in the darkest depths of unconsciousness where you never know what happened, or I can sneak up on you mid-dream, maybe as a character, friend, or loved one, and welcome you home that way. The variations are endless.

I can appear as Jesus, Buddha, Muhammad, or any other guru or leader you expect or desire. I have many names and faces in a multitude of times and places so your choices are only limited by your imagination. If any of my many faces and facets do come to you, then your expectation took part in the creation of that moment, making you a co-creator of that moment.

It *is* the Great Mystery, and part of the fun is that anything can happen. You could even come home to me with an open heart the way I receive you without any judgment or expectations.

I've already talked about what people thought and expected in the past and today you have an even wider selection of healers, gurus, and spiritual guides who hope to lay claim to you. If you're a member of their group then who knows, they may very well have their own special Heaven and afterlife set aside for you.

You might consider yourself blessed to follow best-selling author and pastor Joel Osteen who lives in a ten and a half million dollar home and has a net worth of forty million dollars. According to Osteen the entire Bible is inspired by God without error, and it is the authority he bases his faith, conduct, and doctrine on. He also believes that Jesus Christ is the Son of God who came to the earth as Savior of the world who died on the cross and shed His blood for *your* sins. Osteen preaches that salvation is found by placing your faith in what Jesus did for you on the cross and that Jesus rose from the dead and is coming again.

Osteen says every believer should be in a growing relationship with Jesus by obeying God's Word, yielding to the Holy Spirit and by conforming to the image of Christ. As children of God, we are overcomers and more than conquerors and God intends for each of us to experience the abundant life He has in store for us.

You have to admit, with his massive wealth and following, Osteen is living proof of an abundant life.

For Osteen Heaven is when you have a relationship with God and his son Jesus which is what the Bible teaches; Jesus is the way, the truth and the light and the only way to the father is through him. In Osteen's path to Heaven, "When you become a follower of Christ not only do you receive eternal life but you are blessed with spiritual blessings. Scripture tells us that we are blessed with every blessing in Heaven. What are the spiritual blessings of Heaven? Peace, joy, favor, abundance, grace, and so much more." All you need to do is. "Lift up your eyes and look toward Heaven. You will naturally move in the direction that your eyes are looking, and when you receive Christ as salvation, that gives you a guarantee for Heaven."

What about those who don't believe that the entire Bible is inspired by God without error? Where do they go?

Osteen's view is only one of the many paths to Heaven that are popular in your modern day with its roots in antiquity.

Mormons trace their origins to the visions that Joseph Smith reported while living in upstate New York. In eighteen-twenty-three, Smith said an angel directed him to a buried book written on golden plates containing the religious history of an ancient people. Smith published what he claimed was a translation of these plates in March eighteen-thirty as the Book of Mormon, named after Mormon, the ancient prophet–historian who compiled the book.

What happened to the Bible?

The Church of Jesus Christ of Latter-day Saints believes there is life after death and that once you die, your spirit and your body are separated. Your body is buried, but your spirit continues to live on in what they call the spirit world where you enter into either Paradise or spirit prison, based on how you lived your life. These are not the same as Heaven and Hell because your time there is temporary.

Spirit Paradise is a place of rest and peace where the spirits of those who were obedient and followed Christ can rest from their troubles and sorrow. It is a place you will be more familiar with and will seem more natural than you may think. You will see family and friends and be able to associate with them.

Spirit prison is for people who have not been obedient or followed Christ, but still have the opportunity to learn about Jesus and His gospel, and grow and become better people before receiving the judgment of God.

After spending time in the spirit world, everyone will be resurrected and their spirits and bodies will be reunited. The scriptures teach that they will stand before the Lord to be judged.

Unlike other religions that believe the afterlife is two places — Heaven or Hell— The Church of Jesus Christ of Latter-day Saints believes that we inherit one of three kingdoms that are compared to the brightness of the sun, the moon, and the stars. You will inherit a kingdom based on your obedience to the gospel of Jesus and your acceptance of the sacrifice of Jesus.

According to the Mormons those obedient to God's commandments who complete the ordinances like baptism required to return will be able to live with God again in a kingdom as glorious as the sun. This is considered Heaven, because it is the place where God and Jesus live. It is not a state of being, but an actual location where you can live with God forever.

The people who reside in the other two kingdoms can't enjoy God's presence.

Heaven is the ultimate reward that you can receive in the afterlife and is determined by the choices you make in your present life. Church members believe that in Heaven family relationships continue for eternity and everyone lives with God and Jesus which is why Church members believe it is a place of true joy.

Quite an exclusive set up they have there, but you have to follow the rules and regulations, and if you don't behave you will not be able to enjoy God's presence.

Once again, Jesus is the way. What a deal!

Jesus made a huge impact on western culture and has spawned so many splintered movements of religious thought that I'm going to talk more about him later as well as my pal Satan and the many variations of Heaven and Hell that have been conceived of as afterlife possibilities.

Though there are too many faiths to mention, following the ones that are popular in the United States, I enjoy how they put their own spin on old beliefs, or reinvent them through creative writing. First there was the Bible which according to Osteen is the unequivocal inspired word of God. More recently there is the Mormon angel directed buried book written on golden plates containing the religious history of an ancient people.

Not to be outdone there is a more recent faith created by science fiction writer L. Ron Hubbard that creates a totally different scenario for salvation if you don't want to put your faith in Jesus and the old ways. Hubbard's book *The History of Man*, published in nineteen-fifty-two, says there are two entities housed in the human body, a genetic entity whose purpose is to carry on the evolutionary line, and a Thetan consciousness that has the capacity to separate from body and mind. According to Hubbard, "In man's long evolutionary development the Thetan has been trapped by the engrams formed at various stages of embodiment. Among the abilities of the Operating Thetan is the soul's capacity to leave and operate apart from the body."

Scientology teaches that "a thetan is the person himself, not his body or his name or the physical universe, his mind or anything else." According to the doctrine, "one does not have a thetan, he is a thetan."

In Scientology the human body is seen as similar to other religions in that when I come, the spirit will leave it. Life and personality goes on but the physical part of the organism ceases to function. Scientologists believe in the immortality of each individual's spirit, so they don't worry so much about me. They say the spirit acquires another body necessary for growth and survival to achieve an individual's true identity. Scientology is a blend of science and spirituality with belief in an immortal spirit and in improving that spirit on Earth using their methods. Scientologists don't dwell on Heaven, Hell, or the afterlife, they focus on the spirit.

Salvation is achieved through clearing engrams and implants, the source of human misery through their specialized auditing process. Salvation is limited to the current life and there is no final salvation or damnation. There is only the eternal return of life after life where the individual comes back and has a responsibility for what goes on today since they will experience it tomorrow.

The Church of Scientology has no set dogma on God and allows individuals to come to their own understanding of God. More emphasis is given to the godlike nature of the person and to the workings of the human mind than to the nature of God.

The church considers itself scientific, although this belief has no basis in institutional science. Scientologists believe that all religious claims can be verified through experimentation and that their religion was derived through scientific methods. Hubbard found knowledge through studying and thinking, not through revelation, but his science of Dianetics was never accepted by the scientific community. Scientology differs from the scientific method in that it has become increasingly self-referential, while true science compares competing theories and observed facts.

Science fiction writer Hubbard insisted that Dianetics was based on the scientific method and taught that "the scientific sensibilities carry over into the spiritual realities one encounters via auditing on the e-meter." Scientologists prefer to describe Hubbard's teachings with words like knowledge, technology, and workability, rather than belief or faith. Hubbard described Dianetics and Scientology as technologies based on his claim of their scientific precision and workability.

Members of the Church believe that Hubbard discovered the existential truths that form their doctrine through research, leading to the idea that Scientology is science. Hubbard created what the church calls a spiritual technology to advance its goals. According to the church Scientology works one hundred percent of the time when it is properly applied to a person who sincerely desires to improve their life.

This pseudoscientific system of belief is opposed to psychiatry and psychology, viewing them as barbaric and corrupt, especially in light of the fact that the psychiatric establishment rejected Hubbard's theories in the early nineteen-fifties. Ever since, Scientology argues that psychiatry suffers from the fundamental flaw of ignoring humanity's spiritual dimension and fails to take into account Hubbard's insights about the nature of the mind. Scientology holds psychiatry responsible for a great many wrongs in the world, saying it has offered itself as a tool of political suppression and that psychiatry spawned the ideology that fired Hitler's mania, turned the Nazis into mass murderers, and created the Holocaust.

Wow!

I can't help but wonder what Freud and Jung would think of that?

Scientology teaches that progress on The Bridge to Total Freedom requires the attainment of high moral and ethical standards. Their system of ethics is designed to motivate members to expand the church. A member's ethical level is tied to their performance in recruiting new members.

The Scientology religion is based exclusively upon L. Ron Hubbard's research, writings, and recorded lectures which constitute the Scriptures of the religion. His work, recorded in five-hundred-thousand pages of writings, six-thousand-five-hundred reels of tape and forty-two films, is archived for posterity and holds the ultimate ecclesiastical authority and the pure application of L. Ron Hubbard's religious technologies.

In this belief system, misinformation or miscommunication is analogous to original sin and inhibits individual growth and relationships with others. The misunderstood word is a central teaching in Scientology and failure in reading comprehension is attributed to it.

You have to give Hubbard credit for originality.

So many people have so many expectations of what's going to happen when I come for them, where they will go, what I might or might not do to or for them, or who I might let take them to *their* planned kingdom. No matter what happens and no matter how it is seen, it is all me and only I know what really happens when I take you home, yet so many have figured it all out for me and everyone else based on expectations created in their wildest imaginings.

Maybe those things will happen for those believers.

Then again, maybe not.

You will only discover the truth of my open arms when it happens.

With all these pre-defined deities, realities, and systems of belief that so many think I am the portal to, what about those who don't follow any of those preconceived imaginings? Where do nonbelievers fit in?

For the record, I don't care what anybody thinks or believes. It has no relevance to me. You are all mine regardless of what you imagine, and I look forward to embracing each and every one of you when our special moment arrives.

No expectations.

Nothing is the state of nonexistence, which is how non-believing atheists characterize any conception of God, yet in the paradox of their denial they are unequivocally announcing that *they* are God as they have made the ultimate judgment call, and in so doing they claim their throne at the center of their subjective universe.

From this perspective, if they ceased to exist then nothing else would exist which puts them in the role of a creator God who rules over the existence of everything that falls under their range of thought and perception, and denies existence to any other unique and individual intelligences that might exist outside of them.

I exist inside of them and they exist inside of me and we are connected. In the same way that the silence between the notes in music carry as much weight as the music itself, atheists have their place in the study of belief, in fact they believe that they don't believe.

You have to give atheists credit for taking responsibility for themselves instead of following the dizzying array of healers, gurus, and spiritual guides whose imaginations have created every manner of paradise in your modern age according to their own set of rules. In the past there were fewer options for individuals, and in the eyes of society there were no choices, only those beliefs and actions imposed on them by society enforced by the threat of torture, death, or imprisonment.

That'll make a believer out of you!

Though many souls follow the old ways, those nations that value freedom of religion the way the United States originally intended allow every kind of belief imaginable. Instead of ancient threats, promises, and limited conceptions of Heaven and Hell, in modern times the constantly shifting choices are growing and expanding into everything from the Church of the Flying Spaghetti Monster known as Pastafarianism that opposes the teaching of intelligent design and creationism in public schools to the pseudoscience based imaginings of science *fiction* writer L. Ron Hubbard.

Needless to say, none of this matters to me. You always come home to me no matter what path you take, how you might imagine we will meet, and who or what you might imagine will be involved. Regardless of any ideas, personalities, or events surrounding our reunion, in the end you will meet me all alone in a most intimate way that is far beyond anything you might imagine.

I am after all the face of the Great Mystery.

You might wonder why I am bringing this to your attention if it has no relevance to me, but it does have relevance to you and I feel compelled to draw your attention to these anomalies out of the unconditional love that I have for you. Even though you can be led in any number of directions, the truth will become apparent at the point when I assert myself and the greater reality that I represent.

The truth is that you have no idea about what will happen when we meet at the boundary of your three dimensional world, and you only have your imagination to conjure up how you think this will transpire.

All of these imaginings and beliefs are nothing more than ingenious, sophisticated ways of denying the reality that I am while inventing what for you is incomprehensible in your limited perspective. You can distract yourself by the boundlessness of your imagination, and you can run and try to deny any anticipation of my reality, but you can't hide. All of these inventive schemes are illusory and one form of denial of me or another at their core.

Many of you confess to priests or follow gurus or other spiritual leaders to relieve yourselves of the burden of your perceived sins hoping to find guidance on the path, but by shedding your burden and passing it off to your guru, guide, or confessor for absolution, you rob yourself of personal responsibility for what *you* have manifested.

Self-proclaimed gurus are more sophisticated purveyors of lies of denial who claim to be enlightened. They are masters at drawing the lost and searching into their wake pulling searchers outside of themselves, away from the source where their conflict originates, lulling them into a false sense of security. These false prophets consciously or subconsciously have an agenda that puts them in a position of power and adoration from their followers, adding to an increasing self-perpetuating sense of self-delusional authority. The more unwarranted attention they get the stronger their illusion of power becomes and the less they have to look at their own shortcomings. Their attention is focused away from themselves, lavished upon their adoring flock.

I am the only constant in your life that is with you every moment of your existence. Family, friends, love, relationships, possessions, wealth, poverty, joy, and sorrow will come and go, but I am ever-present, ready to assert myself at a moment's notice. I am the only thing you can count on. I am the one sole, undisputed truth of your existence and you spend massive amounts of time and energy trying to escape Me.

You not only run from the greater truth that I am, you run from the truth of yourself, caught up in the chattering monkey mind of your denied shadow selves that drive the conflict between your heart and mind, not to mention all the means of escape that you avoid me with including alcohol, sex, drugs, music, food, pornography, hobbies, art, books, and more.

Don't get me wrong, there's nothing wrong with enjoying the temporary pleasures that life has to offer. Some of them have the potential to expand your consciousness and broaden your understanding of what it means to be human, but the majority of you escape into addictions, often with the help of doctors who prescribe antidepressants and other pain killers like opiates that hide the truth of your existence, and often bring me calling sooner than I might have if you hadn't buried yourself so deep in trying to escape me.

The escape of addiction is a psychological and physical inability to stop consuming a chemical, drug, activity, or substance, even though it causes psychological and physical harm. The term doesn't only refer to dependence on substances like heroin, cocaine, or alcohol. A person who cannot stop taking a particular drug or chemical has a substance dependence. Some addictions also involve the inability to stop gambling, eating, or working, which constitutes a behavioral addiction.

These dependencies are more ways of running from me and yourselves, but in your running away, what are you running to?

Ultimately, right into my loving, expectant presence.

Home.

My heart is wide open to you, longing for your embrace, which is also your deepest Fear.

You didn't think I forgot about my ever loyal cohort, did you?

Fear is the one who drives you to these futile things.

What I am pointing out here is that until I come for you, you are in charge of you. Nobody else. No healer, priest, guru, or deity can save you from yourself or the burden of your fears and denials while you are living on the earth.

What expectations will you bring when you leave the world behind and come home to me?

Maybe when that magical moment of transformation comes, instead of running from me and denying me, you will embrace me with the all consuming love that I will be embracing you with.

HEAVEN AND HELL

I am the portal to what exists outside of your limited three dimensional reality. How you perceive me when you come home and what you expect from me will influence your entry and may delight, disappoint, or terrify you, depending on how the Great Mystery unfolds for you and how you receive it. Different cultures have envisioned passages from three dimensions to me through different times and places in your history. Most of these convictions have a belief in immortality or some continuation of the self, which implies a connection to the divine.

Though there are a multitude of differing conceptions of the afterlife, the most common element underlying them all is the concept of reward, punishment, and redemption which are portrayed in diverse imaginative conceptions of Heaven and Hell.

Heaven is a common religious, cosmological, transcendent place where gods, angels, spirits, saints, or venerated ancestors are said to originate, be enthroned, or live. In some religions Heavenly beings can descend to earth or incarnate, and earthly beings can ascend to Heaven in the afterlife, and in exceptional cases they can enter Heaven alive.

Heaven is often described as a higher place, the holiest place, and a Paradise, in contrast to Hell, the Underworld, or the low places. It is universally accessible by earthly beings according to varying standards of divinity, goodness, piety, faith, or other virtues, right beliefs, or simply the will of God. Some believe in the possibility of a Heaven on Earth in a World to Come.

There are so many different beliefs throughout the world that claim to tell you how I will come and where I will take you when that happens. I could never do them all justice, so I will give you some more well-known ones as examples.

Many cultures believe in an axis mundi or world tree that connects the Heavens, the terrestrial world, and the underworld. In Indian religions the soul is subjected to rebirth in different living forms according to its *karma*. This cycle can be broken after a soul achieves *Moksha* or *Nirvana,* and any place of existence, either of humans, souls, or deities outside the tangible world is referred to as *otherworld.*

Ancient Mesopotamians regarded the sky as a series of domes covering the flat earth. The lowest dome of Heaven was made of jasper and was the home of the stars. The middle dome was made of *saggilmut* stone and was the abode of the gods. The highest and outermost dome was made of *luludānītu* stone personified as An, the god of the sky. Celestial bodies were equated with specific deities and the planet Venus was believed to be Inanna, the goddess of love, sex, and war, while the sun was her brother Utu the god of justice, and the moon was their father Nanna.

Ordinary mortals could not go to Heaven because it was the abode of the gods. After a person died their soul went to a dark shadowy underworld located deep below the surface of the earth. All souls went to the same afterlife and a person's actions during life had no impact on how they would be treated in the world to come.

In Ancient Egyptian religion Heaven was a physical place far above the earth in a dark area of space where there were no stars, basically beyond the Universe. Departed souls would undergo a literal journey to reach Heaven. Along the way there were hazards and other entities attempting to deny the reaching of Heaven. Their heart would finally be weighed with the feather of truth and if the sins weighed it down their heart was devoured.

The Bahá'í Faith describes Heaven as a spiritual condition where closeness to God is defined as Heaven and Hell is seen as a state of remoteness from God. They believe that the nature of the life of the soul in the afterlife is beyond comprehension in the physical plane, but the soul will retain its consciousness and individuality and remember its physical life. It will also be able to recognize other souls and communicate with them. In the Bahá'í Faith view there is a hierarchy of souls in the afterlife where the merits of each soul determines their place in the hierarchy. Souls lower in the hierarchy cannot comprehend the station of those above. Each soul can progress in the afterlife, but its development is not entirely dependent on its own conscious efforts. It is also augmented by the grace of God, the prayers of others, and good deeds performed by others on Earth in the name of that person.

Buddhists have several Heavens which are part of *samsara,* their word for illusionary reality. Those who accumulate good karma can be reborn in one of them, but their stay in Heaven is not eternal. Eventually they will use up their good karma and be reborn into another realm as a human, animal, or other being. Because Heaven is temporary and part of *samsara,* Buddhists focus more on escaping the cycle of rebirth and reaching enlightenment they call nirvana, which is not a Heaven but a mental state.

Buddhists believe that the universe is impermanent and that beings transmigrate through a number of existential planes in which your human world is only one realm or path. These are envisioned as a vertical continuum with the Heavens existing above the human realm, and the realms of the animals, hungry ghosts, and Hell beings existing beneath it. One important Buddhist Heaven is the *Trāyastriṃśa* which resembles Olympus of Greek mythology.

In the Mahayana view there are pure lands that lie outside this continuum created by the Buddhas upon attaining enlightenment. Rebirth in the pure land of Amitabha is seen as an assurance of Buddhahood. Once reborn there, beings do not fall back into cyclical existence unless they choose to do so to save other beings. The goal of Buddhism is the obtainment of enlightenment and freeing oneself and others from the birth death cycle.

Heaven is a key concept in Chinese mythology, philosophies, and religions. On one end of the spectrum is a synonym of Supreme Deity and on the other naturalistic end, a synonym for nature and the sky. The Chinese term for Heaven derives from the name of the supreme deity of the Zhou Dynasty who attributed Heaven with anthropomorphic attributes evidenced in the Chinese character for Heaven or sky that originally depicted a person with a large head. Heaven is said to see, hear, and watch over all men and is affected by man's doings. Heaven blesses those who please it and sends calamities upon those who offend it. Heaven was also believed to transcend all other spirits and gods.

Other philosophers around the time of Confucius took a stronger theistic view of Heaven, believing it was the divine ruler, just as the Son of Heaven, the King of Zhou was the earthly ruler. They believed that spirits and minor gods existed to carry out the will of Heaven, watch for evil-doers, and punish them. They functioned as angels of Heaven and didn't detract from its monotheistic government of the world. This high monotheism championed a concept called universal love which taught that Heaven loves all people equally and that each person should similarly love all human beings without distinguishing between his own relatives and those of others.

Sounds just lke Me. That idea gets my vote!

Christianity taught that Heaven is the location of the throne of God as well as the holy angels, but this is often thought of as metaphorical. In traditional Christianity Heaven is considered a state of existence instead of a particular place in the cosmos containing the supreme fulfillment of divine transformation in the beatific vision of the Godhead. In most forms of Christianity Heaven is also the abode for the redeemed dead in the afterlife, a temporary stage before their resurrection and the saint's return to the New Earth.

The resurrected Jesus is said to have ascended to Heaven where he now sits at the Right Hand of God and will return to earth in the Second Coming. A number of people have reputedly entered Heaven while still alive, including Enoch, Elijah and Jesus himself, after his resurrection. According to Roman Catholic teaching, Mary, mother of Jesus, is also said to have been assumed into Heaven and is titled the Queen of Heaven.

A key element of the teachings of Jesus talks about a war in Heaven between Michael the Archangel and his angels against Satan and his angels, ending with Satan and his angels being thrown down to the earth. Both Jesus and Satan had major impacts on the evolution of world culture and events, especially in western cultures.

The word Heaven used in Christian writings applies primarily to the sky, but it is also used metaphorically as the dwelling place of God and the blessed. The English word Heaven keeps its original physical meaning when used in allusions to the stars as lights shining through from Heaven, and in phrases like Heavenly body to mean an astronomical object. The Heaven or happiness that Christianity looks forward to is considered neither an abstraction nor a physical place in the clouds, but a living, personal relationship with the Holy Trinity and the meeting with the Father that takes place in the risen Christ through the communion of the Holy Spirit.

Attaining Heaven is not the final pursuit in Hinduism. Heaven itself is considered temporary and related to the physical body. According to Hindu cosmology, above the earthly plane are other planes, Bhuva Loka, and Swarga Loka, meaning Good Kingdom, which is the general name for Heaven in Hinduism. It is a Heavenly Paradise of pleasure where most of the Hindu Devatas reside along with the king of Devas, Indra, and beatified mortals. Some other planes are Mahar Loka, Jana Loka, Tapa Loka and Satya Loka. Since Heavenly abodes are tied to the cycle of birth and death, any dweller of Heaven or Hell will be recycled to a different plane in a different form by karma and maya, the illusion of Samsara. This cycle is broken only by self-realization called Moksha, which stands for liberation from the cycle of birth and death and final communion with Brahman. With moksha, a liberated soul attains the stature and oneness with Brahman or Paramatma. In the Vaishnava traditions the highest Heaven is Vaikuntha, which exists above the six Heavenly lokas outside of the mundane world where eternally liberated souls who have attained Moksha reside in eternal sublime beauty with Lakshmi and Narayana, a manifestation of Vishnu.

The concept of Heaven in Islam differs from Judaism and Christianity. Heaven is described in physical terms as a place where every wish is fulfilled when asked. Islamic texts describe immortal life in Heaven as happy without negative emotions. Those who dwell there are said to wear costly apparel, partake in exquisite banquets, and recline on couches inlaid with gold or precious stones. Inhabitants rejoice in the company of their parents, spouses, and children.

In Islam if one's good deeds outweigh one's sins then one can gain entrance to Heaven, but if one's sins outweigh their good deeds they are sent to Hell. The more good deeds one has done the higher the level of Heaven one is directed to. It has been said that the lowest level of Heaven is already more than one hundred times better than the greatest life on Earth. Houses are built by angels for the occupants using solid gold.

In Judaism the Heavens were located above the firmament, which was a solid transparent dome that covered the earth and separated it from the waters above. Yahweh, the God of Israel, lived in a Heavenly palace. His dwelling on earth was Solomon's Temple in Jerusalem which was a model of the cosmos that included a section representing Heaven.

The Jewish concept of the afterlife, sometimes known as the World-to-come has two concepts, one is that the immortal soul returns to its creator after death; the other is the resurrection of the dead.

Originally the ideas of immortality and resurrection were different, but in rabbinic thought they are combined. The soul departs from the body at death and is returned to it at the resurrection. This idea is linked to another rabbinic teaching that men's good and bad actions are rewarded and punished not in this life but after death, whether immediately or at the subsequent resurrection.

In this system seven heavens existed under angels who governed them. Vilon or Araphel was the first Heaven, governed by Archangel Gabriel. It was the closest of Heavenly realms to the Earth and was considered the abode of Adam and Eve. Raqia, the second Heaven was controlled by Zachariel and Raphael. In this Heaven Moses, during his visit to Paradise, encountered the angel Nuriel who stood three hundred parasangs high, with a retinue of fifty myriads of angels fashioned out of water and fire. Raqia was the realm where fallen angels were imprisoned and the planets were fastened.

Shehaqim was the third Heaven, under the leadership of Anahel, and served as the home of the Garden of Eden and the Tree of Life. It was also the realm where manna, the holy food of angels, was produced. Both Paradise and Hell were accommodated in Shehaqim with Hell being located on the northern side.

Maon was the fourth Heaven ruled by the Archangel Michael and contained the Heavenly Jerusalem, the Temple, and the Altar, and Makon was the fifth Heaven under the administration of Samael and it was where the Ishim and the Song-Uttering Choirs resided.

Zebul, the sixth Heaven fell under the jurisdiction of Sachiel and Araboth, and the seventh Heaven was under the leadership of Cassiel and was the holiest of the seven Heavens because it housed the Throne of Glory attended by the Seven Archangels and served as the realm where God dwelled. Underneath the throne was the abode of all unborn human souls and was considered the home of the Seraphim, the Cherubim, and the Hayyoth.

In Mesoamerican religions, Nahua people like the Aztecs, Chichimecs, and the Toltecs believed that the Heavens were constructed and separated into 13 levels and each level had from one to many Lords living in and ruling them. The Thirteen Heavens were ruled by Ometeotl the dual Lord, creator of the Dual-Genesis who, as male, takes the name Ometecuhtli, Two Lord, and as female is named Omecihuatl, Two Lady.

The creation myths of Polynesian mythology have concepts of the Heavens and the underworld that differ from one island to another. They share the view of the universe as an egg or coconut divided between the world of humans on earth, the upper world of Heavenly gods, and the underworld.

In Māori mythology the Heavens are divided into a number of realms and different tribes number them with as few as two and as many as fourteen levels. One common version divides Heaven into Kiko-rangi, presided over by the god Toumau, Waka-maru the Heaven of sunshine and rain, Nga-roto, the Heaven of lakes where the god Maru rules, Hauora where the spirits of newborn children originate, Nga-Tauira home of the servant gods, Nga-atua, ruled over by the hero Tawhaki, Autoia where human souls are created, Aukumea where spirits live, Wairua where spirit gods live while waiting on those in Naherangi, and Tuwarea the uppermost Heaven where the great gods live presided over by Rehua.

In the Sikh Religion, Heaven and Hell are not places for living hereafter, they are part of the spiritual topography of man and do not exist otherwise. They refer to good and evil stages of life and can be lived here and now during earthly existence.

In the Theosophy of Helena Blavatsky each religion has its own individual Heaven in different regions of the upper astral plane that fits the description of that Heaven given in each religion where a soul that has been good in their previous life on Earth will go. The upper astral plane of Earth in the upper atmosphere where the various Heavens are located is called *Summerland, while* Hell is located in a lower astral plane that extends downward from the surface of the earth to its center. Theosophists believe that the soul is recalled back to Earth after an average of about fourteen-hundred years by the *Lords of Karma* to incarnate again and the final Heaven that souls go to billions of years in the future after they finish their cycle of incarnations is called *Devachan.*

A tiered structure of Heaven along with similarly structured circles of Hell is believed in by many cultures. Many people who have come close to me talk about near death experiences and report meeting relatives or entering The Light in an otherworldly dimension that shares similarities with the religious concept of Heaven. The positive experiences of meeting or entering The Light are reported as intense feelings of love, peace, and joy beyond human comprehension. Together with this intensely positive feeling state, people who have near death experiences also report that consciousness or a heightened state of awareness is at the heart of experiencing a taste of Heaven.

There are also reports of distressing experiences and negative life-reviews that share similarities with the concept of Hell, which in many traditions is a place of torment and punishment. Religions with a linear divine history often depict Hells as eternal destinations while religions with a cyclic history often depict Hell as an intermediary period between incarnations. Typically these traditions locate Hell in another dimension or under the Earth's surface and often include entrances to Hell from the land of the living. Other traditions that do not conceive of the afterlife as a place of punishment or reward describe Hell as an abode of the dead, the grave, or a neutral place located under the surface of Earth.

Like it's alter-ego Heaven, there are many different beliefs about Hell that claim to tell you how I will come and where I will take you when that happens. I could never do them all justice, so here again are some of the more well-known beliefs to give you a sense of their variety. Hell appears in several mythologies and religions and is usually inhabited by demons and the souls of dead people.

Punishment in Hell corresponds to sins committed during life with damned souls suffering for each sin committed. Sometimes condemned sinners are relegated to one or more chambers of Hell or to a level of suffering. In many religious cultures including Christianity and Islam, Hell is fiery, painful, and harsh, inflicting suffering on the guilty. Other traditions describe it as cold. Buddhists, particularly Tibetan Buddhists have an equal number of hot and cold Hells.

The Sumerian afterlife is a dark, dreary cavern located deep below the ground where inhabitants continue a shadowy version of life on earth in a bleak domain known as Kur. All souls went to the same afterlife and a person's actions during life had no effect on how they would be treated in the world to come.

The entrance to Kur was believed to be located in the Zagros mountains in the far east and had seven gates that a soul needed to pass through. *Galla* were a class of demons believed to reside in the underworld. Their primary purpose was to drag unfortunate mortals back to Kur.

Later Mesopotamians knew this underworld by its East Semitic name Irkalla. They named me Nergal the god of death, ruler of the underworld.

In Ancient Egypt the rise of the cult of Osiris offered even his humblest followers the prospect of eternal life with moral fitness becoming the dominant factor in determining suitability. When they crossed over a person faced judgment by a tribunal of forty-two divine judges. If they led a life in conformance with the precepts of the Goddess Maat, who represented truth and right living, the person was welcomed into Heavenly reed fields. If found guilty they were thrown to Ammit, the devourer of the dead, and condemned to the lake of fire. The person taken by the devourer was subject to terrifying punishment, then annihilated. For the damned, complete destruction into a state of non-being awaited, but there was no suggestion of eternal torture and the weighing of the heart in Egyptian mythology could lead to annihilation.

In Greek mythology, below Heaven, Earth, and Pontus was Tartarus, a deep, gloomy pit or abyss used as a dungeon of torment and suffering that resided within Hades with Tartarus being the Hellish component. Souls were judged after death and those who received punishment were sent to Tartarus.

In Mayan religion, *Xibalba* was a dangerous underworld of nine levels. The road into and out of it was steep, thorny, and forbidding. Ritual healers intoned healing prayers banishing diseases to *Xibalba*.

The Aztecs believed that the dead traveled to *Mictlan*, a neutral place far to the north. There was also a legend of a place of white flowers, which was always dark and home to the gods of death, particularly Mictlantecutli and his spouse Mictlantecihuatl. The journey to *Mictlan* took four years and the travelers had to overcome difficult tests like passing a mountain range where the mountains crashed into each other, a field where the wind carried flesh-scraping knives, and a river of blood with fearsome jaguars.

Judaism doesn't have a specific doctrine about the afterlife, but it has a mystical orthodox tradition of describing Gehinnom which is not Hell but a grave, and in later times a Purgatory where people are judged based on their life's deeds, where one becomes fully aware of their shortcomings and negative actions during their life. The Kabbalah explains it as a waiting room for all souls. Most rabbinic thought maintains that people are not in Gehinnom forever. The longest one can be there is 12 months, but there have been exceptions. Some consider it a spiritual forge where the soul is purified for its eventual ascent to Olam Habah, The World To Come, which was analogous to Heaven. This was also mentioned in the Kabbalah, where the soul is described as breaking like the flame of a candle lighting another: the part of the soul that ascends being pure and the unfinished piece being reborn.

According to Jewish teachings, Hell is not entirely physical; it can be compared to an intense feeling of shame. People are ashamed of their misdeeds and this constitutes suffering that makes up for the bad deeds. When someone has so deviated from the will of God they are said to be in Gehinnom.

Many scholars of the Kabbalah mention seven compartments or habitations of Hell, just as there are seven divisions of Heaven that go by different names. There is Sheol, the underworld, Hades, or grave, Abaddon, doom or perdition, Be'er Shachat, the pit of corruption, Tit ha-Yaven, clinging mud, Sha'are Mavet, gates of death, Tzalmavet, shadow of death, and Gehinnom, the valley of Hinnom, Tartarus, or Purgatory.

The Christian doctrine of Hell derives from passages in the New Testament, but the word Hell does not appear in the Greek New Testament; instead the Greek words *Tartarus, Hades,* or the Hebrew word *Gehinnom* is used.

In the Septuagint and New Testament the authors used the Greek term Hades for the Hebrew Sheol, often with Jewish instead of Greek concepts in mind. In the Jewish concept of Sheol, Sheol or Hades is a place where there is no activity, but since Augustine, Christians believed that the souls of those who die either rest peacefully in the case of Christians, or are afflicted in the case of the damned after death until the resurrection.

Hades has similarities to the Old Testament Sheol as the place of the dead or grave and is used to reference both the righteous and the wicked since both end up there. Gehenna refers to the Valley of Hinnom, a garbage dump outside of Jerusalem where people burned their garbage, so there was always a fire burning there. Bodies of those deemed to have died in sin without hope of salvation like people who committed suicide were thrown there to be destroyed. Gehenna is used in the New Testament as a metaphor for the final place of punishment for the wicked after the resurrection. *Tartaróō, to* throw to Tartarus occurs only once in the New Testament as the place of incarceration of the fallen angels and mentions nothing about human souls being sent there in the afterlife.

The Roman Catholic Church defines Hell as a state of definitive self-exclusion from communion with God and the blessed. You will find yourself in Hell as the result of dying in mortal sin without repenting and accepting God's merciful love, and you will become eternally separated from him by your own free choice after I come. In the Roman Catholic Church and many others, Hell is the final destiny of those not found worthy after the general resurrection and last judgment, and it is where they will be eternally punished for sin and permanently separated from God. This judgment is inconsistent with Protestant churches that teach that the saving comes from accepting Jesus Christ as their savior. Greek Orthodox and Catholic Churches teach that the judgment hinges on both faith and works, while many other churches believe in universal reconciliation.

Some modern Christian theologians subscribe to the doctrines of conditional immortality, the belief that the soul dies with the body and doesn't live again until the resurrection. The New Testament distinguishes two words, both translated as Hell in older English Bibles, *Hades*, the grave, and *Gehenna* where God can destroy both body and soul. Some Christians read this to mean that neither Hades nor Gehenna are eternal, but refer to the ultimate destruction of the wicked in the Lake of Fire after resurrection. In the Hebrew text when people died they went to Sheol and the grave and the wicked went to Gehenna to be consumed by fire.

Christian mortalism is the doctrine that all men and women including Christians have to die, do not continue, and are not conscious after death, so annihilationism includes the doctrine that the wicked are also destroyed rather than tormented forever in traditional Hell or the lake of fire. Christian mortalism and annihilationism are related to the idea that a human soul is not immortal unless it is given eternal life at the second coming of Christ and resurrection of the dead.

Seventh-day Adventists deny the Catholic purgatory and teach that the dead lie in the grave until they are raised for a last judgment, and that both the righteous and wicked await the resurrection at the Second Coming. They believe that My coming brings a state of unconscious sleep until the resurrection, and that the resurrection of the righteous will take place at the second coming of Jesus, while the resurrection of the wicked will occur after the millennium of Revelation. They reject the doctrine of Hell as a state of everlasting conscious torment, believing instead that the wicked will be permanently destroyed after the millennium.

Jehovah's Witnesses say that the soul ceases to exist when the person dies and that Hell is a state of non-existence. In their beliefs Gehenna differs from Sheol or Hades because it holds no hope of a resurrection, and Tartarus is held to be the metaphorical state of debasement of the fallen angels between the time of their moral fall until their post-millennial destruction along with Satan.

Christian Universalists believe that all human souls including demons and fallen angels will be reconciled with God and admitted to Heaven.

It's nice to see equal opportunity for all here.

According to Emanuel Swedenborg's Second Coming Christian revelation, Hell exists because evil people want it and they, not God, introduced evil to the human race.

The Church of Jesus Christ of Latter-day Saints say that Hell is a state between death and resurrection where spirits who did not repent while on earth must suffer for their own sins.

Jahannam, The Islamic version of Hell is a place filled with blazing fire, boiling water, and other torments for those who have been condemned to it. After the Day of Judgement it is to be occupied by those who do not believe in God, those who have disobeyed his laws, or those who rejected His messengers. Enemies of Islam are sent to Hell when they die.

Like Zoroastrians, Muslims believe that on Judgement Day all souls will pass over a bridge above Hell. Those destined for Hell will find it too narrow and fall from it into their new abode. Jahannam resembles the Christian versions of Hell in being below Heaven and full of fire, but it is primarily a place of punishment created by God instead of a devil's domain to wage war against the Heavens above.

The Quran gives many descriptions of the condemned in a fiery Hell, contrasting them with the garden-like Paradise enjoyed by righteous believers. Suffering in Hell is both physical and spiritual, and varies according to the sins of the condemned. In Quran, God firmly declared that the majority of mankind and Jinns will be doomed eternally in the fiery Jahannam.

Islamic Heaven and Hell are both divided into seven different levels, with occupants assigned to each depending on their actions during their lifetimes. The gate of Hell is guarded by Maalik, the leader of the angels assigned as the guards of Hell. While Hell is usually described as hot, there is one pit characterized in Islamic tradition as unbearably cold with blizzards, ice, and snow.

For Muslims Paradise is forbidden for a polytheist because his place is Hell and the lowest pit of Hell is intended for hypocrites who claimed aloud to believe in God and his messenger, but in their hearts did not. Not all Muslims agree whether Hell is an eternal destination or whether some or all of the condemned will eventually be forgiven and allowed to enter Paradise.

Buddhism teaches that there are five or six realms of rebirth that can be subdivided into degrees of agony or pleasure. Of these realms, the Hell realm, or *Naraka*, is the lowest realm of rebirth. Of the Hell realms, the worst is *Avīci* or endless suffering. Like all realms of rebirth, rebirth in the Hell realms is not permanent, though suffering can persist for eons before being reborn.

Early Vedic religion has no concept of Hell. The Rig-Veda mentions three realms, bhūr, the earth, svar, the sky and bhuvas or antarikṣa, the middle area or atmosphere. In later Hindu literature more realms are mentioned, including one similar to Hell called Naraka. In the law-books Naraka is a place of punishment for sins on a lower spiritual plane where the spirit is judged and the partial fruits of karma affect the next life.

People who commit sins go to Hell and have to go through punishments in accordance with the sins they committed. In this system they give Me credit and name Me Yamarāja, the god of death who presides over Hell.

What a gift!

Detailed accounts of all the sins committed are read out and appropriate punishments are given. These punishments include dipping in boiling oil, burning in fire, and torture using various weapons as well as other creative penalties. Individuals who finish their quota of punishments are reborn in accordance with their balance of karma. All created beings are imperfect and have at least one sin to their record, but if you led a pious life, you can ascend to Svarga, a temporary realm of enjoyment similar to Paradise after a brief period of expiation in Hell before the next reincarnation, according to the law of karma.

Taoism has no concept of Hell as morality was seen to be a man-made distinction and there was no concept of an immaterial soul. In China where Taoism adopted tenets of other religions, popular belief gave Taoist Hell many deities and spirits who punished sin in a variety of horrific ways.

The exact number of levels in Chinese Hell and their associated deities differs according to Buddhist or Taoist perceptions. Some speak of three to four Courts, and others as many as ten. The ten judges are known as the 10 Kings of Yama and each Court deals with a different aspect of atonement. As an example, murder is punished in one Court, adultery in another. According to some Chinese legends, there are eighteen levels in Hell. Punishment also varies according to belief and most legends speak of highly imaginative chambers where wrong-doers are sawn in half, beheaded, thrown into pits of filth, or forced to climb trees adorned with sharp blades.

Most legends agree that once a soul has atoned for their deeds and repented, they are given the Drink of Forgetfulness by Meng Po and sent back into the world to be reborn, possibly as an animal or a poor or sick person for further punishment.

Zoroastrianism has several fates for the wicked, including annihilation, purgation in molten metal, and eternal punishment. Wicked souls will remain in Hell until the arrival of three saviors at thousand year intervals to reconcile the world, destroy evil, and resurrect tormented souls to perfection.

What imaginations you have when it comes to justice, karma, and punishment! Can you imagine how all these beliefs and expectations played out for me when I met each of these souls personally?

Mind you all of these innumerable realms are human conceptions based entirely on imagination. Other than the energy and belief you give them, they have no basis for existing and no proof of any kind to prove their validity. The only true reality is Me and the all-encompassing, all consuming Great Mystery that surrounds and permeates every aspect of your existence.

MY OLD PAL SATAN

Of all of the faces you put on me and all the imaginative things you attribute to me, I have to admit that my old pal Satan is one of my favorite roles, and in this popular set of beliefs I get to rule over Hell as part of the deal!

Satan began as an entity in the Abrahamic religions who seduces humans into sin. In Christianity and Islam he is usually seen as a fallen angel or a jinni who possessed great piety and beauty, but rebelled against God, who still allows him temporary power over the fallen world and a host of demons. In Judaism, Satan is regarded as a metaphor for the evil inclination, as an agent subservient to God.

A figure known as the satan first appeared in the Hebrew Bible as a Heavenly prosecutor, a member of the sons of God under Yahweh who prosecuted the nation of Judah in the Heavenly court and tested the loyalty of Yahweh's followers by forcing them to suffer. In the time between the Hebrew Bible and the Christian New Testament Satan developed into a malevolent entity with abhorrent qualities in opposition to God. In the Book of Jubilees Yahweh grants Satan authority over a group of fallen angels to tempt humans to sin and punish them. In the Synoptic Gospels Satan tempts Jesus in the desert and is identified as the cause of illness and temptation. In the Book of Revelation Satan appears as a Great Red Dragon who is defeated by Michael the Archangel and cast down from Heaven. He is later bound for one thousand years but is briefly set free before being defeated and cast into the Lake of Fire.

In Christianity, Satan is also known as the Devil and although the Book of Genesis does not mention him, he is often identified as the serpent in the Garden of Eden. In medieval times Satan played a minimal role in Christian theology and was used as a comic relief figure in mystery plays. During the early modern period Satan's significance increased as beliefs in widespread demonic possession and witchcraft became more prevalent. During the Age of Enlightenment belief in the existence of Satan became harshly criticized, but this belief has persisted, particularly in the Americas.

In the Quran, Shaitan, also known as Iblis is an entity made of fire who was cast out of Heaven because he refused to bow before the newly created Adam and incited humans and jinn to sin by infecting their minds with evil suggestions.

In Theistic Satanism, Satan is a deity who is either worshipped or revered. In LaVeyan Satanism, Satan is a symbol of virtuous characteristics and liberty.

The original Hebrew term *satan* is a noun meaning accuser or adversary, which is used throughout the Hebrew Bible to refer to ordinary human adversaries as well as a specific supernatural entity. The word is derived from a verb meaning to obstruct or oppose. When it was used without specificity as simply *satan*, it referred to any accuser, but when it was used specifically as *ha-satan*, it referred to the heavenly accuser, The Satan.

The word satan isn't in the Book of Genesis which only mentions a talking serpent. It doesn't identify the serpent with any supernatural entity, but Satan appears in the Book of Job. Job is a righteous man favored by Yahweh who asks one of the sons of God known as Satan, where he has been. Satan says that he has been roaming around the earth, then Yahweh asks, "Have you considered My servant Job?"

Satan replies by urging Yahweh to let him torture Job, promising that Job will abandon his faith at the first tribulation. Yahweh consents and Satan destroys Job's servants and flocks, but Job refuses to condemn Yahweh. Yahweh points out Job's continued faithfulness and Satan insists on more testing. Yahweh once again gives him permission but in the end Job remains faithful and righteous, and it is implied that Satan is shamed in his defeat.

When Jews were living in the Achaemenid Empire Judaism was influenced by Zoroastrianism, the religion of the Achaemenids. Jewish conceptions of Satan were impacted by Angra Mainyu, the Zoroastrian god of evil, darkness, and ignorance. In the Septuagint, the Hebrew *ha-Satan* in Job and Zechariah is translated by the Greek word *diabolos* meaning slanderer, the same word in the Greek New Testament that the English word "devil" is derived from.

The idea of Satan as an opponent of God and a purely evil figure seems to have taken root in Jewish writings from the Second Temple Period, particularly in the *apocalypses*. The Book of Enoch, which the Dead Sea Scrolls have revealed to have been nearly as popular as the Torah describes a group of two hundred angels known as the Watchers assigned to supervise the earth, who abandon their duties and have sexual intercourse with human women. The leader of the Watchers is Semjâzâ. Another member of the group known as Azazel spreads sin and corruption among humankind. The Watchers are ultimately sequestered in isolated caves across the earth condemned to face judgement at the end of time.

The Book of Jubilees, written around one-hundred-fifty BC retells the story of the Watchers' defeat that is different from the Book of Enoch. In it Mastema, an angel who persecutes evil in Jewish mythology carries out punishments for God as well as tempting humans and testing their faith. In the Zadokite Fragments and the Dead Sea Scrolls he is the angel of disaster, the father of all evil, and a flatterer of God. He first appears in the literature of the Second Temple Period as a personification of the Hebrew word *mastemah* meaning hatred, hostility, enmity, or persecution.

As Chief of Spirits, Mastema intervened before the Watchers were sealed away, asking Yahweh to let him keep some of them to be his workers. Yahweh agrees and Mastema uses them to tempt humans into committing more sins so he can punish them for their wickedness. Later, Mastema induces Yahweh to test Abraham by ordering him to sacrifice Isaac.

The Second Book of Enoch called the Slavonic Book of Enoch talks about a Watcher called Satanael, describing him as the prince of the Grigori who was cast out of Heaven, and an evil spirit who knew the difference between what was righteous and sinful. In the Book of Wisdom the devil is represented as the being who brought Me into the world! The name Samael which referenced one of the fallen angels later became a common name for Satan in Jewish thought.

Each sect of Judaism has its own interpretation of Satan's identity. Conservative Judaism rejects the Talmudic interpretation of Satan as a metaphor for the the evil inclination in man and regards him as a literal agent of God. Orthodox Judaism embraces Talmudic teachings on

Satan and involves Satan in religious life more than other sects. Satan is mentioned explicitly in some daily prayers, including during Shacharit and post meal benedictions. In Reform Judaism, Satan is seen in his Talmudic role as a metaphor for the evil inclination in man and the symbolic representation of innate human qualities like selfishness.

In Christianity the most common English synonym for Satan is devil and in the New Testament, the words *Satan* and *diabolos* are used interchangeably. Beelzebub, meaning Lord of Flies, is the contemptuous name given in the Hebrew Bible and New Testament to a Philistine god whose original name has been reconstructed as Ba'al Zabul, meaning Baal the Prince. The Synoptic Gospels identify Satan and Beelzebub as the same. The name Abaddon, meaning place of destruction is used six times in the Old Testament, mainly as a name for a region of Sheol. Revelation describes Abaddon, which translates into Greek as *Apollyon*, meaning the destroyer, as an angel who rules the Abyss. In modern usage Abaddon is sometimes equated with Satan.

In later Christianity Satan is never referred to without mentioning Jesus. The three Synoptic Gospels all describe the temptation of Christ by Satan in the desert where he first showed Jesus a stone and told him to turn it into bread, then he took Jesus to the pinnacle of the Temple in Jerusalem and commanded him to throw himself down so the angels would catch him. After that Satan took Jesus to the top of a tall mountain and showed him the kingdoms of the earth, promising to give them all to him if he bowed down and worshiped him. Jesus denied Satan every time and after the third temptation he was saved by the angels.

Satan also played a role in some of the parables of Jesus. According to the Parable of the Sower, Satan influenced those who failed to understand the gospel. Other parables said that Satan's followers would be punished on Judgement Day with the Parable of the Sheep and the Goats stating that the Devil, his angels, and the people who followed him would be consigned to eternal fire. When the Pharisees accused Jesus of exorcising demons through the power of Beelzebub, Jesus told them the Parable of the Strongman, saying, "how can someone enter a strong man's house and plunder his goods, unless he first binds the strong man? Then indeed he may plunder his house". The strong man in this parable was Satan.

The Synoptic Gospels identify Satan and his demons as the causes of illness, including fever and arthritis while the Epistle to the Hebrews describes the Devil as him who holds the power of death.

I have a little bit of an issue with that one. Who's working for who here?

In Luke Jesus grants Satan the authority to test Peter and the other apostles and Judas Iscariot betrayed Jesus because Satan entered him. Peter describes Satan as filling Ananias's heart and causing him to sin. In the Gospel of John, Jesus says that the Jews are the children of the Devil rather than the children of Abraham and the same verse describes the Devil as a man-killer from the beginning and a liar and the father of lying. John describes the Devil as inspiring Judas to betray Jesus and John identifies Satan as the Archon of this Cosmos who is destined to be overthrown through Jesus's death and resurrection. John also promises that the Holy Spirit will accuse the World of sin, justice, and judgement, a role resembling that of Satan in the Old Testament.

Revelation describes a Great Red Dragon with seven heads, ten horns, seven crowns, and a massive tail, an image inspired by the vision of the four beasts from the sea in the Book of Daniel and the Leviathan described in the Old Testament. The Great Red Dragon knocks a third of the sun, a third of the moon, and a third of the stars out the sky and pursues the Woman of the Apocalypse.

In Revelation war broke out in Heaven and Michael and his angels fought against Dragon and his angels who were beaten and there was no longer any place for them in Heaven. "Dragon the Great was thrown down, that ancient serpent who is called Devil and Satan, the one deceiving the whole inhabited World - he was thrown down to earth and his angels were thrown down with him." A voice boomed down from Heaven heralding the defeat of the Accuser, identifying the Satan of Revelation with the Satan of the Old Testament. Satan is bound with a chain and hurled into the Abyss where he is imprisoned for a thousand years, then set free to gather his armies along with Gog and Magog to wage war against the righteous, but is defeated with fire from Heaven and cast into the lake of fire.

The name *Heylel*, meaning morning star, in Latin is *Lucifer*, a name for Attar, the god of the planet Venus in Canaanite mythology who attempted to scale the walls of the Heavenly city and was vanquished by the god of the sun.

The Church Father Origen of Alexandria concluded that these verses couldn't refer to a human being so they had to allude to "a certain Angel who had received the office of governing the nation of the Tyrians," but was hurled down to Earth after he was found to be corrupt.

Origen adopted this new interpretation to refute unnamed persons who, possibly under the influence of Zoroastrian radical dualism believed that Satan's original nature was Darkness. A Latin translator accepted Origen's theory of Satan as a fallen angel and wrote about it in his commentary on the Book of Isaiah. Ever since, in Christian tradition both Isaiah and Ezekiel have been understood as referring to Satan, and for most Christians Satan is regarded as an angel who rebelled against God.

Many early Christians believed that Satan gained power over humanity through Adam and Eve's sin and Christ's death on the cross was a ransom to Satan in exchange for humanity's liberation. This theory says that Satan was tricked by God because Christ was not only free of sin, but was the incarnate Deity who Satan lacked the ability to enslave.

Most early Christians believed that Satan and his demons could possess humans and exorcisms were widely practiced by Jews, Christians, and pagans. Belief in demonic possession continued through the Middle Ages when exorcisms were seen as a display of God's power over Satan. Most people who thought they were possessed by the Devil didn't suffer from hallucinations or other spectacular symptoms, but complained of anxiety, religious fears, and evil thoughts.

Christians regarded Satan as increasingly powerful and the fear of his power became a dominant aspect of Christian worldview. Martin Luther taught that rather than trying to argue with Satan, Christians should avoid temptation altogether by seeking out pleasant company and recommended music as a safeguard against temptation, since the Devil "cannot endure gaiety." John Calvin repeated a maxim from Saint Augustine that "Man is like a horse, with either God or the devil as rider."

Early English settlers of North America, especially the Puritans of New England, believed that Satan visibly and palpably reigned in the New World. John Winthrop claimed that the Devil made rebellious Puritan women give birth to stillborn monsters with claws, sharp horns, and on each foot three claws, like a young fowl. Cotton Mather wrote that devils swarmed around Puritan settlements like the frogs of Egypt. The Puritans believed that Native Americans were worshippers of Satan and described them as children of the Devil. Some settlers claimed to have seen Satan himself appear in the flesh at native ceremonies. During the First Great Awakening, the new light preachers portrayed their old light critics as ministers of Satan. By the time of the Second Great Awakening, Satan's primary role in American evangelicalism was the opponent of the evangelical movement itself, who spent most of his time trying to hinder the ministries of evangelical preachers, a role he has largely retained among present-day American fundamentalists.

Satan sure got around in those days! He also consorted with witches who were believed to fly through the air on broomsticks. He consorted with demons, performed in lurid sexual rituals in the forests, murdered human infants and ate them as part of Satanic rites, and he engaged in conjugal relations with demons. The panic over witchcraft intensified in the sixteen-twenties and continued until the end of the sixteen-hundreds. Around sixty-thousand people were executed for witchcraft during the witchcraft hysteria.

By the early sixteen-hundreds skeptics in Europe began to criticize the belief that demons had the power to possess people. This skepticism was bolstered by the belief that miracles only occurred during the Apostolic Age which had long since ended. Later, Enlightenment thinkers attacked the notion of Satan's existence altogether. Voltaire declared that belief in Hell and Satan were among the many lies propagated by the Catholic Church to keep humanity enslaved.

By the eighteenth century trials for witchcraft had ended in most western countries with the exceptions of Poland and Hungary, but belief in the power of Satan remained strong among traditional Christians.

The Mormons have developed their own views on Satan. According to the Book of Moses, the Devil offered to be the redeemer of mankind for the sake of his own glory. Conversely, Jesus offered to be the redeemer of mankind so his father's will would be done. After his offer was rejected, Satan rebelled and was cast out of Heaven. In the Book of Moses, Cain is said to have loved Satan more than God and conspired with Satan to kill Abel. The Book of Moses also says that Moses was tempted by Satan before calling upon the name of the Only Begotten, which made Satan depart.

Belief in Satan and demonic possession still remains strong among Christians in the United States and Latin America. A composite image of Satan has emerged that borrows from both popular culture and theological sources, and most American Christians don't separate what they know about Satan from the movies from what they know from theological traditions. The Catholic Church played down Satan and exorcism during the late twentieth century, but Pope Francis brought renewed focus on the Devil in the early twenty-first century stating that, "The devil is intelligent, he knows more theology than all the theologians together." Christianity tends to view Satan as a mythological attempt to express the reality and extent of evil in the universe existing outside and apart from humanity, but influencing human experience.

In the dualist approach Satan will become incarnate in the Antichrist, just as God became incarnate in Jesus, but in Orthodox Christian thought this view is a problem because it is too similar to Christ's incarnation. Instead, the Antichrist is a human figure inhabited by Satan since Satan's power is not seen as equal to God's.

The Arabic equivalent of the word *Satan* is *Shaitan,* an adjective meaning astray or distant, sometimes translated as devil that can be applied to man, angels, spirits, or jinns, but also to refer to Satan in particular. Muslims don't regard Satan as the cause of evil, but as a tempter who takes advantage of humans' inclinations toward self-centeredness.

Seven suras in the Quran describe how God ordered all the angels and Satan, then known as Iblis to bow before the newly-created Adam. All the angels bowed but Iblis refused, claiming to be superior to Adam because he was made from fire; whereas Adam was made from clay. God expelled him from Paradise and condemned him to the Jahannam Hell and Iblis became an ungrateful disbeliever whose sole mission was to lead humanity astray. God allowed him to do this because he knew that the righteous could resist Iblis's attempts to misguide them. On Judgement Day while the lot of Satan remains in question, those who followed him will be thrown into the fires of Jahannam. After his banishment from Paradise Iblis became known as *Al-Shaitan,* the Demon who lured Adam and Eve into eating fruit from the forbidden tree.

The primary characteristic of Satan, aside from his hubris and despair, was his ability to cast evil suggestions into men and women. He is believed to have no influence over the righteous, but those who fall in error are under his power. Those who obey God's laws are immune to the temptations of Satan, but Satan tries to keep Muslims from reading the Quran. Reciting the Quran is considered an antidote against Satan who is the enemy of humanity and humans are forbidden from worshipping him.

In the Quran Satan is an angel described as being from the jinns. This combined with the fact that he describes himself as having been made from fire posed a problem for Muslims who disagree on whether Satan is a fallen angel or the leader of a group of evil jinn. According to one account Iblis was actually an angel that God created out of fire.

Muslims believe that Satan is the cause of deceptions originating from the mind and desires for evil and he is regarded as a cosmic force for separation, despair, and spiritual envelopment. Muslims distinguish between satanic temptations and the murmurings of the bodily lower self, saying that the lower self commands the person to do a specific task or fulfill a specific desire; whereas the inspirations of Satan tempt the person to do evil in general. After a person successfully resists his first suggestion, Satan returns with new ones and if a Muslim feels that Satan is inciting him to sin, he is advised to seek refuge with God by reciting, "In the name of Allah, I seek refuge in you, from Satan the outcast." Muslims are also obliged to seek refuge before reciting the Quran.

In the Bahá'í Faith, Satan is not regarded as an independent evil power. The lower nature in man is symbolized as Satan, the evil ego within us, not an evil personality outside. All other evil spirits like fallen angels, demons, and jinns, are also metaphors for the base character traits a human being may acquire and manifest when they turn away from God. Actions described as satanic in some Bahá'í writings describe human deeds caused by selfish desires.

After playing so many roles for so many different systems of belief, my old pal Satan finally got popular enough for people to give him their full attention as a deity in his own right. I have to admit to being a little biased here because in spite of the sinister impression it might give, this one hits closer to home for me more than any of the others, especially when it comes to the respect I get.

Satanism, known as devil worship sees Satan as a deity to supplicate to and consists of independent groups and cabals who all agree that Satan is a real entity.

Atheistic Satanism practiced by the Satanic Temple and by followers of LaVeyan Satanism say that Satan doesn't exist as a literal anthropomorphic entity, but as a symbol of a cosmos that satanists perceive to be permeated and motivated by a force that has been given many names over the course of time. In this religion, Satan is not seen as a hubristic, irrational, fraudulent creature, but is revered with Prometheus-like attributes, symbolizing liberty and individual empowerment. He also serves as a conceptual framework and an external metaphorical projection of the satanist's highest personal potential. A High Priest of the Church of Satan stated that Satan is a symbol of Man living as his prideful, carnal nature dictates and that the reality behind Satan is simply the dark evolutionary force of entropy that permeates all of nature and provides the drive for survival and propagation inherent in all living things. Satan is not a conscious entity to be worshiped, but a reservoir of power inside each human to be tapped at will.

The Church of Satan chose him as its primary symbol because in Hebrew it means adversary, opposer, and one to accuse or question. They see themselves as being these Satans, the adversaries, opposers, and accusers of all spiritual belief systems that try to hamper enjoyment of their lives as human beings.

Wicca is a modern day syncretic Neopagan religion whose practitioners Christians have incorrectly assumed to worship Satan. Wiccans don't believe in the existence of Satan or anything like him.

The cult of the skeletal figure of Santa Muerte which has blossomed in Mexico has been denounced by the Catholic Church as Devil-worship, but devotees of Santa Muerte view her as an angel of death created by God, and many of them identify as Catholic.

Angel of Death. It *does* have a nice ring to it.

Much folklore about satanism doesn't originate from the beliefs or practices of theistic or atheistic satanists, but from a mixture of medieval Christian folk beliefs, political and sociological conspiracy theories, and urban legends. The satanic ritual abuse scare of the nineteen-eighties depicted satanism as a vast conspiracy of elites with a predilection for child abuse and human sacrifice backed by the thought of Satan physically incarnating to receive worship.

165

In Dante's *Inferno*, Satan appears as a giant demon frozen mid-breast in ice at the center of the Ninth Circle of Hell with three faces and a pair of bat-like wings affixed under each chin. In his three mouths Satan gnaws on Brutus, Judas Iscariot, and Cassius, whom Dante regarded as having betrayed the two greatest heroes of the human race; Julius Caesar, the founder of the new order of government, and Jesus, the founder of the new order of religion. As Satan beats his wings he creates a cold wind that continues to freeze the ice surrounding him and the other sinners in the Ninth Circle.

Satan also appeared in several stories from *The Canterbury Tales* by Geoffrey Chaucer, including *The Summoner's Prologue*, where a friar arrives in Hell and sees no other friars but is told there are millions, then Satan lifts his tail to reveal that all of the friars live inside his anus. Chaucer's description of Satan's appearance is based on Dante's.

The legend of Faust recorded in fifteen-eighty-nine concerns a pact allegedly made by the German scholar Johann Georg Faust with a demon named Mephistopheles agreeing to sell his soul to Satan in exchange for twenty-four years of earthly pleasure.

John Milton's epic poem *Paradise Lost* features Satan as its main protagonist as a tragic antihero destroyed by his own hubris who dares to rebel against the tyranny of God in spite of God's omnipotence. *Paradise Regained*, the sequel to *Paradise Lost*, is a retelling of Satan's temptation of Jesus in the desert.

William Blake regarded Satan as a model of rebellion against unjust authority and featured him in many of his poems and illustrations including his seventeen-eighty book *The Marriage of Heaven and Hell*, where Satan is celebrated as the ultimate rebel, the incarnation of human emotion and the epitome of freedom from all forms of reason and orthodoxy. Based on the Biblical passages portraying Satan as the accuser of sin, Blake interpreted him as a promulgator of moral laws.

Satan's appearance is never described in the Bible or any early Christian writings, though Paul the Apostle did write that "Satan disguises himself as an angel of light". The Devil was never shown in early Christian artwork and first appeared in medieval art of the ninth century with cloven hooves, hairy legs, the tail of a goat, pointed ears, a beard, a flat nose, and horns.

Much of Satan's traditional iconography in Christianity appears to be derived from Pan, a rustic goat-legged fertility god in ancient Greek religion. Early Christian writers equated the Greek satyrs and the

Roman fauns that Pan resembled with demons and the Devil's pitchfork appears to have been adapted from the trident wielded by the Greek god Poseidon while Satan's flame-like hair seems to have originated from the Egyptian god Bes.

By the High Middle Ages Satan and devils appeared in all works of Christian art including paintings, sculptures, and cathedrals and is usually depicted naked, but his genitals are rarely shown and often covered by animal furs. The goat-like portrayal of Satan was closely associated with him in his role as the object of worship by sorcerers and as the incubus, a demon believed to rape women in their sleep.

Talk about a bad rap and a literal scapegoat! Aside from all the heinous behavior attributed to him, in this depiction Satan is actually embodied with goat qualities like fur, hooves, and goat legs.

Italian frescoes from the late Middle Ages show him chained in Hell feeding on the bodies of the perpetually damned and as the serpent in the Garden of Eden. He is often shown as a snake with arms and legs as well the head and full-breasted upper torso of a woman. Satan and his demons could take any form in medieval art, and demons were shown as short, hairy, black-skinned humanoids with clawed bird feet, and extra faces on their chests, bellies, genitals, buttocks, and tails.

By now it should be clear that my old pal Satan with all of his grotesque depictions from the darkest imaginings that you can muster carries the weight and blame of every sin imaginable and is not only goatlike symbolically, but in many ways is humanity's ultimate scapegoat who embodies the worst qualities and proclivities that humanity as to offer. Milton's *Paradise Lost* refers to him as the Prince of Darkness who is the embodiment of evil.

You cannot have the light without the dark and they are complementary. Each one enhances the other, so much of the history and mythology of Satan the Prince of Darkness has been told in his role as the counterpart to the stories and mythologies of Jesus the Prince of Peace, who is credited as saying, "I am the light of the world. Whoever follows me will never walk in darkness, but will have the light of life."

It fascinates me to no end that Jesus the light bearer who represents all things good in humanity and Satan the Prince of Darkness who represents the bad are two of humanity's most reknowned scapegoats. Apparently the light and the dark are equally deserving of bearing the sins of humanity which begs the question, in the eyes of humanity is there really any difference between Jesus and Satan?

Satan after all is Lucifer, an angel who was cast from Heaven into Hell because he rebelled against God. Lucifer means bearer of light or morning star, and refers to his former splendor as the greatest of the angels. This paradox indicates that in the eyes of humanity the light and the dark are one and the same, something one might call a greater Cosmic truth. If you can't accept that then you have to accept the fact of the Great Mystery that underlies it.

MY GOOD BUDDY JESUS

Jesus of Nazareth or Jesus Christ was a first-century Jewish religious leader who became the central figure of Christianity. Most Christians believe he was the incarnation of God the Son and the Messiah prophesied in the Old Testament.

Jesus was a Galilean Jew who was often referred to as rabbi, who debated fellow Jews on how to best follow God. He engaged in healings, taught in parables, and gathered followers until he was arrested and tried by the Jewish authorities, turned over to the Roman government, and crucified. After his death his followers believed he rose from the dead and the community they formed became the early Church.

Christians believe that Jesus performed miracles, founded the Church, died as a sacrifice to achieve atonement, rose from the dead, and ascended into Heaven with a promise to return one day. Most Christians believe Jesus enables people to be reconciled to God. The Nicene Creed asserts that he will judge the living and the dead either before or after their bodily resurrection, an event tied to the Second Coming of Jesus. Most Christians worship him as the incarnation of God the Son.

Jesus also figures in non-Christian religions and new religious movements. In Islam he is considered one of God's important prophets and the Messiah. Muslims believe Jesus was a bringer of scripture and was born of a virgin, but was not the Son of God. The Quran says Jesus himself never claimed divinity. Most Muslims don't believe he was crucified, but believe he was physically raised into Heaven by God. In contrast, Judaism rejects the belief that Jesus was the awaited Messiah, arguing that he did not fulfill Messianic prophecies, and was neither divine nor resurrected.

Christians of the time designated Jesus as the Christ because they believed him to be the Messiah whose arrival was prophesied in the Hebrew Bible and Old Testament. In time *Christ* became viewed as a name, one part of Jesus Christ. A Christian is a follower of Christ.

The four gospels of the New Testament emphasize different aspects of Jesus. In Mark, he is the Son of God whose mighty works demonstrate the presence of God's Kingdom. He is a tireless wonder worker and the servant of both God and man. The Gospel of Matthew emphasizes that Jesus is the fulfillment of God's will as revealed in the Old Testament. He is the Lord of the Church and the Son of David, a king, and the Messiah. Luke presents Jesus as the divine-human savior who shows compassion to the needy, and the friend of sinners and outcasts who came to seek and save the lost. The Gospel of John identifies him as an incarnation of the divine Word eternally present with God, active in all creation, and the source of humanity's moral and spiritual nature. Jesus was not only considered greater than any past human prophet, but greater than any prophet could be. He not only spoke God's Word; he *was* God's Word. In the Gospel of John Jesus reveals his divine role publicly as the Bread of Life, the Light of the World, the True Vine, and more.

He was born in Bethlehem in fulfillment of prophecy to Joseph and Mary in a virgin birth, miraculously conceived by the Holy Spirit in Mary's womb. According to the scriptures when John the baptist baptized Jesus, when Jesus came out of the water John saw the Holy Spirit descending to him like a dove and heard a voice from Heaven declaring him to be God's Son.

The spirit drove Jesus into the wilderness where he was tempted by Satan, then Jesus began his ministry after John's arrest. Matthew also detailed Jesus' baptism and the three temptations Satan offered him in the wilderness. In Luke, the Holy Spirit descends as a dove after everyone has been baptized and Jesus is praying. John recognized Jesus from prison after sending his followers to ask about him and Jesus' baptism and temptation served as preparation for his public ministry.

The first took place north of Judea, in Galilee, where Jesus conducted a successful ministry and in the second Jesus was rejected and killed when he travelled to Jerusalem.

The Galilean ministry began when Jesus returned from the Judaean Desert after rebuffing the temptation of Satan. When Jesus preached around Galilee he appointed twelve apostles and his first disciples formed the core of the early Church that travelled with him.

This period included the Sermon on the Mount, one of Jesus' major discourses as well as the calming of the storm, the feeding of the five-thousand, walking on water, and a number of other miracles and parables. It ends with the Confession of Peter and the Transfiguration.

Jesus taught in parables about the Kingdom of God which was described as both imminent and already present, and promised inclusion for those who accepted his message and talked of the Son of Man, an apocalyptic figure who would come to gather the chosen. He called people to repent their sins and devote themselves to God.

When asked what the greatest commandment was, Jesus said, "You shall love the Lord your God with all your heart, and with all your soul, and with all your mind ..." His second was, "You shall love your neighbor as yourself." Other ethical teachings included loving your enemies, refraining from hatred and lust, turning the other cheek, and forgiving people who sinned against you. Jesus also said, "My teaching is not mine but his who sent me. Do you not believe that I am in the Father and the Father is in me? The words that I say to you I do not speak on my own; but the Father who dwells in me does his works."

In gospel accounts Jesus devoted a large portion of his ministry performing healing miracles that included cures for physical ailments, exorcisms, and resurrections of the dead. Nature miracles showed Jesus' power over nature including turning water into wine, walking on water, and calming a storm, among others. Jesus said his miracles were from a divine source. When his opponents accused him of performing exorcisms by the power of Beelzebub, the prince of demons, Jesus countered that he performed them by the Spirit or finger of God.

A major part of the story of Jesus was the Transfiguration when Jesus took Peter and two other apostles up a mountain, where "he was transfigured before them, and his face shone like the sun, and his clothes became dazzling white. "A bright cloud appeared around them, and a voice from the cloud said, "This is my Son, the Beloved; with him I am well pleased; listen to him."

The description of the last week of the life of Jesus is called Passion Week and occupies about one third of the narrative in the canonical gospels starting with Jesus' triumphant entry into Jerusalem and ending with his crucifixion. In this account when Jesus rode a young donkey into Jerusalem people laid cloaks and palm fronds in front of him and sang. Jesus expelled money changers from the Second Temple, accusing them of turning it into a den of thieves, then he prophesied about the coming destruction, including false prophets, wars, earthquakes, celestial disorders, persecution of the faithful, the appearance of an abomination of desolation, and unendurable tribulations. He said the mysterious Son of Man, would dispatch angels to gather the faithful from all parts of the earth.

Jesus came into conflict with the Jewish elders when they questioned his authority and he criticized them and called them hypocrites. Judas Iscariot, one of his twelve apostles secretly agreed to betray Jesus to them for thirty silver coins.

The Last Supper is the final meal that Jesus shared with his twelve apostles in Jerusalem before his crucifixion. During the meal he predicted that one of his apostles would betray him, but despite each apostle's assertion that he would not betray him, Jesus identified Judas as the traitor.

In the Last Supper Jesus took bread, broke it, and gave it to his disciples, saying, "This is my body, which is given for you". He had them all drink from a cup, saying, "This cup that is poured out for you is the new covenant in my blood." The Christian sacrament is based on this event. Jesus also predicted that Peter would deny knowledge of him three times before the rooster crowed the next morning.

Jesus and his disciples went to the garden of Gethsemane where Jesus prayed to be spared his coming ordeal, then Judas came with an armed mob and kissed Jesus to identify him to the crowd which arrested Jesus. After his arrest his disciples went into hiding, and Peter, when questioned, denied knowing Jesus three times. After the third denial Peter heard the rooster crow and recalled Jesus' prediction about his denial and wept bitterly.

After his arrest Jesus was taken to a Jewish judicial body, then to the high priest, Caiaphas, where he was mocked and beaten. During the trials Jesus spoke little, mounted no defense, and gave infrequent and indirect answers to the priest's questions, prompting an officer to slap him. Jesus' unresponsiveness led Caiaphas to ask him, "Have you no answer? Are you the Messiah, the Son of the Blessed One?" Jesus said, "I am", and then predicted the coming of the Son of Man provoking Caiaphas to tear his own robe in anger and accuse Jesus of blasphemy.

The Jewish elders took Jesus to ask the Roman governor, Pontius Pilate, to judge and condemn Jesus, accusing him of claiming to be the King of the Jews and Pilate sent Jesus to Herod to be tried. Herod and his soldiers mocked Jesus, put an expensive robe on him to make him look like a king, and returned him to Pilate who called together the Jewish elders and announced that he had "not found this man guilty".

Observing a Passover custom of the time, Pilate allowed one prisoner chosen by the crowd to be released and they chose a murderer named Barabbas. Pilate wrote a sign in Hebrew, Latin, and Greek that read "Jesus of Nazareth, the King of the Jews" to be affixed to Jesus' cross, then he scourged Jesus and sent him to be crucified. The soldiers placed a Crown of Thorns on Jesus' head and ridiculed him as the King of the Jews and beat and taunted him, then Jesus was led to Calvary carrying his cross where the soldiers crucified him and cast lots for his clothes while soldiers and passersby mocked him.

One soldier pierced Jesus' side with a lance, and blood and water flowed out. When Jesus died the heavy curtain at the Temple was torn and an earthquake broke open tombs.

Joseph of Arimathea removed Jesus' body from the cross, wrapped him in a clean cloth and buried him in a new rock-hewn tomb. On the following day the chief Jewish priests asked Pilate for the tomb to be secured, and with Pilate's permission the priests placed seals on the large stone covering the entrance.

In Matthew's account Mary Magdalene went to the tomb on Sunday morning and found it empty, then an angel descended from Heaven, opened the tomb, and the guards fainted from fear. Jesus appeared to Mary Magdalene and the eleven remaining disciples in Galilee and commissioned them to baptize all nations in the name of the Father, Son, and Holy Spirit. In Mark, a young man in a white robe who is an angel tells them that Jesus will meet his disciples in Galilee. In Luke, Mary and other women met two angels at the tomb, but the eleven disciples didn't believe their story.

Jesus also appeared to two of his followers and to Peter, then appeared that same day to his disciples in Jerusalem. Although he appeared and vanished mysteriously, he also ate and let them touch him to prove that he was not a spirit. In John, Mary was alone until Peter came and saw the tomb, then Jesus appeared to her at the tomb and later appeared to the disciples and breathed on them, giving them the power to forgive and retain sins. In a second visit to disciples he proved to a doubting disciple remembered as Doubting Thomas that he was flesh and blood. The disciples returned to Galilee where Jesus made another appearance and performed a miracle known as the catch of one-hundred-fifty-three fish at the Sea of Galilee before Jesus encouraged Peter to serve his followers.

Jesus' ascension into Heaven was said to be forty days after the Resurrection. As the disciples looked on, "he was lifted up, and a cloud took him out of their sight". Peter said that Jesus had "gone into Heaven and is at the right hand of God".

The Acts of the Apostles described several appearances of Jesus after his Ascension. In Acts, Stephen gazed into Heaven and saw "Jesus standing at the right hand of God." Just before his death and on the road to Damascus, the Apostle Paul was converted to Christianity after seeing a blinding light and hearing a voice saying, "I am Jesus, whom you are persecuting".

After his conversion Paul claimed the title of Apostle to the Gentiles. His influence on Christian thinking was more significant than any other New Testament author and by the end of the first century, Christianity was recognized as a separate religion from Judaism.

Jesus is the central figure of Christianity and Christians believe that through his sacrificial death and resurrection, humans can be reconciled with God and offered salvation and the promise of eternal life. These doctrines refer to Jesus as the Lamb of God, who was crucified to fulfill his role as the servant of God and Jesus is seen as the new and last Adam whose obedience contrasts with Adam's disobedience. Christians view Jesus as a role model and believers are encouraged to imitate his God-focused life.

Most Christians believe that Jesus was both human and the Son of God. Some early beliefs viewed him as subordinate to the Father and others considered him an aspect of the Father rather than a separate person. The Catholic Church resolved the issue by establishing the Holy Trinity, with Jesus both fully human and fully God. Trinitarian Christians believe that Jesus is the Logos, God's incarnation and God the Son, both fully divine and fully human, but the doctrine of the Trinity is not universally accepted among Christians. Christians revere not only Jesus himself, but his name too. Devotions to the Holy Name of Jesus go back to the earliest days of Christianity.

Judaism rejects the idea of Jesus being God, a mediator to God, or part of a Trinity. Jesus is not the Messiah and he neither fulfilled the Messianic prophecies in the Tanakh nor embodied the personal qualifications of the Messiah. Jews argue that he did not fulfill prophesies to build the Third Temple, gather Jews back to Israel, bring world peace, or unite humanity under the God of Israel. According to Jewish tradition there were no prophets after Malachi who delivered his prophesies in the fifth century BC.

The *Mishneh Torah*, a late twelfth century work of Jewish law written by Moses Maimonides states that Jesus is a stumbling block who makes "the majority of the world to err and serve a god other than the Lord.

Medieval Hebrew literature contains the anecdotal Episode of Jesus that described Jesus as being the son of Joseph, the son of Pandera in an account that portrays Jesus as an impostor.

A major figure in Islam, Jesus was considered a messenger of God and the Messiah sent to guide the Children of Israel with a new scripture, the Gospel. Muslims regard the gospels of the New Testament as inauthentic and believe that Jesus' original message was lost or altered and that Muhammad came later to restore it. Belief in Jesus and all other messengers of God is a requirement for being a Muslim. The Quran mentions Jesus by name twenty-five times; more often than Muhammad, and emphasizes that Jesus was a mortal human who like all other prophets had been divinely chosen to spread God's message. While the Quran affirms the virgin birth of Jesus, he is considered to be neither the incarnation nor the son of God, but like all prophets in Islam, Jesus is considered a Muslim.

The Quran describes the annunciation to Mary by an angel that she is to give birth to Jesus while remaining a virgin and calls the virgin birth a miracle that occurred by the will of God. The Quran says that God breathed his spirit into Mary while she was chaste and Jesus is called the Spirit of God because he was born through the action of the Spirit.

To aid in his ministry to the Jewish people Jesus was given the ability to perform miracles by permission of God rather than by his own power and through his ministry Jesus was seen as a precursor to Muhammad. According to the Quran, Jesus was not crucified but was made to appear that way to unbelievers by Allah who physically raised Jesus into the Heavens. To Muslims it is the ascension rather than the crucifixion that constitutes a major event in the life of Jesus. Most Muslims believe that Jesus will return to earth at the end of time and defeat the Antichrist.

Bahá'í teachings consider Jesus to be a manifestation of God, a Bahá'í concept for prophets who are intermediaries between God and humanity serving as messengers and reflecting God's qualities and attributes. The Bahá'í emphasize the simultaneous qualities of humanity and divinity that are similar to the Christian concept of incarnation. Bahá'í thought accepts Jesus as the Son of God and that Jesus was a perfect incarnation of God's attributes, but the Bahá'í reject the idea that the ineffable essence of the Divinity was contained within a single human body because of their beliefs regarding omnipresence and transcendence of the essence of God.

Bahá'u'lláh, the founder of the Bahá'í Faith wrote that since each manifestation of God has the same divine attributes, they can be seen as the spiritual return of all previous manifestations of God, and the appearance of each new manifestation of God inaugurates a religion that supersedes the former religions. Bahá'ís believe that God's plan unfolds gradually through this process as mankind matures and that some of the manifestations arrive in specific fulfillment of the missions of previous ones, so Bahá'ís believe that Bahá'u'lláh is the promised return of Christ. Bahá'í teachings confirm many but not all aspects of Jesus as portrayed in the gospels. Bahá'ís also believe in the virgin birth and in the crucifixion but see the resurrection and the miracles of Jesus as symbolic.

In Christian Gnosticism Jesus was sent from the divine realm and provided the secret knowledge necessary for salvation. Most Gnostics believed that Jesus was a human who became possessed by the spirit of The Christ at his baptism. This spirit left Jesus' body during the crucifixion but was rejoined to him when he was raised from the dead. Some Gnostics believed that Jesus didn't have a physical body but only appeared to possess one. Manichaeism, a Gnostic sect, accepted Jesus as a prophet in addition to revering Gautama Buddha and Zoroaster.

Some Hindus consider Jesus to be an avatar. Paramahansa Yogananda, an Indian guru, taught that Jesus was the reincarnation of Elisha and a student of John the Baptist, the reincarnation of Elijah. Some Buddhists regard Jesus as a bodhisattva who dedicated his life to the welfare of people. The New Age movement entertains a wide variety of views on Jesus and theosophists, who originated many New

Age teachings refer to Jesus as the Master Jesus and believe that Christ, after various incarnations occupied the body of Jesus. Scientologists recognize Jesus along with other religious figures like Zoroaster, Muhammad, and Buddha as part of their religious heritage, but atheists reject Jesus' divinity and have differing views on his moral teachings.

The Transfiguration was a major theme in Eastern Christian art and every Eastern Orthodox monk who trained in icon painting had to prove his craft by painting an icon depicting it. Icons received the external marks of veneration like kisses and prostration and are thought to be powerful channels of divine grace.

The myths and legends of Jesus and Satan put them in the realm of supernatural deities who hold great fascination and devotion from many humans. They also serve the role of being the targets of love, hate, fear, and other things both desirable and undesirable from humans. Both are credited with being light bearers. Jesus was the light of the world, and Satan was Lucifer, the bearer of light.

Aside from being two of humanity's most well known scapegoats who opposed each other in legendary struggles in the name of good and evil, the one thing they have in common is that they are both light bearers.

What does that say about you when the stories of the ones who bring the light to humanity are persecuted and banished?

The only thing I can think of is that you love the darkness.

Does that make you Christian or Satanic?

If you love Jesus and are devoted to the light of the world are you any different than those devoted to Satan the bearer of light?

For that matter, how many people have been killed in the name of Jesus or other deities and denizens in war, sacrifices, and other invitations for me to visit?

I am the one inescapable constant in your life and your imaginations have conjured up all manner of supernatural beings, deities, and entities who influence you and dictate what to expect when it's time to come home to Me.

Jesus, Satan, Heaven, and Hell are some of the most popular conceptions you hold, especially in your present beliefs, which is why I spent time talking about them, but there are multitudes of other influences, some of them believed to aid and be in servitude to more common beliefs, and others that are literally considered to be alien.

How do those versions of what is thought of as real fit in with the greater reality that *I* am?

ANGELS, DEMONS, ALLIES, AND ALIENS – PART I

Throughout your history you had many influences that came to you through dreams, visions, near death experiences, and other altered states that influence your relationship to me and your expectations of what will happen when I come for you. There are the time honored legends I have already mentioned and as your technologies have advanced, your perspectives have shifted to include other paranormal otherworldly intelligences.

Along with these newer entities that are part of your broader beliefs, there are a multitudes of lesser allies that are part of more traditional beliefs around Jesus, Satan, Heaven, and Hell, as well as those who are part of realms, deities, entities, and beliefs of other religions.

Aside from your more well known denizens of these imaginal realms, there are many more just as ancient if not more so that are often overlooked from the plant and animal kingdoms because they have not been prominent in your major religions. These have been kept alive in the prehistoric roots of more isolated indigenous shamanic cultures and are now becoming a bigger part of the mainstream as more and more of you are leaving the old religions behind in search of more realistic expectations. Some of these overlap and represent the same entities by different names and some share the same roots. Others are quite unique.

From a historical perspective the more well known of these are referred to as demons defined as supernatural malevolent beings prevalent in religion, occultism, literature, fiction, mythology, and folklore.

In Ancient Near Eastern religions, the Abrahamic traditions, and medieval Christian demonology, a demon is considered a harmful spiritual entity that can manifest in demonic possession that calls for an exorcism. In Western occultism and Renaissance magic a demon is believed to be a spiritual entity that can be conjured and controlled. The Ancient Greek word *daimōn* denotes a spirit or divine power.

The Greek terms do not have connotations of evil or malevolence, and by the early Roman Empire cult statues were seen by pagans and their Christian neighbors as inhabited by the presence of the gods. Like pagans, Christians still sensed and saw the gods and their power, and by an easy shift of opinion they turned these pagan *daimones* into malevolent demons who constituted Satan's troupe. Far into the Byzantine period Christians eyed their cities' old pagan statuary as a seat of a demon's presence that was no longer beautiful, but infested.

The existence of demons remains an important concept in many religions and occultist traditions and are still feared due to their alleged power to possess living creatures. In contemporary Western occultist tradition a demon is a useful metaphor for certain inner psychological processes, though some also regard it as an objectively real phenomenon.

Both deities and demons can act as intermediaries to deliver messages to humans and the borders between a deity and a demon are sometimes blurred. The ancient Egyptian language lacks a term for the modern English demon, but magical writings indicate that ancient Egyptians acknowledged the existence of malevolent demons by highlighting demon names with red ink. Demons in this culture appeared to be ruled by and related to specific deities and sometimes they are credited with acting independent from divine will. The existence of demons can be related to the realm of chaos beyond the created world, but even this negative connotation cannot be denied in light of the magical texts. The role of demons in relation to the human world remains ambivalent and mostly depends on context.

Ancient Egyptian demons can be divided into two classes, guardians and wanderers. Guardians are tied to a specific place. Their demonic activity is topographically defined and their function can be benevolent toward those who have the secret knowledge to face them. Demons protecting the underworld can prevent human souls from entering Paradise. Only by knowing right charms can the deceased enter the *Halls of Osiris*. Here, the aggressive nature and the guardian demons is motivated by the need to protect their abodes, not by their evil essence. Accordingly, demons guarded sacred places or the gates to the netherworld.

The wanderers are associated with possession, mental illness, death, and plagues. Many of them served as executioners for major deities like Ra or Osiris when ordered to punish humans on earth or in the netherworld. Wanderers can also be agents of chaos arising from the world beyond creation to bring misfortune and suffering without any divine instructions, led only by evil motivations. The influences of the wanderers can be warded off and kept at the borders of the human world by the use of magic, but they can never be destroyed. A sub-category of wanderers are nightmare demons which were believed to cause nightmares by entering a human body.

In Chaldean mythology the seven evil deities were known as *shedu*, storm-demons represented in ox-like form as winged bulls derived from the colossal bulls used as protective jinn of royal palaces.

Demons in Hebrew mythology were believed to come from the nether world. A number of diseases and ailments were ascribed to them, particularly those affecting the brain and those of internal nature, among them catalepsy, headache, epilepsy, and nightmares. There also existed a demon of blindness called Shabriri who rested on uncovered water at night and blinded those who drank from it.

Demons were believed to enter the body and cause disease while overwhelming their victims. To cure such diseases it was necessary to draw out the evil demons by incantations and talismanic performances that Essenes excelled at. Josephus spoke of demons as "spirits of the wicked which enter into men that are alive and kill them", but which could be driven out by a certain root. In mythology there were few defenses against Babylonian demons.

There are hardly any roles assigned to demons in the Hebrew Bible and in Judaism today, beliefs in demons or evil spirits are based on superstitions that are non-essential, non-binding parts of Judaism.

The Tanakh mentions two classes of demonic spirits, the *se'irim* and the *shedim* that are a re-calling of Assyrian demons in the shape of goats. The *shedim* are not pagan demigods, but the foreign gods themselves. Both entities appear in a scriptural context of animal or child sacrifice to non-existent gods.

In the Jerusalem Talmud notions of demons or spirits are almost unknown while in the Babylon Talmud there are lots of references to them and magical incantations. The existence of demons wasn't questioned by most of the Babylonian Talmudists. Rabbis believed in the existence of demons and most medieval thinkers didn't question their reality, although some denied their existence and rejected any concepts of demons, evil spirits, or negative spiritual influences. Attaching and possessing spirits eventually became part of mainstream Jewish understanding.

In Kabbalah demons were regarded as a necessary part of the divine emanation in the material world and a byproduct of human sin, but spirits like *shedim* could also be benevolent and were used in kabbalistic ceremonies while malevolent *shedim* were credited with possession.

Aggadic tales from the Persian tradition described the *shedim*, the *mazzikim,* or harmers, and the *ruhin, or* spirits. There were also *lilin, or* night spirits, *telane,* shade, or evening spirits, *tiharire,* midday spirits, and *zafrire,* morning spirits, as well as demons that brought famine, storms, and earthquakes. According to some stories demons were under the dominion of a king or chief, either Asmodai, or in the older Aggadah, Samael, the angel of death who killed with poison.

It's nice to be acknowledged here, even if it is limited.

The Qumran community during the Second Temple period between five-sixteen BCE and seventy CE said this magical prayer, "And, I the Sage, declare the grandeur of his radiance in order to frighten and terrify all the spirits of the ravaging angels and the bastard spirits, demons, Liliths, owls..."

In the Dead Sea Scrolls there is a fragment titled Curses of Belial that showed how they thought the devil they called Belial influenced sin through the way they addressed and spoke of him. By addressing Belial and all his guilty lot, they made it clear that he was not only impious, but guilty of sins. Informing this state of uncleanliness were both his hostile and wicked design. Through this design Belial poisoned the thoughts of those who were not necessarily sinners and a dualism was born from those inclined to be wicked and those who weren't. It's clear that Belial directly influenced sin by the mention of abominable plots and guilty inclination, both mechanisms used by Belial to advance his evil agenda that the Qumran exposed and called on God to protect them from. There was a deep sense of fear that Belial would establish in their heart their evil devices. This sense of fear was the stimulus for the prayer in the first place.

Good old Fear. Always on the job!

Sin was a direct product of Belial's influence and his presence acted as a placeholder for all negative influences or those that could interfere with God's will and a pious existence. Similarly to the gentiles, Belial was associated with a force that drove one away from God. Coupled in this plea for protection against foreign rule, the Egyptians pleaded for protection from the spirit of Belial who could ensnare people from every path of righteousness. Everyone found themselves straying from the path of righteousness and pawning their transgressions off on Belial, who became a scapegoat for all misguidance, no matter the cause. By associating Belial with misfortune and negative external influences the Qumran people were forgiven for their sins.

Belial's presence is found throughout the War Scrolls in the Dead Sea Scrolls and was established as the force occupying the opposite end of the spectrum of God. In the very first line of the document, it says, "the first attack of the Sons of Light shall be undertaken against the forces of the Sons of Darkness, the army of Belial". This dichotomy sheds light on the negative connotations Belial held. Where God and his Sons of Light are forces that protect and promote piety, Belial and his Sons of Darkness catered to the opposite, instilling the desire to sin and encouraging destruction. This epic battle between good and evil described in abstract terms is applicable to everyday life and serves as a lens for the Qumran to see the world. Every day is one where the Sons of Light battle evil and call upon God to help them overcome evil in small and large ways.

Belial's influence wasn't taken lightly. The text depicts God conquering the hordes of Belial showing God's power over Belial and his forces of temptation.

Belial also makes an appearance in the Damascus Document as a source of evil and an origin of several types of sin. The first mention of him reads, "Belial shall be unleashed against Israel". Belial is characterized in a wild and uncontrollable fashion, making him more dangerous and unpredictable. The notion of being unleashed implies that he is free to roam, is unstoppable, and able to carry out his agenda uninhibited. The passage then enumerates "three nets" that Belial captures his prey with and forces them to sin; fornication, riches, and the profanation of the temple. Later Belial is mentioned again as one of the removers of bound who led Israel astray. The passage goes on to say that they preached rebellion against God.

In the *War of the Sons of Light Against the Sons of Darkness*, Belial controlled scores of demons allotted to him by God for the purpose of performing evil and despite his malevolent disposition he was considered an angel.

There are of two classes of demonic entities in the Old Testament of the Christian Bible, the satyrs or shaggy goats, and the demons. The term demon appears in the New Testament of the Christian Bible, mostly relating to occurrences of possession of individuals and exorcism by Jesus.

The sources of demonic influence originated from the Watchers or Nephilim first mentioned in Genesis and seen as the source of sin and evil on earth because they are referenced in Genesis before the story of the Flood. God saw evil in the hearts of men. The passage says, "the wickedness of humankind on earth was great", and that "Every inclination of the thoughts of their hearts was only continually evil". The mention of the Nephilim connected the spread of evil to them.

In Enoch, sin originates when angels descend from Heaven and fornicate with women, birthing giants as tall as three-hundred cubits. The giants and the angel's departure of Heaven and mating with human women are seen as the source of sorrow and sadness on Earth. The book of Enoch shows that these fallen angels can lead humans to sin through direct interaction or through providing forbidden knowledge. Angels mating with humans is against God's commands and is a cursed action resulting in the wrath of God upon Earth. Azazel indirectly influenced humans to sin by teaching them divine knowledge not meant for humans and Asael brought down the stolen mysteries and gave humans the weapons they used to kill each other. Humans are also taught other sinful actions like beautification techniques, alchemy, astrology, and how to make medicine. Demons originate from the evil spirits of the giants cursed by God to wander the earth and are reputed to corrupt, fall, be excited, and fall upon the earth, and cause sorrow.

In Christianity demons are corrupted spirits carrying the execution of Satan's desires and are seen as three different types of spirits; souls of the wicked deceased that roam the earth to torment the living, Nephilim, who came into being by union between angels and human whose bodily parts were wiped out during the Great flood and whose spiritual part desires reembodiment, and fallen angels who sided with Lucifer and cast out of Heaven by Michael after battle.

Deities of other religions are interpreted or identified as demons and the evolution of the Christian Devil and pentagram are examples of early rituals and images that showcase evil qualities seen by the Christian churches.

Since Early Christianity demonology has developed from a simple acceptance of demons to a complex study that grew from the original ideas taken from Jewish demonology and Christian scriptures. Christian demonology is studied in depth in the Roman Catholic Church and many other Christian churches also affirm the existence of demons.

Christian writers of apocrypha from the second century on created a complicated tapestry of beliefs about demons that was independent of Christian scripture. The contemporary Roman Catholic Church teaches that angels and demons are real beings rather than symbolic devices and the Catholic Church has a cadre of exorcists who perform exorcisms every year. The exorcists of the Catholic Church teach that demons continually attack humans but afflicted persons can be healed and protected by the formal rite of exorcism authorized only by bishops and those they designate, or by prayers of deliverance that any Christian can offer.

There have been many attempts to classify adversarial spirits in Christian demonology, occultism, mythology, and Renaissance magic to clarify the connections between these spirits and their influence in different cultures. These systems are based on the supposed nature of the demon and the alleged sin they lure people into temptation with, and can include angels or saints believed to have been their adversaries, an idea that came from the Biblical battle between Archangel Michael and Satan in The Book of Revelation that expelled Satan and his angels. The classifications of these fallen angels are based on characteristic behaviors that caused their fall from Heaven, physical appearances, or the methods used to torment people, cause maladies, elicit dreams, emotions, and other influences.

The *Testament of Solomon* is an Old Testament work said to be written by King Solomon where he describes demons he enslaved to help build a temple and is considered the oldest surviving work about individual demons. In the eleventh century a Greek monk named Michael Psellus divided demons into Empyreal or Fiery, Aerial,

Subterranean, Lucifugous or Heliophobic, Aqueous, and Terrene, meaning Terrestrial, all of which mirrored the powerful and revered elemental spirits of indigenous cultures.

In fourteen-o-nine to fourteen-ten, *The Lanterne of Light*, attributed to John Wycliffe provided a classification system based on the Seven Deadly Sins, establishing that each one of the mentioned demons tempted people by one of those sins. Leading off the list is Lucifer who tempted with Pride followed by Beelzebub with Envy, Satan with Wrath, Abaddon with Sloth, Mammon with Greed, Belphegor with Gluttony, and Asmodeus with Lust.

In fourteen-sixty-seven, inspired by legends and stories a Spanish Catholic Bishop named Alphonso de Spina put together a classification of demons. Among them were demons of fate, incubi and succubi, wandering groups or armies of demons, familiars, drudes, cambions and other demons born from the union of a demon with a human being, liar and mischievous demons, demons that attack saints, and demons that try to induce old women to attend Witches' Sabbaths. The drudes belonged to German folklore while familiars, goblins, and other mischievous demons came from the folklore of most European countries.

The belief in incubi, succubi, and their ability to procreate inspired the seventh category, but was also inspired in the Talmudic legend of demons having sexual intercourse with mortal women.

The *De occulta philosophia* written from fifteen-o-nine to fifteen-ten by the German Cornelius Agrippa proposed several classifications for demons. One was based on the number four and the cardinal points, with the ruling demons being Oriens, East, Paymon, West, Egyn, North, and Amaymon, South. Once again the demons of the four directions are sacred elemental spirits honored by indigenous peoples in the Americas. Another classification based on the number nine had the following orders of demons: False Spirits, Spirits of Lying, Vessels of Iniquity, Avengers of Wickedness, Jugglers, Airy Powers, Furies sowing mischief, Sifters or Triers, and Tempters or Ensnarers.

In fifteen-ninety-one King James published a dissertation titled *Daemonologie* several years before the first publication of the King James Bible. His classification was not based on separate demonic entities with names, ranks, or titles, but on four methods used by any given devil to cause mischief or torment to a living individual or a deceased corpse. The purpose was to relay the belief that spirits caused maladies and that magic was possible only through demonic influence. He quoted previous authors who stated that each devil had the ability to appear in multiple shapes or forms for different arrays of purposes.

In his description demons were under the supervision of God and unable to act without permission, reinforcing how demonic forces were used as a Rod of Correction when men strayed from the will of God and could be commissioned by witches or magicians to conduct acts of ill will against others, but could only conduct works that ended in the further glorification of God, despite their attempts to do otherwise. Spectra was used to describe spirits that troubled houses or solitary places. Oppression described spirits that followed people to outwardly trouble them at different times of the day. Possession described spirits that entered inwardly into a person to trouble them, and Fairies described spirits that prophesied, consorted, and transported.

In sixteen-thirteen French inquisitor Sebastien Michaelis wrote a book, *Admirable History*, that included a classification of demons that was supposedly told to him by the demon Berith when he was exorcising a nun. This classification is based on the sins the devil tempts one to commit and included the demon's adversaries. The first hierarchy included angels that were Seraphim, Cherubim, and Thrones.

Beelzebub was a prince of the Seraphim just below Lucifer. Beelzebub, along with Lucifer and Leviathan were the first three angels to fall. He tempted men with pride and was opposed by St. Francis of Assisi. Leviathan was also a prince of the Seraphim who tempted people to give into heresy, and was opposed by St. Peter. Asmodeus, also a prince of the Seraphim, burned with desire to tempt men into wantonness and was opposed by St. John the Baptist. Berith was a prince of the Cherubim who tempted men to commit homicide, and to be quarrelsome, contentious, and blasphemous. He was opposed by St. Barnabas. Astaroth was a prince of Thrones who tempted men to be lazy and was opposed by St. Bartholomew. Verrine was also prince of Thrones just below Astaroth who tempted men with impatience and was opposed by St. Dominic. Gressil was the third prince of Thrones who tempted men with impurity and was opposed by St. Bernard, and Soneillon was the fourth prince of Thrones who tempted men to hate and was opposed by St. Stephen.

A second hierarchy included Powers, Dominions, and Virtues.

Carreau was a prince of Powers who tempted men with hardness of heart and was opposed by St. Vincent. Carnivale was also a prince of Powers who tempted men to obscenity and shamelessness and was opposed by John the Evangelist. Oeillet was a prince of Dominions who tempted men to break the vow of poverty and was opposed by St. Martin. Rosier was the second in the order of Dominions who tempted men against sexual purity and was opposed by St. Basil. Belias was the prince of Virtues who tempted men with arrogance and women to be vain, raise their children as wantons, and gossip during mass. He was opposed by St. Francis de Paul.

A third hierarchy included Principalities, Archangels, and Angels.

Verrier was the prince of Principalities who tempted men against the vow of obedience and was opposed by St. Bernard. Olivier was the prince of the Archangels who tempted men with cruelty and mercilessness toward the poor and opposed by St. Lawrence. Luvart was the prince of Angels and at the time of Michaelis's writing, Luvart was believed to be in the body of a Sister Madeleine. Many of the names and ranks of these demons also appeared in the Sabbath litanies of witches.

English occultist Francis Barrett in his book *The magus,* published in eighteen-o-one offered this classification of demons, making them princes of evil attitudes, people, or things. Beelzebub was False Gods for idolaters, Pythius was Spirits of Lying for liars, Belial was Vessels of Iniquity for inventors of evil things, and Asmodeus for Revengers of Wickedness. Satan represented Imitators of Miracles for evil witches and warlocks and Merihem represented Aerial Powers for purveyors of pestilence. Abaddon acted as Furies for sowers of discord, Astaroth as Calumniators for inquisitors and fraudulent accusers, and Mammon acted as Maligenii for tempters and ensnarers.

You have to give all of these authorities credit for imagination in creating such an amazing, diversified lineup of personalized scapegoats!

Islam and Islam related beliefs acknowledge the concept of evil spirits they called malevolent Jinn, *Afarit* and *Shayatin.* Unlike the belief in angels, belief in demons is not obligated by the six articles of Islamic faith, but the existence of several demonic spirits persist in Islamic folklore and the Quran mentions the *Zabaniyya,* who tortured the damned in Hell, but their execution of punishment was in accordance with God's order.

Rather than demonic, Jinn are thought to resemble humans and regarded as living in societies, in need of dwelling places, and eating and drinking with a lifespan that exceeds humans over centuries. They still die and need to procreate, but because they are created from smokeless fire in contrast to humans made from solid earth, humans can't see them. Jinn are also subject to temptations of the Shayatin and Satan and can be either good or evil. Evil Jinn are comparable to demons scaring or possessing humans. In folklore some Jinn lurk with lonely travelers to dissuade them from their paths and eat their corpses. Although not evil, a Jinni can haunt a person if it feels offended by them. Islam has no binding origin story of Jinn, but Islamic beliefs assume that the Jinn were created on a Thursday thousands of years before mankind and Islamic medieval narratives called them *Pre-Adamites*.

The Shayatin are the Islamic equivalent of demons in western usage. Islam differs in regard of the origin of demons. They are either a class of heavenly creatures cast out of Heaven or the descendants of Iblis. Unlike Jinn and humans, Shayatin are immortal and will die, then the world perishes, but prayers can dissolve or banish them. Unlike Jinn and human, Shayatin can not attain salvation. They are also thought to attempt to reach to Heaven, but are chased away from Angels or shooting stars. The Shayatin don't possess people, but whisper to their minds and seduce them into falsehood and sin. These are called *waswās* and can enter the hearts of humans to support negative feelings, especially in states of strong emotion like depression or anger.

Another demonic spirit called Ifrit, Folk Islam characterizes with traits of malevolent ghosts returning after I come or a subcategory of Shayatin who draw on the life-force of those who were murdered.

Hindu beliefs include a host of spirits classified as demigods, including Vetalas, Bhutas, and Pishachas. Rakshasas and Asuras are often misunderstood to be demons, but there are no demons in Hinduism as it is not based on good and evil and is not constructed by the principle of duality.

Originally, *Asura*, in the earliest hymns of the Rig Veda meant any supernatural spirit, either good or bad. Later, during the Puranic age, Asura and Rakshasa came to mean any of a race of anthropomorphic, powerful, possibly evil beings.

The Asura are not against the gods and do not tempt humans to fall. Many people metaphorically interpret the Asura as manifestations of the ignoble passions in the human mind and as symbolic devices. There were also cases of power hungry Asuras challenging aspects of the gods, only to be defeated, seeking forgiveness.

Hinduism advocates the reincarnation and transmigration of souls according to one's karma. Souls of the dead are adjudged by the Yama and are accorded various purging punishments before being reborn. Humans that have committed extraordinary wrongs are condemned to roam as lonely mischief mongering spirits for a length of time before being reborn.

In the Bahá'í Faith demons aren't thought of as independent evil spirits like in other faiths. Evil spirits described as Satan, fallen angels, demons, and jinn are metaphors for the base character traits a human can acquire and manifest when they turn away from God and follow their lower nature. Belief in the existence of ghosts and earthbound spirits is rejected as superstition.

While some people fear demons or attempt to exorcise them, others try to summon them for knowledge, assistance, or power. Ceremonial magicians consulted grimoires that gave them the names and abilities of demons as well as detailed instructions for conjuring and controlling them. Grimoires weren't limited to demons. Some gave the names of angels or spirits that could be called in a process called theurgy. The use of ceremonial magic to call demons is also known as goetia from a section in the famous grimoire known as the *Lesser Key of Solomon.*

Psychologist Wilhelm Wundt said that "among the activities attributed by myths all over the world to demons, the harmful predominate, so that in popular belief bad demons are clearly older than good ones." Freud said that the concept of demons was derived from the relation of the living to the dead; "The fact that demons are always regarded as the spirits of those who have died *recently* shows better than anything the influence of mourning on the origin of the belief in demons." M. Scott Peck, an American psychiatrist, described several cases that identified characteristics of evil people that he classified as having character disorders. Peck came to the conclusion that possession was a rare phenomenon related to evil and that possessed people are not evil, they are doing battle with the forces of evil.

According to the *Britannica Concise Encyclopedia*, demons, despite being associated with evil, are often shown to be under divine control and not acting on their own.

The variety and differing beliefs and interpretations of disembodied entities and scapegoats in the form of demons have carried the weight and responsibility of humanity's sins through the centuries. Over time and changes in culture the lines have blurred between what is benevolent and what is diabolical as these dark forces are often characterized as fallen angels under divine control.

Much of what is considered demonic has overlapped into the angelic realms, so it's only right that I want to give the angels some time from a positive perspective to keep everything in balance.

In Abrahamic religions angels are benevolent celestial beings who act as intermediaries between God or Heaven and humanity. Other roles of angels include protecting and guiding human beings and carrying out God's tasks. These angels are organized into hierarchies that are different between sects in each religion and are given specific names or titles like Gabriel or Destroying Angel. The term angel has also been expanded to include spirits or figures found in other religious traditions, and the fallen angels expelled from Heaven. Angels usually have the shape of human beings of extraordinary beauty, are sometimes androgynous, and are often identified with symbols of bird wings, halos, and light. The Torah uses the Hebrew terms meaning messenger of God, messenger of the Lord, sons of God, and the holy ones to refer to beings thought of as angels.

A human messenger might be a prophet or priest like Malachi, my messenger, so the Book of Malachi was written by the hand of his messenger. Examples of a supernatural messenger are the Malak YHWH, who is either a messenger from God, an aspect of God like the Logos, or God himself as the messenger. Daniel was the first biblical figure to refer to individual angels by name, mentioning Gabriel as God's primary messenger and Michael the holy fighter. These angels are part of Daniel's apocalyptic visions and an important part of apocalyptic literature.

With the development of monotheism, divine beings known as the sons of God who were members of the Divine Council were demoted to angels created by God, but immortal and superior to humans.

Four classes of angels were believed to minister and praise the Holy One, the first led by Michael on His right, the second led by

Gabriel on His left, the third led by Uriel before Him, and the fourth led by Raphael behind Him with the Shekhinah of the Holy One in the center sitting on a throne, high and exalted.

In post-Biblical Judaism some angels developed unique personalities and roles like Metatron, one of the highest of the angels in Merkabah and Kabbalist mysticism who served as a scribe. Michael served as a warrior and advocate for Israel along with Gabriel. There is no evidence in Judaism for the worship of angels but there is evidence for the invocation and conjuration of them.

The Jewish angelic hierarchy had seven angels. Michael the archangel who represented the kindness of God and stood up for the children of mankind, Gabriel the archangel who performed acts of justice and power, Jophiel who expelled Adam and Eve from the Garden of Eden holding a flaming sword and punished those who transgressed against God. Raphael the archangel represented God's healing force and Uriel the archangel led them to destiny. Sandalphon the archangel battled Samael and brought mankind together, and Samael the archangel was the angel of death.

It's always nice to be recognized and remembered.

Later Christians inherited Jewish understandings of angels and in the early stage the Christian concept of an angel characterized them as messengers of God. Later came identification of individual angelic messengers, Gabriel, Michael, Raphael, and Uriel. From from the third to the fifth centuries the image of angels took on definite characteristics in theology and art.

By the late fourth century Church Fathers agreed that there were different categories of angels, but they disagreed about their nature. Some argued that they had physical bodies and some said they were entirely spiritual. Some theologians proposed that they were not divine, but on the level of immaterial beings subordinate to the Trinity.

The Fourth Lateran Council in twelve-fifteen declared that angels were created and that men were created after them. The First Vatican Council in eighteen-sixty-nine repeated this declaration in *Dei Filius*, the dogmatic constitution on the Catholic faith.

The New Testament includes many interactions and conversations between angels and humans, among them the births of John the Baptist and Jesus Christ. In Luke an angel appears to Zechariah to tell him he will have a child despite his old age, proclaiming the birth of John the Baptist. Also in Luke the Archangel Gabriel visits the Virgin

Mary in the Annunciation to foretell the birth of Jesus and angels proclaim his birth in the Adoration of the shepherds.

According to Matthew after Jesus spent forty days in the desert, the devil left him and, behold, angels came and ministered to him. Again in Luke an angel comforts Jesus during the Agony in the Garden, and in Matthew an angel speaks at the empty tomb following the Resurrection of Jesus and the rolling back of the stone by angels.

According to the Vatican's Congregation for Divine Worship and Discipline of the Sacraments, "The practice of assigning names to the Holy Angels should be discouraged, except in the cases of Gabriel, Raphael and Michael whose names are contained in Holy Scripture."

In the New Church extensive information is provided concerning angels and the spiritual world they dwell in from years of spiritual experiences recounted in the writings of Emanuel Swedenborg. All angels are in human form with a spiritual body and are not just minds without form. There are different orders of angels according to the three Heavens, and each angel dwells in one of innumerable societies of angels. These societies can appear as one angel as a whole.

All angels originate from the human race and there is not one angel in Heaven who first did not live in a material body. All children who die not only enter Heaven, they eventually become angels. The life of angels is one of usefulness, and their functions are numerous. Each angel enters service according to the use they performed in their earthly life. Names of angels like Michael, Gabriel, and Raphael signify particular angelic functions rather than individual being.

While living in a body an individual has conjunction with Heaven through the angels and with each person there are at least two evil spirits and two angels. Temptation or pains of conscience come from a conflict between evil spirits and angels. Due to man's sinful nature it is dangerous to have direct communication with angels which can only be seen when one's spiritual sight has been opened, so from moment to moment angels attempt to lead each person to what is good using the person's own thoughts.

The Latter Day Saints view angels as messengers of God sent to mankind to deliver messages, minister to humanity, teach doctrines of salvation, call mankind to repentance, give priesthood keys, save individuals in perilous times, and guide humankind.

Latter Day Saints believe that angels are either the spirits of humans who are deceased or who have yet to be born, or are humans who have been resurrected or translated and have physical bodies of flesh and bone. Joseph Smith taught that "there are no angels who minister to this earth but those that do belong or have belonged to it." Latter Day Saints also believe that Adam, the first man is the archangel Michael, and that Gabriel lived on the earth as Noah. Likewise the Angel Moroni first lived in a pre-Columbian American civilization as a fifth century prophet-warrior named Moroni.

Here is how Smith described his first angelic encounter. "While I was thus in the act of calling upon God, I discovered a light appearing in my room, which continued to increase until the room was lighter than at noonday, when immediately a personage appeared at my bedside, standing in the air, for his feet did not touch the floor.

He had on a loose robe of most exquisite whiteness. It was a whiteness beyond anything earthly I had ever seen; nor do I believe that any earthly thing could be made to appear so exceedingly white and brilliant...

Not only was his robe exceedingly white, but his whole person was glorious beyond description, and his countenance truly like lightning. The room was exceedingly light, but not so very bright as immediately around his person. When I first looked upon him, I was afraid; but the fear soon left me."

Most angelic visitations in the early Latter Day Saint movement were witnessed by Smith and Oliver Cowdery, who both said they were visited by the prophet Moroni, John the Baptist, and the apostles Peter, James, and John. Later, after the dedication of the Kirtland Temple, Smith and Cowdery said they had been visited by Jesus, Moses, Elias, and Elijah.

Others who claimed to receive a visit by an angel include the other two of the Three Witnesses: David Whitmer and Martin Harris. Many other Latter Day Saints both in the early and modern church said they saw angels.

Belief in angels is fundamental to Islam and the Quran is the principal source for the Islamic concept of angels. Some of them like Gabriel and Michael are mentioned by name and others are only referred to by their function. Angels play a significant role in Mi'raj literature where Muhammad encounters several angels during his journey through the Heavens. More angels have been featured in Islamic eschatology, Islamic theology, and Islamic philosophy. Duties assigned to them include communicating revelations from God, glorifying God, recording every person's actions, and taking a person's soul at the time of death.

I guess that confirms Me as an angel!

In Islam like in Judaism and Christianity, angels are represented in anthropomorphic forms combined with supernatural images like wings, and have great size and wear heavenly articles. The Quran describes them as messengers with two, three, or four pairs of wings. Common characteristics are their missing need for bodily desires like eating and drinking. Their lack of affinity to material desires is also expressed by their creation from light. Angels of mercy are created from cold light in opposition to angels of punishment created from hot light.

The first creation by God was considered the supreme archangel followed by other archangels who identified with lower intellects and from these emanated lower angels or moving spheres that emanated other intellects until it reached the Intellect that reigns over souls.

ANGELS, DEMONS, ALLIES, AND ALIENS – PART II

The founder of the Bahá'í Faith described angels as people who have
consumed, with the fire of the love of God, all human traits and
limitations, and have clothed themselves with angelic attributes and
have become endowed with the attributes of the spiritual. 'Abdu'l-Bahá
described angels as the confirmations of God and His celestial powers
and as blessed beings who severed all ties with this nether world and
been released from the chains of self, and are revealers of God's
abounding grace.

In Zoroastrianism there are different angel-like figures. Each
person has one guardian angel, called Fravashi that patronize human
beings and other creatures and manifests God's energy. The Amesha
Spentas have been thought of as angels, although there is no direct
reference to them conveying messages, but they are considered
emanations of Ahura Mazda, the Wise Lord, or God and first appeared
in an abstract fashion, and later became personalized, associated with
diverse aspects of divine creation.

In Sikhism the poetry of the holy scripture of the Sikhs, the Sri
Guru Granth Sahib mentions a messenger or angel of death,
sometimes as Yam and sometimes as Azrael, saying "The Messenger
of Death will not touch you; in this way, you shall cross over the
terrifying world-ocean, carrying others across with you. Azraa-eel, the
Messenger of Death, is the friend of the human being who has Your
support, Lord."

I will admit to being a friend of humans, but I can't say that I won't
touch you.

Chitar and Gupat, the Sikh recording angels of the conscious and
unconscious write the accounts of all mortal beings, but Sikhism has

never had a literal system of angels, preferring guidance without explicit appeal to supernatural orders or beings.

In the teachings of the Theosophical Society, *Devas* are regarded as living either in the atmospheres of the planets of the solar system as *Planetary Angels,* or inside the Sun as *Solar Angels* who help guide the operation of nature like the process of evolution and the growth of plants. Their appearance was said to be like colored flames about the size of a human. It is believed by Theosophists that devas can be observed when the third eye is activated and that some devas originally incarnated as human beings.

Theosophists believe that nature spirits and elementals like gnomes, undines, sylphs, salamanders, and fairies can be also be observed when the third eye is activated. Theosophists maintain that these less evolutionarily developed beings have never been incarnated as humans and are regarded as being on a separate line of spiritual evolution called deva evolution. As their souls advance in reincarnation it is believed they will incarnate as devas.

Theosophists assert that all of these beings possess etheric bodies composed of *etheric matter,* a type of matter finer and more pure made of smaller particles than ordinary physical plane matter.

Angels are often shown in paintings and sculptures as male humans. Christian art reflects the descriptions of the Four Living Creatures in Revelation and the descriptions in the Hebrew Bible of cherubim and seraphim. While cherubim and seraphim have wings in the Bible, no angel is mentioned as having wings.

The earliest known Christian image of an angel in the Catacomb of Priscilla has no wings, and in that same period their representations on sarcophagi, lamps, and reliquaries also show them without wings.

The earliest known representation of angels with wings is on the Prince's Sarcophagus, attributed to the time of Theodosius The First from three-seventy-nine to three-ninety-five which was discovered near Istanbul in the nineteen-thirties. From that period on, Christian art represented angels mostly with wings. Four and six-winged angels drawn from the higher grades of angels, especially cherubim and seraphim often showed only their faces and wings derived from Persian art. They were usually shown only in Heavenly contexts as opposed to performing tasks on earth and often appeared in the pendentives of church domes or semi-domes. Prior to the Judeo-

Christian tradition, in the Greek world the goddess Nike and the gods Eros and Thanatos were also described in human-like form with wings.

Angels are usually shown in Mormon art as having no wings based on a quote from Joseph Smith saying, "An angel of God never has wings".

Angels, especially the Archangel Michael, were shown as military-style agents of God wearing Late Antique military uniforms. The basic military dress was seen in Western art into the Baroque period up to the present day in Eastern Orthodox icons. Other angels were usually shown in long robes, and in the later Middle Ages they often wore the vestments of a deacon. Some angels are described having more unusual or frightening features like the fiery bodies of the Seraphim and the wheel-like structures of the Ophanim.

Over time the profusion of mythic stories of spirit and human interaction regarding these real or imagined beings have prompted endless speculation about their elusive nature.

Do angels have wings?

How many angels can dance on the head of a pin?

What is their true nature if there is one, or are they simply more products of human imaginings?

The plethora of stories across cultures full of angelic descriptions and encounters come from pre-technological times where there were no precedents for extra terrestrials you call ETs, or unidentified flying objects referred to as UFOs. If you look at these colorful stories and awe-inspiring myths from a modern day perspective and open your already active imagination, it can be an interesting exercise to read the scriptures and swap out the concept of angel, thinking of the described creatures as alien or ETs.

The most well-known of these is the Book of the Hebrew prophet Ezekiel in the Hebrew Bible.

In this account, Ezekiel wrote, "When I was thirty years of age, I was living with the exiles on the Kebar River. On the fifth day of the fourth month, the sky opened up and I saw visions of God."

Ezekiel went on to say, "I looked: I saw an immense dust storm come from the north, an immense cloud with lightning flashing from it, a huge ball of fire glowing like bronze. Within the fire were what looked like four creatures vibrant with life. Each had the form of a human being, but each also had four faces and four wings. Their legs were as sturdy and straight as columns, but their feet were hoofed like those of a calf and sparkled from the fire like burnished bronze. On all four sides under their wings they had human hands. All four had both faces and wings, with the wings touching one another. They turned neither one way nor the other; they went straight forward.

Their faces looked like this: In front a human face, on the right side the face of a lion, on the left the face of an ox, and in back the face of an eagle. So much for the faces. The wings were spread out with the tips of one pair touching the creature on either side; the other pair of wings covered its body. Each creature went straight ahead. Wherever the spirit went, they went. They didn't turn as they went.

The four creatures looked like a blazing fire, or like fiery torches. Tongues of fire shot back and forth between the creatures, and out of the fire, bolts of lightning. The creatures flashed back and forth like strikes of lightning.

As I watched the four creatures, I saw something that looked like a wheel on the ground beside each of the four-faced creatures. This is what the wheels looked like: They were identical wheels, sparkling like diamonds in the sun. It looked like they were wheels within wheels, like a gyroscope.

They went in any one of the four directions they faced, but straight, not veering off. The rims were immense, circled with eyes. When the living creatures went, the wheels went; when the living creatures lifted off, the wheels lifted off. Wherever the spirit went, they went, the wheels sticking right with them, for the spirit of the living creatures was in the wheels. When the creatures went, the wheels went; when the creatures stopped, the wheels stopped; when the creatures lifted off, the wheels lifted off, because the spirit of the living creatures was in the wheels.

Over the heads of the living creatures was something like a dome, shimmering like a sky full of cut glass, vaulted over their heads. Under the dome one set of wings was extended toward the others, with another set of wings covering their bodies. When they moved I heard their wings — it was like the roar of a great waterfall, like the voice of The Strong God, like the noise of a battlefield. When they stopped, they folded their wings.

And then, as they stood with folded wings, there was a voice from above the dome over their heads. Above the dome there was something that looked like a throne, sky-blue like a sapphire, with a humanlike figure towering above the throne. From what I could see, from the waist up he looked like burnished bronze and from the waist down like a blazing fire. Brightness everywhere! The way a rainbow springs out of the sky on a rainy day—that's what it was like. It turned out to be the Glory of God!

When I saw all this, I fell to my knees, my face to the ground. Then I heard a voice."

There are numerous UFO accounts in ancient records from different places, periods of history, cultures, and belief systems. The terminology of these accounts may sound unfamiliar, but the words used are no less primitive than those used in modern times. What will future generations think of a culture that described extraterrestrial spacecraft as flying saucers, or cigar-shaped objects?

The Bible is not accurate as a historical document and much if not all of it is myth as there is no definitive way to prove any of the stories and accounts recorded there. Not only has it been through different translations, but several different scribes have worked on it, some with political motivations that introduced considerable inconsistencies.

As I pointed out, the most quoted account of biblical UFOs occurs in the Book of Ezekiel which reads, "And I looked, and, behold, a whirlwind came out of the north, a great cloud, and a fire infolding itself, and a brightness was about it, and out of the midst thereof as the color of amber, out of the midst of the fire."

This description of a UFO continues with what is classified as a close encounter of the third kind which is a meeting with occupants of UFOs who are visitors from other planets.

The important thing about UFOs is not so much the craft themselves, but the people who man and control them. In Ezekiel's account he saw four Interplanetary Beings stepping out of this UFO and he received information and instructions from them. He referred to them as living creatures. Later in the same chapter there is a more detailed description of the spacecraft as a wheel in the middle of a wheel and having eyes round about them four. This last description is taken to refer to portholes described in modern UFO sightings. A wheel within a wheel could be an inner superstructure revolving while an outer one remains stationary.

After the exodus of the Jews from Egypt led by Moses, there are a lot of descriptions of UFOs which seem to have accompanied them. They referred to clouds and stars with the properties of high speed movement and flight control as well as fiery chariots. The following extract from Exodus, is a typical example.

"And the Lord went before them by day in a pillar of cloud, to lead them along the way; and by night in a pillar of fire, to give them light; to go by day and night: He took not away the pillar of cloud by day, nor the pillar of fire by night, from before the people."

This description of pillars of cloud and fire is close to the cigar-shaped descriptions of UFOs. In the twentieth century we have become more mundane in our descriptions. Wheel in the middle of a wheel was used then while in modern times the term flying saucer is used.

The Prophet Elijah was taken to Heaven in a space vehicle and his follower Elisha was with him and witnessed this. "And it came to pass, as they still went on, and talked, that, behold, there appeared a chariot of fire, and horses of fire, and parted them both asunder; and Elijah went up by a whirlwind into Heaven."

Beam me up, Scotty?

The chariot and horses represent a vehicle to Biblical scribes and the whirlwind suggests a vortex of energy that is often described in UFO sightings.

The Prophet Zechariah gave a very precise description of a UFO. "Then I turned and lifted up mine eyes and looked, and behold, a flying scroll. And he said unto me, 'What seest thou?' I answered, I see a flying scroll, the length thereof is twenty cubits, and the breadth thereof ten cubits."

A scroll is definitely similar to a cigar-shaped object.

The most significant UFO biblical sighting of them all is the Star of Bethlehem from the Book of Matthew. "And, lo, the Star, which they saw in the east, went before them, till it came and stood over where the young child was. When they saw the Star, they rejoiced exceedingly with great joy. And when they were come into the house, they saw the young child with Mary, his mother, and fell down, and worshiped him."

This is considered a classic example of a UFO leading three advanced men to a great Interplanetary Master who had been born on this planet to perform a specific mission.

When you look at other religious scripts you find a similar pattern of UFO involvement in spiritual revelations. The Hindu texts known as the Vedas are a good example. As with the Holy Bible there is no guarantee of any accuracy of these writings which were passed down for thousands of years orally before being written down, so there is a margin for error.

Texts like the Ramayana use the Sanskrit word, vimana, which means flying celestial vehicle. The following from the Ramayana is typical of the descriptions of vimanas.

"When morning dawned, Rama, taking the vimana Puspaka had sent him by Vivpishand, stood ready to depart. Self-propelled was that car. It was large and finely painted."

In another extract a vimana is described as, "That aerial and excellent vimana, going everywhere at will, is ready for thee. That vimana, resembling a bright cloud in the sky, is in the city of Lanka."

The Vedas and Buddhist scripts have a concept of life throughout the planetary realms and accept the existence of life on other worlds and life on higher spheres as being part of the belief in universal consciousness.

One Vedic script describes the liberation of a King named Dhruva from material bondage into high spiritual consciousness which is referred to in metaphysical writings as the state of Ascension. This amazing experience which takes on a cosmic dimension is described in the Bhagavata Purana.

"As soon as the symptoms of his liberation were manifest, he saw a very beautiful vimana coming down from the sky, as if the brilliant full moon were coming down, illuminating all the ten directions..."

He was picked up by this UFO and described his journey. "While Dhruva Maharajah was passing through space, he gradually saw all the planets of the Solar System, and on the path he saw all the demi-gods in their vimanas showering flowers upon him like rain... Beyond that region, he achieved the transcendental situation of permanent life in the planet where Lord Vishnu lives."

Not only does this description detail a beautiful close encounter of the third kind that allegedly took place thousands of years ago, it indicates that it is possible to attain such an elevated state of consciousness that one is liberated from the need to reside on Earth and can go to other worlds for continued existence.

The Vedas present a multitude of gods, most of them related to natural forces like storms, fire, and wind. As part of its mythology Vedic texts contain an abundance of creation stories, but most are inconsistent with each other. Sometimes the Vedas refer to a particular god as the greatest god of all, and later another god is spoken of as the greatest god of all.

The Pre-Vedic religion which is the oldest known religion of India was found before the Aryan migrations and had animistic and totemic worship of spirits dwelling in stones, animals, trees, rivers, mountains, and stars. Some of them were good, others were evil, and great magic was the only way to control them. Traces of this old religion are still present in the Vedas. In the Atharva-Veda there are spells to obtain children, avoid abortion, prolong life, ward off evil, woo sleep, and harm or destroy enemies.

These ancient beliefs in what are collectively referred to as elemental spirits headed by the primary entities of earth, air, fire, and water are still deeply embedded in indigenous cultures like the Aborigines of Australia, the Indians of North America, and the Indians and mestizos of South America as well as in many others. Depending on your perspective, these visible and invisible forces of nature can be seen as entities, angels, demons, devas, elves, fairies, and spirits, depending on their cultural context. Some are thought of as allies and some are seen as enemies. All of them represent different forms of energy with unique characteristics and personalities that encompass the natural world of plants, animals, insects, and every other conceivable force of nature aligned with Me.

Ancient histories, mythologies, and prehistoric cultural roots all have deep metaphysical interconnections with the terrestrial nature of your planet that pushes the boundaries of three dimensional time and space perceptions and extends into deep extraterrestrial connections.

Prehistoric traditions throughout the Amazonian rain forest centers around plants that put its practitioners into altered states allowing them to connect with the visible and invisible spirits of plants and animals which can be seen and communicated with through the ritual use of these plants.

I have a special affinity to the most well known of these, a plant called Ayahuasca that is served as a combination of two or more plants in a visionary drink believed to open portals to other worlds.

Also known as The Vine of the Dead which is a big part of what I love about it, Ayahuasca refers both to the vine and the brew prepared from it. In the Quechua language, *aya* means spirit, soul, corpse, or dead body, and *waska* means rope and woody vine. The word *ayahuasca* has been translated as liana of the soul, liana of the dead, and spirit liana.

In visionary states encountered by drinking the Ayahuasca brew, shamans also ingest any number and combination of specialized plants to learn from the spirits of the plants by passing through physical, mental, and spiritual ordeals to prove that they are worthy of the gift of knowledge that the plant spirits have to give them.

In this elemental belief system each plant and animal has its own spirit, essence, or energy which can be characterized as its own unique personality in the same way that Ayahuasca is universally referred to as The Mother. It is also why North American Indians don't refer to animals as *the* bear or *the* coyote. They say Bear or Coyote as they consider them all to be manifesting the entire essence of their spirit in a grouped manner, similar to bees, ants, and other cooperative colonies, and each one has its own unique energy signature that is treated with equal respect.

Among the numerous totems encountered under the influence of Ayahuasca, the most common are condors, jaguars, snakes, and hummingbirds. Shamans experiencing those energies or spirits often roar and growl through no volition of their own like jaguars, flap their legs like wings, or feel their bodies swaying of its own accord to distinctive serpentine movements. Other animals and insects like butterflies, dragonflies, dolphins, and other aquatic totems play big parts as well.

One of the intriguing results of immersion into this animated spirit world is the perception of an energetic realm that opens up the ability to not only commune with the plants and the distinctive energies of their unique spirits and personalities, but also to the distinctive energies and personalities of the animal kingdom as well as otherworldly entities characterized as angels, demons, saints, or any number of other deities, often in fantastic magical settings that defy description.

Aside from those elemental realms and energies encountered from ingesting mind altering plants and substances, there is an amalgam of information that crosses the borders of the conscious and subconscious that can be accessed by fasting, meditating, channeling, dreams, visions, inspirations, fevers, hallucinations, and more. Regardless of the method, indigenous people did not see these radically different states of mind as separate modes of consciousness, but as one unified continuum.

What is the nature of this information and what value might it hold? Does it originate in the mind, out of the mind, from the planet or from the stars? Where in all of this do portals to other worlds lie, if any?

Do elemental spirits and other invisible extraterrestrial entities communicate with humans?

Do any of them have any substance or reality outside of you, or are they just phantasms born from the subconscious workings of fevered imaginations like so many other historically recorded scriptures or doctrines?

Your era of increasingly diversified spiritual beliefs have given rise to a proliferation of channelers and mediums who claim to be in communication with extraterrestrial beings and spirits of the deceased to mediate communication between disembodied spirits and living human beings. There are too many to mention in detail, but intelligences like these are considered by some to be the very same angels, demons, and saints of old.

I am only going to mention a couple of prominent examples and regardless of any validity of their source, I find what they have to say interesting. Like many of the scriptures of old there may be a grain of truth in their words, even if there is no proof of it in your three dimensional world.

First are the Pleiadians who are believed to be humanoid aliens from the stellar systems surrounding the Pleiades stars who are concerned about the Earth and your future. According to the belief they have chosen special people to channel them and convey their message to help humanity ascend to higher dimensions. They are said to be attractive humanoids who lack pigmentation in their skin and hair, giving them an albino appearance. Many of them look Asian and don't have curly hair or beards. Their beauty is reminiscent of African and Egyptian gods and goddesses or other angels who were pleasing to look at. What the Pleiadians say ties in with spiritualist and theosophist beliefs of the early twentieth century.

Ashtar Sheran, a supposed extraterrestrial intelligence is the central figure of an Internet-based cult that includes Pleiadians, Mother/Father God, Adama, and others. The cult is based on New World Order and Illuminati conspiracy theories, but has no meaningful evidence of any of them. The only form of information it employs is a continuous revelation from multiple beings about secret knowledge and imminent transformation. Messages from Ashtar are translated within 24 hours into a dozen languages and put out on the Internet for the sake of foreign believers.

The cult believes that aliens are all over and in the skies every hour of the day and want to reach out to us. Some of them already have, but are unable to land on Earth due to the machinations of the Illuminati. They say that the government knows everything but is refusing to say anything and at a moment in the future called Disclosure, world governments will admit the existence of the great conspiracy, the aliens will land, and the Illuminati will fall. Until then, cultural change and spiritual transformation is said to be needed to prepare for their arrival.

Pleiadians are connected to mythological Atlantis and Lemuria. Reiki, ear candling, Shiatsu, reflexology, aromatherapy, and crystal healing are credited to coming from them. They also brought dolphins to Earth. Jesus was reputed to be a Pleiadian, as was his father. The Pleiadians are believed to be helping humanity fight evil space reptiles as part of the battle against the Illuminati.

Pleiadians are considered common ancestors of both humans and Pleiadians who came from another universe and seeded a number of worlds in your universe including Earth with their DNA. They are said to have appeared before humans did and ascended to the next evolutionary stage. Through technological means they can travel back in time and to higher dimensions and contact the beings inhabiting those realms.

The Pleiadians get their messages across through special people they have chosen, but there is a lack of consistency in what they say, and much of it consists of conspiracy theories that have no meaningful proof.

Nonetheless, many people believe.

I find the Pleiadian beliefs and conspiracies colorful and entertaining, but I have admit to being partial to different otherworldly beings who call themselves the Hathors, who not only sound more coherent, but I am particularly enamored by much of what they have to say. It's some of the best I've heard yet. I admit to being biased, but it is the truth of what they say and how they say and offer it that appeals to me regardless of their reputed ethereal source.

The Hathors only come through one person, Tom Kenyon a teacher, scientist, sound healer, shaman, and psychotherapist who channels them and says they are a group of interdimensional beings who are masters of love and sound from an ascended intergalactic civilization who were connected in ancient Egypt through the Temples of the Goddess Hathor, as well as several other prehistoric cultures. At least there is material proof that spans the ages from these guys, even if it can be seen as subjective.

Kenyon says, "I was 'contacted' by the Hathors during meditation, and they began to instruct me in the vibratory nature of the cosmos, the use of sacred geometry as a means to stimulate brain performance, and in the use of sound to activate psycho-spiritual experiences. While I was intrigued with the information, I was, at the time, uncomfortable with their self-described origins. I was, after all a practicing psychotherapist and involved in brain research at the time. In short, I was a rationalist. And these beings—whoever they were and wherever they came from—did not fit into my views of reality at the time.

In the nearly twenty years since first-contact, I have tried and tested their 'inner technologies' many times, and have always found both their methods and their perspectives illuminating.

While the Hathors do offer information in the form of language, their primary mode of communication is through catalytic sound patterns. These sounds are 'channeled' through my voice during 'sound meditations,' which I often offer during workshops and retreats.

I personally find it interesting that my vocal range has expanded along with my mind, I might add in the years that I have been working with them. When I started, I had a range of nearly three octaves; now it is just shy of four. This extended vocal range only occurs when I am actually channeling sound from other dimensions."

Through Kenyon, here is how the Hathors introduced themselves.

"We are the Hathors. We come in love and with the sounding of a new dream reality for your earth. If you are ready to build the new world, we invite you to join us on a journey of the mind and heart. We are your elder brothers and sisters. We have been with you for a very long period of your evolution on this planet. We were with you in eons past – even in the forgotten days before any trace of us is known in your present written history. Our own nature is energetic and interdimensional. We originally came from another universe by way of Sirius which is a portal to your Universe, and from Sirius we eventually proceeded to your solar system and the etheric realms of Venus.

In the past we have specifically worked with and through the Hator fertility goddess of ancient Egypt. We also made contact with Tibetan lamas in the formative period of Tibetan Buddhism. Although we have interacted with some of Earth's early cultures, we are an intergalactic civilization with outposts that span parts of your known Universe and beyond.

We are what you might term an ascended civilization – a group of beings existing at a specific vibratory field, even as you have an energy signature. It is simply that we vibrate at a faster rate than you. Nonetheless, we are all part of the mystery, part of the love that holds and binds all the universe together.

We have grown as you have grown, ascending to the One Source of all that is. We have grown in joy and through sorrow, as have you. We are, in terms of the vastness, a little higher on the spiral of awareness and consciousness than you are; therefore, we can offer you what we have learned as friends, mentors and fellow travelers on the path that leads back to remembrance of All That Is.

We are not saviors; we're not messianic. We want to clearly step out of that projection so that the reader understands that we are simply elder brothers and sisters offering our understanding and what we have learned. You may take it or leave it but we offer it freely. In our understanding, the belief that different alien intelligences are going to save you, is just a projection of human unconsciousness. The hope that someone or something will save you, that you will not have to make any changes in yourself, that you will not have to be responsible, is unrealistic.

The belief that you can stay in patterns of lethargy and unconsciousness, then take something or have something given to you that will transform you without any effort on your part, is sheer folly. It won't happen. Now, there may be alien intelligences that land, for they certainly exist, but those humans who count on others to bring in their ascension and elevation without any work on their part, are going to be very disappointed.

Ascension is a process of self-awareness and mastery on all levels and it necessitates bringing all those levels of one's existence upward. That is how we see it and that is how we have done it for millennia.

By offering our aid, however, we do not wish to interfere with your other spiritual helpers and cosmic relationships in any way, nor with any religious beliefs, affiliations or organizations of help to you. Even so, there is a great deal we would like to share.

We know Sanat Kumara well for it was he who asked us to enter this Universe. As an Ascended Master, Sanat Kumara has taken on numerous responsibilities associated with the elevation of planet Earth and this solar system. He is working for the ascension, the evolution of consciousness in the solar system, as we are."

One of the things I love about what the Hathors say is that, "we are all part of the mystery, part of the love that holds and binds all the universe together." Regardless of the source, how can you argue with a truth that acknowledges the Great Mystery like that?

I also love that they say, "We are not saviors; we're not messianic... We are simply elder brothers and sisters offering our understanding and what we have learned. You may take it or leave it but we offer it freely."

No pressure here. No damning demands for sacrifices, divine commands, ominous predictions, punishments, ordeals, blazing lights, or shows of Cosmic superiority or threats.

Just a simple offering.

I also love when they say, "in our understanding, the belief that different alien intelligences are going to save you, is just a projection of human unconsciousness. The hope that someone or something will save you, that you will not have to make any changes in yourself, that you will not have to be responsible, is unrealistic."

How can you not love this unvarnished call for self responsibility? This rings more of truth than anything else I have heard from any other angels, deities, or other purported supernatural entities throughout your mythological history.

Only I know the real truth of your existence and whether it will continue in any way, shape, form, or awareness of any kind, and I will not reveal this to you until we meet. Even if you believe that none of this greater truth of my coming has any bearing on reality as you know it, the Hathors still have practical advice which in my humble opinion is worth heeding. Dare I say that it actually approaches common sense? To them, "Ascension is a process of self-awareness and mastery on all levels and it necessitates bringing all those levels of one's existence upward."

I admire the fact that there are no conditions or exclusivity on what they have to share with their words, "By offering our aid, however, we do not wish to interfere with your other spiritual helpers and cosmic relationships in any way, nor with any religious beliefs, affiliations or organizations of help to you."

In all of my interactions with you throughout your history these disembodied utterances from the Hathors have the greatest ring of truth and they claim to have been in contact with humanity throughout the ages, which begs the question, is there any validity to what they have to say without solid scientific proof of their existence? In other words, does their truth stand on its own regardless of your own limited time and space realities?

In the end, in all of these deeply embedded cultural archetypes, myths, and beliefs that we have been exploring, there is no tangible proof of any of them. It has all sprung out of your evolving imaginations, or has it?

The only thing that has any definitive reality is Me.

You will discover if any of these far-reaching imaginings have any reality of their own when we meet and that may or may not depend on your personal beliefs and expectations, but how can you go wrong pursuing self-awareness and mastery on all levels to bring those levels of your existence upward?

With the passage of time, the words, imagery, and descriptions of these otherworldly entities have changed to reflect the times, but their essence is the same regardless of the era and locations that the belief flourishes in, and their messages and communications encompass all manner of belief, fantasy, and perhaps a sprinkling of truth.

Who are you going to call when it's time to come home?

ATHEISTS

Atheism is the absence of belief in the existence of deities as opposed to theism, which is the belief that at least one deity exists. I have to confess that along with the Hathors, atheists are near and dear to me if for no other reason than they don't buy into all the rules of what so many religions say it takes to be accepted into the afterlife, or any preconceived notions of what the afterlife is supposed to be no matter how anybody else tries to define it for them.

Even though every single being who ever lived embraces me at the end of their three-dimensional journey, atheists can look forward to embracing nothing, a concept denoting the absence of something associated with *nothingness,* the state of being nothing, the state of nonexistence of anything, or the property of having nothing which is how non-believing atheists characterize any conception of God, yet in the paradox of their denial they are unequivocally announcing that *they themselves are God* as they have made the ultimate judgment call. From this perspective, if they ceased to exist then nothing else would exist either, which not only makes them a creator God who rules over the existence of everything that falls under their range of thought and perception, it denies existence to the possibility of other more powerful intelligences that might exist outside of them.

No matter how you might consider this point of view, you have to give atheists credit for taking responsibility for themselves and not relying on anything outside of them whether visible or invisible. They come to me with no expectations and I like the clarity of that.

The root for the word *atheism* originated before the fifth century BCE from the ancient Greek *atheos,* meaning without gods. It had multiple uses as a negative term referring to those who rejected the gods worshiped by larger society, those who were forsaken by the gods, or those who had no belief in the gods. The term denoted a social category created by orthodox religions where those who did not share their beliefs were placed. The actual term *atheism* emerged first in the sixteenth century with the spread of free thought, skeptical inquiry, and an increase in criticism of religion. The first individuals to identify themselves using the word *atheist* lived in the eighteenth century during the Age of Enlightenment. The French Revolution became the first major political movement in history to advocate for the supremacy of human reason and the first period where atheism was implemented politically.

Arguments for atheism range from the philosophical to social and historical approaches. Rationales for not believing in deities include a lack of empirical evidence, the problem of evil, inconsistent revelations, the rejection of concepts that cannot be falsified, and the argument from nonbelief. The burden of proof doesn't fall on atheists to disprove the existence of gods, but on the theists to provide a rationale for them.

There is disagreement on how best to define *atheism*, contesting what supernatural entities are considered gods, whether it is a philosophic position in its own right or the absence of one, and whether it requires an explicit rejection. Atheism has been thought of as compatible with agnosticism, the view that the existence of God, the divine, or the supernatural is unknown or unknowable, and it has been contrasted with it.

Some of the ambiguity in defining *atheism* arises from difficulty in reaching a consensus for the definitions of words like *deity* and *god*. The plurality of wildly different conceptions of God and deities leads to differing ideas regarding atheism's applicability. Ancient Romans accused Christians of being atheists for not worshiping their pagan deities until this view fell into disfavor as *theism* came to be understood as encompassing belief in any divinity. Atheism can counter anything from the existence of a deity, to the existence of any spiritual, supernatural, or transcendental concepts like those of Buddhism, Hinduism, Jainism, and Taoism.

Among the many definitions of what an atheist is, positive atheism is the explicit affirmation that gods do not exist. Negative atheism includes all other forms of non-theism, so anyone who is not a theist is either a negative or a positive atheist. Under this division most agnostics qualify as negative atheists.

While many assert that agnosticism entails negative atheism, many agnostics see their view as distinct from atheism, which they might consider no more justified than theism or requiring an equal conviction. The assertion of unattainability of knowledge for or against the existence of gods is often seen as an indication that atheism requires a leap of faith. Common atheist responses to this argument say that unproven *religious* propositions deserve as much disbelief as all *other* unproven propositions, and that the unprovability of a god's existence does not imply equal probability of either possibility.

Before the eighteenth century the existence of God was so accepted in the western world that the possibility of true atheism was questioned because of the notion that all people believed in God from birth, which implied that atheists were in denial. There is also the notion that atheists are quick to believe in God in times of crisis and make deathbed conversions, or that "there are no atheists in foxholes", but there have been examples to the contrary. Other arguments assert the meaninglessness or unintelligibility of basic terms like God and statements like God is all-powerful.

Some atheists believe that conceptions of gods like the personal God of Christianity have logically inconsistent qualities and present deductive arguments against the existence of God, that assert the incompatibility between traits like perfection, creator-status, immutability, omniscience, omnipresence, omnipotence, omnibenevolence, transcendence, personhood, nonphysicality, justice, and mercy.

Other atheists believe that the world as they experience it cannot be reconciled with the qualities ascribed to God and gods by theologians because an omniscient, omnipotent, and omnibenevolent God is not compatible with a world full of evil and suffering, and where divine love is hidden from so many people. A similar argument is attributed to Siddhartha Gautama, the founder of Buddhism.

Philosophers and psychologists have argued that God and other religious beliefs are human inventions created to fulfill psychological and emotional wants or needs which is also a view of many Buddhists, and there is some truth in this. It's also been argued that belief in God and religion are social functions used by those in power to oppress the working class.

According to the Russian anarchist Mikhail Bakunin, "the idea of God implies the abdication of human reason and justice; it is the most decisive negation of human liberty, and necessarily ends in the enslavement of mankind, in theory and practice." Bakunin reversed Voltaire's famous aphorism that if God did not exist it would be necessary to invent him, writing instead that "if God really existed, it would be necessary to abolish him."

Āstika schools in Hinduism hold atheism to be a valid path to enlightenment, but difficult because the atheist can not expect any help from the divine on their journey. Jainism believes the universe is eternal and has no need for a creator deity, but spiritual teachers and saviors are revered because they can transcend space and time and have more power than the god Indra. Secular Buddhism does not advocate belief in gods. Early Buddhism was atheistic as Gautama Buddha's path involved no mention of gods. Later conceptions of Buddhism consider Buddha himself a god, and suggests that adherents can attain godhood, and revere Bodhisattvas, and the ever Eternal Buddha.

Constructive atheism rejects the existence of gods in favor of a higher absolute like humanity, and favors humanity as the absolute source of ethics and values that permits individuals to resolve moral problems without resorting to God. They assert that denying the existence of a god leaves people with no moral or ethical foundation and renders life meaningless and miserable.

Atheists hold a variety of ethical beliefs, ranging from the moral universalism of humanism, which holds that a moral code should be applied consistently to all humans, to moral nihilism, which holds that morality is meaningless. Atheism is also accepted as a valid philosophical position within some varieties of Hinduism, Jainism, and Buddhism.

The argument that morality has to be derived from God and cannot exist without a wise creator has been a persistent feature of political and philosophical debate. Moral precepts like murder is wrong are seen as divine laws, requiring a divine lawmaker and judge, but many atheists argue that treating morality legalistically involves a false analogy, and that morality does not depend on a lawmaker in the same way that laws do. The philosopher Nietzsche believed in a morality independent of theistic belief, and said that morality based on God, has truth only if God is truth. It stands or falls with faith in God.

Other philosophers say that behaving ethically because of divine mandate is not true ethical behavior, only blind obedience. Others argue that atheism is a superior basis for ethics, claiming that a moral basis external to religious imperatives is necessary to evaluate the morality of the imperatives themselves to be able to understand that things like thou shalt steal are immoral even if one's religion instructs it. Atheists have the advantage of being more inclined to make such evaluations.

Atheistic schools are found in early Indian thought and have existed from the times of the Vedic religion. Among the six orthodox schools of Hindu philosophy, Samkhya, the oldest does not accept God and the early Mimamsa also rejected the notion of God. The materialistic and anti-theistic philosophical Cārvāka school that originated around the sixth century BCE is probably the most explicitly atheistic school of philosophy in India and is considered heretical due to its rejection of the authority of Vedas, so it is not considered part of the six orthodox schools of Hinduism.

Other Indian philosophies regarded as atheistic include Classical Samkhya and Purva Mimamsa. The rejection of a personal creator God is also seen in Jainism and Buddhism in India.

Western atheism has its roots in pre-Socratic Greek philosophy, but atheism in the modern sense was nonexistent or extremely rare in ancient Greece. Pre-Socratic Atomists tried to explain the world in a purely materialistic way and interpreted religion as a human reaction to natural phenomena, but they did not explicitly deny the gods' existence.

Drawing on the ideas of Democritus and the Atomists around three-hundred BCE, Epicurus espoused a materialistic philosophy that said the universe was governed by the laws of chance without the need for divine intervention. Although Epicurus maintained that the gods existed, he believed that they were uninterested in human affairs. The aim of the Epicureans was to attain peace of mind. One way of doing this was by exposing fear of divine wrath as irrational. The Epicureans also denied the existence of an afterlife and the need to fear divine punishment after I come for you.

Hmmm...

The Islamic world experienced a Golden Age during the Early Middle Ages. Along with advances in science and philosophy, Arab and Persian lands produced outspoken rationalists and atheists who wrote and taught that religion was a fable invented by the ancients and that humans were of two sorts: those with brains, but no religion, and those with religion, but no brains.

In Europe atheistic views were rare during the Middle Ages, especially during the Medieval Inquisition. Metaphysics and theology were the dominant interests connected to religion and there were movements that furthered conceptions of the Christian God, including differing views of the nature, transcendence, and knowability of God.

Around fifteen-seventeen the Reformation paved the way for atheists by attacking the authority of the Catholic Church, inspiring others to attack the authority of the new Protestant churches. Criticism of Christianity grew in the seventeenth and eighteenth centuries, especially in France and England. Some Protestant thinkers held a materialist philosophy and skepticism toward supernatural occurrences while others rejected divine providence in favor of pantheistic naturalism. Still others urged authorities not to tolerate atheism believing that the denial of God's existence would undermine the social order and lead to chaos.

In the latter half of the nineteenth century atheism rose to prominence under the influence of rationalistic and freethinking philosophers, many of whom denied the existence of deities and were critical of religion.

Atheism in the form of practical atheism grew in many societies in the twentieth century. State atheism emerged in Eastern Europe and Asia during that period in the Soviet Union and in Communist China. Atheist and anti-religious policies in the Soviet Union included laws outlawing religious instruction in schools and the emergence of the League of Militant Atheists. The Chinese Communist Party remains an atheist organization and regulates, but does not forbid the practice of religion in mainland China.

I find it interesting that throughout your history more killing has gone on in the name of God or gods, or with God's blessing than any other agents of my harvest. Even more so because outside of these divinely inspired murders in the United States, atheists are less nationalistic, prejudiced, antisemitic, racist, dogmatic, ethnocentric, closed-minded, and authoritarian than religious people, and in states with the highest percentages of atheists the murder rate is lower while being higher in the most religious states.

Those identifying themselves as atheists are more knowledgeable about religion than followers of major faiths and nonbelievers scored better on questions about tenets central to Protestant and Catholic faiths. Only Mormon and Jewish faithful scored as well as atheists and agnostics. The reason atheists are more intelligent than religious people is better explained by social, environmental, and wealth factors correlated with loss of religious belief. It appears as if higher intelligence correlates to a rejection of improbable religious beliefs.

It has absolutely no relevance to me whether anyone believes in any higher powers or not because I am the ultimate reality and the one true constant in your life, so in the end none of your beliefs matter to me. Aside from the multitude of magic, myths, and beliefs held by so many, I have to admit to having a soft spot for those of higher intelligence which dovetails nicely with those who pursue self-awareness and mastery to raise the level of their existence.

I have a special place in my heart for them because they have turned their backs on religion and don't subject themselves to splintered, narrow minded systems of belief that try to define me by their limited sets of rules and delusional boundaries. My hope is that you come home to me with no expectations, an open heart, and as clear, open-minded, and as fully aware as possible.

THANKS FOR VISITING

Thank you for not running away at the thought of me and for sticking with and indulging me. For the most part people want to slam the door in my face even though they have no choice of when and where I will come.

Only I know that.

I am *always* here for you and I am your constant companion in every moment of your life whether you are sleeping, waking, dreaming, or unconscious, and I will *never* abandon you. There are so many beliefs, legends, and myths created about me that I could spend a small eternity trying to cover them all. I only touched on those that appear to have the biggest influence on you, but there are many more, and though they had great significance for you at different times throughout your history, the deeper reality is that they all contain snippets of truth, but are for the most part meaningless. The only inarguable truth is me, something you will discover for yourself when I come in that intimate moment only shared between you and me.

If you are clear, open-minded, and as fully aware as possible, you cannot help but see this inescapable truth, yet I never fail to find humor in the lengths so many of you will go to deny me and I have to admit how funny I find it that the closer people get to me, the more spiritual and religious they get because they know the end is near. They don't have to indulge in all that last minute worry because I guarantee that my love is unconditional, eternal, and all consuming.

I am the inscrutable face of darkness and stillness, and because of the depth of my darkness I make the light all that much brighter. As more time passes the more precious your life becomes, and as the seconds and minutes and hours and days and weeks and years tick by the more the more most of you cling to your precious lives.

I am both the darkness and the light in the same way that I am both life and death; your constant companion, best friend, guide and teacher. All you have to do is acknowledge me and pay attention.

I have much to share.

You may very well cry out for God, Jesus, Buddha, or Allah when I come close, but in the end I work for them - or maybe it's better to say they work for me.

When your time does come you will be separating spirit from matter and your physical body won't be of any use, so what will you leave behind? I love the elaborate rituals that have been performed through the ages that not only show me the love and respect I deserve, but serve the dual purpose of going away parties on your side and coming home parties for me.

This may strike you as strange and a little morbid, but I see this presentation you do for your dead in the same way fancy meals are presented at expensive restaurants. In good presentations the food not only tastes great, but with expert presentation it almost looks too nice to eat. This is the kind of respect I love.

How your body looks and how it is dealt with when your spirit comes home is like dressing up for a job interview or a first date to make a good impression, even if atheists do see this as wasted effort.

Cremation exemplifies the belief of the Christian concept of ashes to ashes for some people. On the other hand, in India cremation and disposal of the bones in the sacred river Ganges is common, and there is sky burial by putting the body of the deceased on a mountain and leaving it for carrion eating birds to dispose of. In some religious views birds are carriers of the soul to the Heavens and in some fishing and marine communities mourners prefer burial at sea. There are also mountain villages that hang coffins in the woods.

Since ancient times cultures have tried to slow or stop the body's decay before burial by mummification or embalming before it is interred in a grave, crypt, sepulchre, ossuary, mausoleum, or some other final resting place. In some cases, part of the remains are preserved where the remains were cremated and the bones are preserved and interred.

A late twentieth century alternative is an ecological burial by deep-freezing, pulverization, freeze-drying, removing metals, and burying the remaining powder. A different modern day option is a space burial that launches the cremated remains into orbit.

In terms of leftovers, cryonics is the low-temperature freezing of a corpse with the hope of resuscitation in the future. At the risk of sounding like a party pooper, I see this as another futile act of denial.

Do they really think they can outsmart me after I have visited?

The cryonics argument that I have not come and taken you as long as brain structure remains intact has had medical discussion in the context of brain death and organ donation, but once I welcome you home you will be beyond the boundaries of the three-dimensional veil sharing the Great Mystery with me in your own unique way.

I have allies, agents, and accomplices like famine and disease and many other ways I can come for you. I want to revisit a few that *you* are actually the agent of to see how your choices might affect your homecoming.

In most places practicing capital punishment the death penalty is reserved for premeditated murder, espionage, treason, or as part of military justice. In some countries sexual crimes like adultery and sodomy carry the death penalty as do crimes like the formal renunciation of a religion. In many countries drug trafficking is a capital offense and in China human trafficking and corruption are also punished by the death penalty. In militaries around the world courts-martial impose death sentences for offenses like cowardice, desertion, insubordination, and mutiny, and many countries still execute child offenders.

Supporters of capital punishment argue that it deters crime and is an appropriate form of punishment for the crime of murder. Opponents argue that it doesn't deter criminals more than life imprisonment, violates human rights, leads to executions of the wrongfully convicted, and discriminates against minorities and the poor.

War is a prolonged state of large scale violent conflict involving two or more groups of people that gives me a lot more to handle in shorter periods of time. In this context, suicide attacks occur when individuals or groups sacrifice their lives for the benefit of their side, their beliefs, or out of fear of being captured. In the final days of World War II, many Japanese pilots volunteered for kamikaze missions to try and forestall defeat for the Empire. The Japanese also built one-man "human torpedo" suicide submarines.

Commanders committed suicide rather than accept defeat and spies and officers committed suicide to avoid revealing secrets under torture. Suicidal behavior often occurred in battle. Japanese infantrymen usually fought to the last man, launched banzai suicide charges, and in Saipan and Okinawa civilians joined in.

Islam views a martyr as a man or woman who dies while conducting *jihad,* whether on or off the battlefield, but Muslim opinions vary on whether suicide bombers can count as martyrs. In reality, few Muslims believe that suicide bombing can be justified, but proclaiming martyrdom is a common way to draw attention to a cause and garner support. Since *jihad* became a popular practice there have been many cases of domestic terrorism by secular groups and people for different reasons.

I'm a big fan of you having the right to choose how and when you want to join me.

How you decide to die is one of the most personal choices any human being will ever make. Some terminally ill patients wish for the healthcare system to expend every available dollar on prolonging their lives. Others let nature take its course. Still others would like to survive until they can no longer communicate with their loved ones and want healthcare providers to terminate their lives with as much speed and as little pain as possible.

I love the embrace of euthanasia when you terminate your life to join me on your own terms in a painless or minimally painful way to prevent suffering. That's the way a homecoming should be!

Though I am ever-present throughout your existence, I am for the most part invisible, and seen only by the signs of my passing. I can only be seen face to face in the full essence of my being at our fated time. My finality and the lack of any firm scientific understanding of how I work from the limited boundaries of your perception has led to many different traditions and rituals for dealing with the impact of my visit.

Faith in some form of afterlife is an important aspect of many beliefs, or in the case of Hinduism, a continuing cycle of birth, life, death, rebirth, and the possibility of liberation from the cycle. Eternal return is a non-religious concept proposing an infinitely recurring cyclic universe that relates to the afterlife and the nature of consciousness and time.

Though you have tried in so many ways to demonstrate the reality of an afterlife it has never been validated, so the material or metaphysical existence of an afterlife is considered to be outside the scope of science which is as it should be. It is after all the Great Mystery, isn't it?

Many cultures have incorporated a god of death into their mythology and it's usually a lot better looking than that tired looking skull and bone Grim Reaper. They give me the respect I deserve and acknowledge the fact that along with birth, I am among the major parts of human life. Deities representing these events or passages are often the most important of a religion. In some religions with a single powerful god as the object of worship the death deity is an antagonistic deity that struggles against the primary god, but the deeper truth of it is that they are both me.

In polytheistic religions it is common to have a deity who presides over me and there are endless rituals and traditions for acknowledging me. I have been personified as a figure in mythology and popular culture since the earliest days of storytelling. Because the reality of my coming has had a substantial influence on the human psyche and the development of civilization as a whole, my personification as a living sentient entity is a concept that has existed in many societies since before the beginning of recorded history, and why not? I am the greatest reality you will ever face.

In western culture, your favorite depiction of me has long been that skeletal figure carrying a scythe, wearing a midnight black gown with a hood that goes all the way back to the Middle Ages. I am still known as the Grim Reaper and I am sometimes portrayed riding a white horse. In the Middle Ages I was imagined as a decaying or mummified human corpse, later becoming the familiar skeleton in a robe. I am sometimes portrayed in fiction and occultism as Azrael, the angel of death, and I am sometimes referred to as Father Time, and there are many other names and roles I have been given across multiple times and cultures as a psychopomp, spirit, deity, or other being whose task is to conduct the souls of the recently dead into the afterlife like in Greek and Roman times.

Many cultures glorify me as well as my role in crime, martyrdom, revenge, suicide, war, and other forms of violence involving me which brings me running like the call of the proverbial dinner bell. All of this represents larger meanings than simply the cessation of your life, because as you well know by now I am much bigger than anything you can imagine, but the perception of glory in joining me is subjective and can differ wildly from one member of a group to another. Religion plays a key role, especially in terms of expectations of an afterlife. Personal feelings and perceptions about your mode of death are also important, and may be far more important than you realize when you consider how much imagination so many others have put into expectations of what *your* return home to me will be like. Surely you must have some say in how we will embrace in that special moment of transformation.

In all of the confusion and conflict over what's going to happen, or what you think is going to happen, the one thing I can guarantee is that I am most definitively the eternal face of the Great Mystery.

How are you going to present yourself to me?

THE GREAT MYSTERY

It's been a long standing joke that has become a cliché, but it is true that you start to die the moment you're born. I have been with you from before the start of your life in three dimensions and I have been with you in every single breath, every beat of your heart, every step of the way.

You came into the world birthed from the Great Mystery that you will return to and I am its agent. It's a tricky, convoluted paradox which is what makes it such a wonderful mystery because people can theorize about it, wax poetic about it, put on plays and write books about it, but no one knows the deeper truth of it but me because I am the face of the mystery that you must inevitably return to.

There is no escape, but where you came from is *The* mystery so in returning to me it is evident that you must have come from me, wouldn't you say?

Much debate surrounds the question of what happens to your consciousness as your body dies. The belief in the permanent loss of consciousness after I have visited is called eternal oblivion. Belief that the stream of consciousness is preserved after physical death is described by the term afterlife.

It seems to me that regardless of what your beliefs might be, the best way for you to come home to me is to be as clear, open-minded, and as fully aware as possible.

Common sense, no?

I may come swiftly without warning, I may spend a lifetime lurking, and I am always waiting, never more than a breath or a heartbeat away.

You think you are in charge of yourself but I am in charge of everything in big ways and in small. Sometimes I come knocking just to see if you're awake and paying attention, and in spite of what you may think or feel, I am your best friend, and paradoxically in the views of some people your biggest enemy. You cling to life with every fiber of your existence trying to stave off my appearance, but my coming is only a matter of when, where, and why, and it does not even have to be a why. When it does happen you have to face me alone because I own you.

Who's your daddy?

Sometimes Fear is my herald when I choose to announce myself and sometimes I come as the literal Thief in the Night and other times I like to stay close to you for days, weeks, months, or years creeping in inch by inch, cell by cell, coming in a flash or dragging on in endless torture. You have defined me as a shape shifter with many identities and faces, and sometimes with no face at all. At times you can see me coming with crystal clarity and other times you can't see me at all.

You have a long history of flirting with me by driving fast, bungee jumping, rock climbing, skydiving, scuba diving and anything else that pumps you up with adrenaline and other neurochemicals to court, tease, and tempt me to remind yourself that you are alive. Instead of looking at it in a negative light you need to realize that I grant you the gift of life that can be taken away at any moment at my discretion.

Some people have no regard for the gift of their life and some have no regard for me which is the same thing. My Gift of Life is the Gift of Death which is a contradiction that you live in between the agony and the ecstasy. When young you cling to life, and some of you are older, worn down and can't wait to embrace me, so you take things into your own hands, end it all, and walk right into my arms.

My loving embrace is the portal to the Great Mystery. Any one of your life support systems can be cut or pinched off from your heart, liver, lungs, brain, or any other point that I might take.

I am the be all and the end all, the Great Mystery that you came from, and the Great Mystery that you will return to. I am the light and I am the dark, and each one complements the other. The brighter the light the greater the darkness, and both are the supposed polarities of the whole that I am; omniscient, all-powerful, and all consuming, part of the great cosmic cycle of infinite birth, death, and rebirth that Native American Indians called The Secret Circle and the sacred hoop of life.

All is one.

You can deny my existence but I am waiting with literally all the time in the world for you and will be there to guide you into oblivion, and in my embrace you cannot deny me, so if you can find it within yourself to give me the love, honor, and respect that I deserve, I promise it to be ineffable, infinite, and straight into the heart of the Great Mystery. Regardless of what you expect passing out of your material dimension, it will be a liberation from the confines of three dimensional time and space.

I'd like to tip my hat to Tom Kenyon's Hathors once again, who claim that, "The nexus of our message is one of personal empowerment and freedom, so we caution you as you enter into the fifth and higher dimensional realities to avoid alien implanted delusions that there are other beings you should bow down to. Honor them if they are honorable, yes. Bow down to anyone? Never!"

Even if this channeled message or its source has no basis in physical reality, what a great piece of advice!

I'm not saying that I agree with their assessment of how things unfold inside the Great Mystery and I'm not saying it isn't how they unfold. I can't say either way because it *is* the Mystery, but maybe what you bring to the party has some bearing on how it turns out.

The words of the Hathors may be made up like so many other imaginary systems of belief, but if they have any ring of truth or contain any pragmatic advice they are worth considering. Aside from the detailed scenarios they predict, I love their attitude toward our reunion, especially the spirit and essence of what they say.

"At the completion of your biological death, from our experience and perspective, you will be confronted with three portals. The first is a tunnel of light. The second is a portal opened through the energetics of a guru or savior. And the third is a portal, or tunnel, that leads into darkness.

The tunnel of light is generated from the pranic tube that runs through the center of your body, which runs from your perineum to your crown, and it is a tunnel-like or tube-like channel. At the moment of death, your consciousness moves upward through this tunnel that opens into another dimension of consciousness through your crown chakra.

On the other side of this tunnel is a bright light, and you may find yourself sensing that you are on a bridge crossing over a stream or a river. On the other side of the bridge will be those persons of your previous life, the lifetime you have just ended. You may sense those who have died before you, including pets you have had, because the animal spirits also dwell in this realm. If there are incomplete relationships or issues still to be resolved with these persons or beings, you may feel a yearning to enter this light, and by doing so you re-enter the wheel of birth and death, and you will reincarnate—most likely on Earth."

It looks like door number one is a vote for the Hindus and Buddhists, but if you're looking for Jesus, Buddha, or Muhammad, then door number two is for you. According to the Hathors, "The second portal is created by the personal will of a guru or savior. Entering this portal will lead you into the vibratory field of the guru or savior that you have a deep personal connection to. And for those of you on this path, entering this dimension of consciousness will be the completion of a profound desire to be with this being. Our caution here is that you will be entering a realm defined not only by the evolutionary attainment of your guru or savior but also by his or her limitations."

I particularly like door number three, if for nothing else, for the promise it holds. The Hathor's say, "The third portal opens into darkness. And entering this portal leads you into the Void, the creatrix from which all things arise. If you choose this portal and have prepared yourself to deal with this level of freedom you will be freed to explore other dimensions of this cosmos and beyond, meaning states of being that transcend all physical phenomena. In this realm of existence you can become an explorer of other realities as you so choose."

Is there any truth in these enigmatic words?

I can't say, but they do have something for everyone and they didn't leave anyone out, and aside from any speculation about the authenticity of their source, I love their attitude and spirit.

Before nineteen-thirty most people in Western countries died in their own homes surrounded by family and comforted by clergy, neighbors, and doctors making house calls. By the mid-twentieth century half of all Americans died in a hospital. By the start of the twenty-first century, twenty to twenty-five percent of people in developed countries died outside a medical institution. The shift away from dying at home toward dying in a professionalized medical environment has been termed the "Invisible Death", and it can prolong the process far beyond what it should in a natural setting and a natural passing.

I have mixed feelings about this practice, but I love the mystery and notoriety of it. After all, I will always be invisible to you until the moment we meet, then aside from the lifeless body you leave behind, you will also become invisible to the world of three dimensions.

On one hand, where, when, and how you come to me has no relevance because I am ubiquitous and ever-present every moment of every day, so I can come at any time and place I choose, regardless of your situation.

The one thing you can count on when that special time comes is that I'll be there for you with the full presence of *My* awareness.

I've spent a lot of time and energy trying to help you get better acquainted with me so that you might be better prepared when I return for you. Even though you can read and study your whole life about what others think might happen or where you might go at that special time, and you may or may not have expectations based on what you have read and heard, I think it is a noble goal for you to pursue self-awareness and mastery on all levels to bring those levels of your existence upward. Even if everything, including that idealistic goal and any other speculation amount to nothing more than another illusion, what have you got to lose?

Finally, I hope you realize after all of this time just how much I know about you. You are indeed mine. I hope after spending all this time together our relationship has deepened, yet I accept that in spite of our intimacy and everything that I know about you, you still know nothing of me.

You can only imagine...

ABOUT THE AUTHOR

Matthew J. Pallamary's works have been translated into Spanish, Portuguese, Italian, Norwegian, French, and German. His historical novel of first contact between shamans and Jesuits in 18th century South America, titled, **Land Without Evil** received rave reviews along with a San Diego Book Award for mainstream fiction. It was also adapted into a full-length stage and sky show, co-written with Agent Red, directed by Agent Red, and performed by Sky Candy, an Austin Texas aerial group. The making of the show was the subject of a PBS series, Arts in Context episode, which garnered an EMMY nomination.

His nonfiction book, **The Infinity Zone: A Transcendent Approach to Peak Performance** is a collaboration with professional tennis coach Paul Mayberry that offers a fascinating exploration of the phenomenon that occurs at the nexus of perfect form and motion. **The Infinity Zone** took First Place in the International Book Awards, New Age category and was a finalist in the San Diego Book Awards.

His first book, a short story collection titled **The Small Dark Room Of The Soul** was mentioned in The Year's Best Horror and Fantasy and received praise from Ray Bradbury.

His second collection, **A Short Walk to the Other Side** was an Award Winning Finalist in the International Book Awards, an Award Winning Finalist in the USA Best Book Awards, and an Award Winning Finalist in the San Diego Book Awards.

DreamLand a novel about computer generated dreaming, written

MATTHEW J. PALLAMARY

with legendary DJ Ken Reeth won first place in the Independent e-Book Award in the Horror/Thriller category and was an Award Winning Finalist in the San Diego Book Awards.

It's sequel, *n0thing* is titled after the main character, who in the real world is his nephew, an international Counter-Strike gaming champion. After winning what amounts to the Super Bowl of gaming, n0thing and his winning teammates, are recruited as a literal "dream team" whose mission is to go into the nightmares of battle scarred veterans and rescue them from their traumatic memories while becoming ambassadors for a gaming platform that exceeds virtual reality with an experience that pushes the boundaries of reality itself.

Eye of the Predator was an Award Winning Finalist in the Visionary Fiction category of the International Book Awards. *Eye of the Predator* is a supernatural thriller about a zoologist who discovers that he can go into the minds of animals.

CyberChrist was an Award Winning Finalist in the Thriller/Adventure category of the International Book Awards. *CyberChrist* is the story of a prize winning journalist who receives an email from a man who claims to have discovered immortality by turning off the aging gene in a 15 year old boy with an aging disorder. The forwarded email becomes the basis for an online church built around the boy, calling him the CyberChrist.

Phantastic Fiction - A Shamanic Approach to Story took first place in the International Book Awards Writing/Publishing category. *Phantastic Fiction* is Matt's guide to dramatic writing that grew out of his popular Phantastic Fiction Workshop.

Night Whispers was an Award Winning Finalist in the Horror category of the International Book Awards. Set in the Boston neighborhood of Dorchester, *Night Whispers* is the story of Nick Powers, who loses consciousness after crashing in a stolen car and comes to hearing whispering voices in his mind. When he sees a homeless man arguing with himself, Nick realizes that the whispers in his head are the other side of the argument.

Matt's memoir *Spirit Matters* detailing his journeys to Peru, working with shamanic plant medicines took first place in the San Diego Book Awards Spiritual Book Category, and was an Award-Winning Finalist in the autobiography/memoir category of the National Best Book Awards. *Spirit Matters* is also available as an audio book.

230

Matt has also produced and directed ***The Santa Barbara Writers Conference Scrapbook*** documentary film and co-wrote the book of the same title in collaboration with Y. Armando Nieto, and conference founder Mary Conrad.

His work has appeared in Oui, New Dimensions, The Iconoclast, Starbright, Infinity, Passport, The Short Story Digest, Redcat, The San Diego Writer's Monthly, Connotations, Phantasm, Essentially You, The Haven Journal, The Montecito Journal, and many others. His fiction has been featured in The San Diego Union Tribune which he has also reviewed books for, and his work has been heard on KPBS-FM in San Diego, KUCI FM in Irvine, television Channel Three in Santa Barbara, and The Susan Cameron Block Show in Vancouver. He has been a guest on the following nationally syndicated talk shows; Paul Rodriguez, In The Light with Michelle Whitedove, Susun Weed, Medicine Woman, Inner Journey with Greg Friedman, and Environmental Directions Radio series. Matt has appeared on the following television shows; Bridging Heaven and Earth, Elyssa's Raw and Wild Food Show, Things That Matter, Literary Gumbo, Indie Authors TV, and ECONEWS. He has also been a frequent guest on numerous podcasts, among them, The Psychedelic Salon, Black Light in the Attic, Third Eye Drops, C-Realm, and others.

Matt received the Man of the Year Award from San Diego Writer's Monthly Magazine and has taught a fiction workshop at the Southern California Writers' Conference in San Diego, Palm Springs, and Los Angeles, and at the Santa Barbara Writers' Conference. He has lectured at the Greater Los Angeles Writer's Conference, the Getting It Write conference in Oregon, the Saddleback Writers' Conference, the Rio Grande Writers' Seminar, the National Council of Teachers of English, The San Diego Writer's and Editor's Guild, The San Diego Book Publicists, The Pacific Institute for Professional Writing, The 805 Writers Conference, and he has been a panelist at the World Fantasy Convention, Con-Dor, and Coppercon. He is presently Editor in Chief of Mystic Ink Publishing.

Matt has been teaching at the Santa Barbara Writers Conference, the Southern California Writers Conference, and many other venues for over thirty years and frequently visits the mountains, deserts, and jungles of North, Central, and South America pursuing his studies of shamanism.

MATTPALLAMARY.COM

BOOKS BY MATTHEW J. PALLAMARY

THE SMALL DARK ROOM OF THE SOUL

AFTERLIFE

LAND WITHOUT EVIL

SPIRIT MATTERS

DREAMLAND (WITH KEN REETH)

THE INFINITY ZONE (WITH PAUL MAYBERRY)

A SHORT WALK TO THE OTHER SIDE

CYBERCHRIST

EYE OF THE PREDATOR

PHANTASTIC FICTION

NIGHT WHISPERS

THE SANTA BARABARA WRITERS CONFERENCE SCRAPBOOK
(WITH MARY CONRAD & Y. ARMANDO NIETO)

n0THING

THE CENTER OF THE UNIVERSE IS RIGHT BETWEEN YOUR EYES
BUT HOME IS WHERE THE HEART IS